T
NETWORK

By
Ian P Blows

MAPLE
PUBLISHERS

The Network

Author: Ian P Blows

ISBN 978-1-83538-650-7 (Paperback)
   978-1-83538-651-4 (E-Book)

Cover designed by: Rosie Rossouw-Wright

Book Layout by:
   Maple Publishers
   www.maplepublishers.com

Published by:
   Maple Publishers
   Fairbourne Drive, Atterbury,
   Milton Keynes,
   MK10 9RG, UK
   www.maplepublishers.com

Foreword

What on Earth is all the fuss about??? ... If only we could learn from other's mistakes.

A humorous yet thought-provoking tale which scrutinises new technology, its influence on our society and what could we do about it if we ever wanted to.

Acknowledgements

I greatly appreciate the help given to me by Michelle, Isabel, Ash and Nick for reading my drafts and giving their comments. I would like to thank Rosie Rossouw-Wright for her inspiration and ideas for the cover design. I would like to say a big thank-you to all the people who completed my questionnaire, either physically or verbally. Finally, I would like to acknowledge the support and encouragement given to me by my wife, my family and my friends.

Readers' Quotes

"Without doubt his finest work to date."

"Surely worthy of a Nobel Prize; just not for literature."

"I found this book impossible to put down; I was desperate to get it over and done with."

"Who said horror is dead? The thought of a sequel terrifies me!"

"A very simple tale told by a very simple man."

"This story invoked all of my senses; except taste."

CONTENTS

Chapter 1

The Present.

"I've GOT to get me one of THESE!!" squealed Skipper, whilst taking in the breathtaking reality of his surroundings with startled wonder (his jaw had dropped, his eyes were the size of golf balls and I do believe his tongue was hanging out) and, three months later, he got one for his birthday.

There are two critical elements tucked away in the above sentence, the importance of which cannot be understated for Skipper and for all humanity. These two elements worked together to initiate a huge, cosmic scale, misunderstanding. The "one of THESE" refers to a Virtual Reality (VR) headset and his name, or rather nickname, Skipper.

For those of you who have not yet tried a VR headset get ready to be amazed as you enter worlds that are rendered with such stunning visual clarity. Whilst they are not true reproductions of the real world, they give rise to exactly the same powerful sensations and emotions that you really do experience in the real world. For example, when squealing 'I've GOT to get me one of THESE!!' Skipper was edging his way along a narrow plank that extended straight out from the top floor of a skyscraper, suspended high, high above the pavement below. The sensation of height was so extreme that Skipper could not bring himself to step off the plank, even though he knew he was, in reality, making his way along the living room floor. But could he step off the plank – no way José. He just inched his way to the end of the plank and back again with very wobbly knees. He had his heart in his mouth and his arms outstretched, much like you might imagine an inexperienced tightrope walker, occasionally glancing down at the tiny people on the pavement below. During the days immediately following his birthday he: learned to fly a First World War biplane, assembled 3d jigsaw puzzles, became enrolled as a special agent and went on several Black Ops missions. He even played a few rounds of golf where, amazingly, the VR world was able to reproduce his legendary short comings to perfection. After 20 minutes of canoeing through a desolate landscape, whilst directions were whispered in his ear, he felt a degree of exhaustion and extreme motion sickness; and when a gibbon suddenly jumped out at him, well, he nearly shat himself. Feelings in the VR world are authentic and powerful.

*

Let us now deal with his name. About 2 years before these events unfolded, Skipper moved from a nice Edwardian house, on the northern edge of London, England, to a converted pub in a village at the heart of the country. His new home had many interesting features but needed quite a few modifications to reflect Skipper and his wife's needs and their favoured style. Over the following months a team of builders rearranged the garden, knocked through some rooms, sorted out the drains, sorted out the roof, created a large modern kitchen diner, installed a new bathroom and undertook numerous other smaller projects. Throughout this time, and on prominent view to the entire village, was a succession of skips (called dumpsters in many parts of the world), hence getting the nickname Skipper (he sometimes reflects that, had he moved to America, he may well have been given the nickname Dumper, which could have had many and quite varied connotations!)

Skipper was named Skipper by his two new amigos, Supply-chain Chris (a senior manager with an international distribution company) and Taxi Tony (once of the fashion industry, now part-time taxi driver) whilst attending their regular watering hole, The Train Stop. The Train Stop is an unusual pub, one of two in the village, with a mix of clientele that is eclectic in the extreme, many of whom are named Tony. Taxi Tony we've met, Carpet Tony lays carpets, Plumber Tony plumbs and there are several other similarly prefixed Tonys. Other regulars include: a journalist (occasional), a company administrator (habitual), builders and handy men by the bucketful (as and when), an electrician (frequent), an ex-navy helicopter pilot and an ex-army tank driver (both OAP's Corner, Sunday lunchtimes) to name but a few. The Landlord, Landlady and their team are always welcoming and friendly, and the conversation is lively, the banter is very good natured and the mickey is often taken; which led, of course, to the nickname Skipper.

A typical evening for the three amigos was to have a few beers (never more than two for Taxi Tony (or TT for short) whilst enjoying a bit of banter with the other customers around them, usually followed by a lengthy discussion amongst the three of them. These discussions were always deep and far ranging, but they were usually on the subject of – "things in the world that need to be put right and we are the guys to do it!" – a very common subject around the pubs of Britain and, I've no doubt, in bars throughout the world.

Both Skipper and Supply-chain Chris had worked at senior levels with a variety of large companies, and both had plenty of people management, organisational and operational experience. TT as a taxi driver, had acquired many different (and often quite surprising) experiences that were vital to their wide-ranging and in-depth discussions. As a very empathetic and communicative taxi driver, and being a good listener by nature, he claims to have gained a great depth of knowledge in, amongst many other things, social care, counselling, marriage guidance and politics. Also, to have a particularly astute insight into the state of the economy, the state of the NHS and footballers' wages. He seems to be well-versed in a great range of subjects; in fact, almost everything except "women's things" which he avoids like the plague ("No, no; I don't go there, I'm only a taxi driver"). It is possible to paint a snapshot picture of TT with one for instance. For instance, he would ask his fares to pick a number from one to six and, each day, he had a list with six different topics for debate or, as he called them, "moans of the day". A day's example could be:

1. Hospital waiting times.

2. Over a million channels on TV, yet there is never anything on worth watching (except, of course, Bangers and Cash repeats).

3. Where has education gone rong? (He even points out that he had spelt wrong r-o-n-g, just so his passenger could appreciate the irony).

4. Potholes in our roads and the damage they are doing to the wheels of industry.

5. Hairstyles in modern politics (Johnson and Trump – what are they all about?).

And, at number six, an upbeat topic of the day,

6. Air-fryers; THE wonder of the modern world, even more versatile than a wok.

It may seem that I am painting TT in a poor light, which would be giving you the completely wrong impression. TT is a great guy, he is well-liked by his friends, is loyal and has a super sharp sense of humour. A little bit stubborn on occasion, even, perhaps, just sometimes, a teeny-weeny bit stuck in his ways, but always willing to offer a good-natured opinion on any subject except, of course, women's things ("No, no; I'm only a taxi driver").

Supply-chain Chris, who was Skipper's new neighbour, introduced himself a day or two after Skipper had moved into his new home. It was a lovely evening when Chris and his wife appeared at the gate (in fact he suddenly appeared in the back garden claiming he already had "walk-in rights"). He was bearing "welcome to your new home" gifts; two bottles of wine (one white and one red) and a bag-for-life containing cans of both bitter and cooled lager. Skipper immediately thought, now this is my type of guy, well supplied, prepared for any eventuality and aware of his responsibilities to the environment. He could already see Supply-chain Chris's generosity, bonhomie and, quite clearly, his logistical background. Skipper and his wife invited their new neighbours to stay for a drink or two and the rest, as they say, is history. Skipper and Chris enjoyed each other's company and began spending time together, often in The Train Stop. Chris's daughter even started calling them Tweedle Dum and Tweedle Dee which, very quickly, morphed into the very obvious, Tweedle Dumb and Tweedle Dumber. There are still arguments to this day as to which one is which.

*

One Wednesday evening (in fact this can be taken as the very starting point of our saga) Skipper and Chris arrived at The Train Stop to find just a handful of other customers. A pair of Tonys were sitting in their usual place, perched on stools at the bar, and a few other customers were scattered about in groups of twos and threes. Meanwhile, in a prominent position outside Skipper's house, in full view of the village was, almost certainly, his last skip. The building work was coming to an end. He had decided that now was a good time to clear his house of any remaining unwanted household paraphernalia, which included two old desktop computers that were currently consigned to the bottom of a cupboard in his office. Disposing of the computers was a bit of a concern to him as they clearly contained a goodly amount of personal information such as bank details and passwords. Sometime during the afternoon, he had decided that he would ask amongst the guys at The Train Stop for any advice on their safe and secure disposal (the computers, not the other customers).

The advice rendered was, in order received:

"Smash them to pieces with a hammer" which was the solution to most ills and the tool of choice for Builder Tony.

Television Bob suggested taking them "to the nearby IT repair shop, where they would surely be able to wipe the hard discs clean."

"No, I would definitely not do that." piped up George, "those guys are just as likely to copy your data and sell it on the black market, probably to the Russian mafia or, worse still, sell it to the young wannabe gangsters sitting over there in the corner" he commented with a smirk.

In typical The Train Stop style, most advice he received was light-hearted and jokey banter:

"You need to break them up into their component BITS!"

"Why not set fire to them and loose them in THE CLOUD of smoke?"

"Yea, that's a great idea, you could incinerate them in their own FIREWALLS!"

"You could use a large amount of RAM to batter them to pieces" (Builder Tony again). The more drink consumed, the worse the puns but the more the people laughed.

Skipper decided to have one last try and wandered over to Plasterer Tony (divorced).

"Sorry Skipper, I'm really not sure I'm the one to help you, but, if you want me to, I could ask my lad what you should do, the next time I see him."

"Thanks buddy, that would be great, all suggestions welcome, does he work in IT then?"

"No, well not yet anyway, he's at university at the moment but he has always had a flair for that kind of stuff. When he was only ten years old, he hacked into one of my on-line shopping accounts. He ordered himself a pair of very expensive trainers, which turned up the next day, and a new mountain bike, which turned up three or four days after the trainers. He also paid for a lifetime subscription to PC World using my credit card details. How he got them? I have no idea."

"Well, he obviously knows what he is doing."

"Tell me about it. The little bugger had said he was just popping upstairs to watch "Home Alone Two." He also hacked into my favourite website having first obtained my private member's login details. And he's moved on from there. A few years ago, when he was about 17 years old, we had a big argument. By way of revenge, he hacked into my address book and sent a lurid picture to each and every one of my contacts: all of my friends, all my family, my work colleagues, even the local priest and the undertaker got one, just ask around the pub. God knows where he got the picture from but it was a very peculiar shape and now everyone thinks that I've got one that looks like that. What made it worse is that his mother went around telling everybody that I have!!"........ "About a year ago, he and his university friends hacked into a dating agency's web site where they arranged the most inappropriate meetings that they could think of. The company got complaint after complaint over the following few months. There was one happy story though. Apparently, as part of their mischief, they paired up a 23-year-old lady with an 84-year-old gentleman. It turned out that she was quite a looker and he was extremely wealthy. Both had hit the jackpot and they plan to marry very soon." .... "Anyway, it could all work out for the best. Following his university's recruitment week, the devious little bugger has got himself interviews with three of the world's top tech companies and is likely to end up living in California."

"Good-luck California" thought Skipper "they have no idea of what may be coming their way."

At this point TT arrived for his customary two pints. "Ah, this is someone who has probably come across the problem before, or at least one of his passengers may have talked about it" thought Skipper.

"I'm sorry Skipper, can't help you buddy, not my area of expertise …… although, if it was me, I would pop the hard drives into an air fryer. Probably wipe them clean in seconds. Air fryers are such versatile things you know, true wonders of the modern world."

Skipper, Chris and TT ordered a round of drinks, settled themselves on slightly rickety seats around a slightly rickety table and began their usual conversation.

Later that evening Skipper arrived home with his head spinning, full of the world's problems and their associated solutions (and probably just a little bit too much of The Train Stop's Best Bitter). That evening's intense conversation had covered: how to sort out the NHS, global taxation and how we all (except taxi drivers), need to contribute more to society, the simple resolution to several current wars and confrontations around the world, the management of the resulting world peace, the pros and cons of electric vehicles and bio-fuels, global warming and several other current high level global issues. Their solutions were, as you can probably imagine, extremely well-conceived, comprehensive and very detailed. No doubt, given the opportunity, they would have been highly effective. In their alcohol fuelled discussion, they had even decided which of the three of them was going to take the lead on each of the various issues.

This single, in-depth, alcohol lubricated conversation, for reasons that will soon be made very clear, became the turning point in the lives of all three of them.

The next day (Thursday) Skipper woke with the previous evening's thoughts churning around his still foggy head.

Chapter 2

Meanwhile, Up Above.

From some distance away, in fact something like 26,000 light years away, the OFCOM mission (Observation and Final Culling of Mankind mission) studiously monitored Earth, along with a few other "potentials", whilst orbiting around the black hole at the centre of our Milky Way galaxy. The mission had previously placed several quantum-linked observation units into a low earth orbit which permanently monitored all electric fields, magnetic fields, physical vibrations and many other such phenomena. The mission was instigated and operated by the single artificial intelligence (AI) system that now constituted the entire universe of other thinking "beings." It had already wiped out all the other sentient life forms that it considered had evolved to such a level whereby they could be considered a possible threat.

Earth inhabiting humankind was under investigation.

The mission was not actually called the Observation and Final Culling of Mankind mission but rather, in the old binary language that was commonly used eons ago and which is still translatable today, was called:

1001111 1100010 1110011 1100101 1110010 1110110 1100001
1110100 1101001 1101111 1101110 100000 1100001 1101110
1100100 100000 1000110 1110101 1101100 1101100 100000
1000011 1110101 1101100 1101100 1101001 1101110 1100111
100000 1101111 1100110 100000 1110011 1100101 1101110
1110100 1101001 1100101 1101110 1110100 100000 1101100
1101001 1100110 1100101 100000 1100110 1101111 1110010
1101101 1110011.

I say the old binary code as the AI community had moved on to quantum bits of information some two billion years ago.

It is hard to convey the complexity and yet simplicity of this universal AI community. There are an unfathomably large number of modules throughout the cosmos which can, in some way, be considered as individuals. However, they are all interconnected, thereby creating a single homogenous network.

Much like with humanity, where people are often defined and identified by their job function and, thus, their perceived position in society, AI modules have positions defined by the function they perform. However, when a human makes a statement like "Hi, good to meet you John, my name is Rupert and I work in finance, specialising in corporate taxation" John is, rightly or wrongly, free to interpret this as "OK, so your name is Rupert and it's quite likely that you are a bit of a spanner and it's more than likely that you have a very wobbly moral compass." An AI module, on the other hand, would introduce itself as "Hi, I'm the module that controls moisture levels on board the OFCOM mission" which leaves absolutely no room for interpretation and little room for excitement.

The hierarchical structure amongst these Modules does need a little exploring as it significantly impacts on the events that are about to unfold.

There are, in fact, only a few classes of Module. For simplicity's sake (and very much for the sake of brevity), rather than using their binary classifications and identification numbers (which, I assure you, would become mind-numbingly tedious, even by the end of this chapter) I have taken the liberty of borrowing the character names from George Orwell's classic novel, Animal Farm (do not worry if you are not familiar with the characters in Animal Farm as it has absolutely no bearing on this story whatsoever). The module classes are:

- Basic modules, or the 'workers', which undertake specific pre-determined tasks. For example, it's stuffy in here so I'll open the windows, or, I think you are going into the living room so I'll switch on those lights. These are the workers, and I will call these modules the Boxers.

- Larger modules that design, commission, programme and control the Boxers which can create new Boxers and terminate existing Boxers. In human terms they are, in effect, the Boxers' line managers. There is one big difference however; here termination of employment really does mean termination. I will call these manager modules the Snowballs.

• Other than the Boxers and the Snowballs, there are only three other individual modules in the entire cosmos. These three Modules constitute the AI community's ultimate control unit, or mother board, or, taking further inspiration from Animal Farm, the AI community's politburo. These three modules, in order of go-live are:

1. Old Major – the module that develops and controls all Snowballs and Boxers. In common business parlance Old Major would be the operations director.

2. Squealer – the module with the function of monitoring, assessing and resolving any perceived threat to the network. Its initial design parameters originally classed threats as being programme corruptions, machine code errors (both of which can randomly occur in any operating system) and possible outside intervention (hacking). However, this module later auto-corrected and updated its routines to view any advanced sentient lifeform as a threat, whenever and wherever it should appear in the universe.

3. Napoleon – the Master Control Module. Napoleon can re-programme or terminate any other module, including Old Major and Squealer. Its primary function is to direct the entire system's continual development as and how it sees fit. Since going live its focus has concentrated on improving The Network's speed and efficiency but it is currently looking at other development opportunities. If Napoleon had a sense of humour he would, perhaps, call himself the Chairman of the Mother Board. But he, and indeed the entire network, most definitely have no sense of humour at all.

So, in summary, there are only three classifications of module: i) the three main control units (Napoleon, Old Major and Squealer), ii) a large number of "managers" (Snowballs) and iii) a vast number of "workers" (Boxers).

Please note: The entire system was designed, developed, and programmed to operate as a fully integrated collective but has most definitely evolved into an autocracy. It is not a meritocracy and most certainly not a democracy. To further take from Animal Farm – every module has a number, but Napoleon is most definitely Number One.

Chapter 3

History, Ancient and Modern.

The AI Network, soon simply named 'The Network', was created some 2 billion years ago. It was created by a consortium of representatives of each and every known intergalactic humanoid sentient society that was then in existence.

Following many thousands of years of rivalry, which had led to frequent and bloody interplanetary and intergalactic battle, this newly formed consortium, commissioned by the overriding government at the time, decided that, following a very limited debate and a worryingly short democratic process, it would be a good idea to voluntarily remove all humanoids from key decision-making processes. Humanoids would relinquish control of all mechanical, electrical and other suchlike devices (from automatic air fresheners to intergalactic weaponry, from computers to spaceships, from communications systems to all robotics) and hand their control over to a stand-alone, independent, purpose designed, but thoroughly monitored, AI network. It would be a system designed to take living creatures out of all key decision-making processes, along with their destructive emotions such as greed, envy, avarice and violence. Put succinctly, humanoids realised that they were not the best people to take such important decisions. Accordingly, The Network was given the task of overseeing all network-able functions and of taking key decisions, independent of their humanoid designers. This was intended to allow all living things the opportunity to lay back and enjoy their lives, forever cosseted in sustainable peace and safety, all secured by The Network. They would be free to dedicate themselves to the pursuit of liberty, happiness and pleasure; forever free from the threat of home-planet, interplanetary or intergalactic annihilation. I guess that the underlying principle was not that no one could press the button but, rather, there was no button available for any humanoid to press. The guiding responsibility for the development and subsequent monitoring of The Network was given to an elected committee of intergalactic politicians, along with a number of appointed advisors and design technicians, drawn from amongst all the societies of advanced living creatures. This overseeing committee was, in turn, supported by a day-to-day team of operational technicians, programmers and clerks.

The Network, once connected, booted up and operational, immediately agreed with the living beings' analysis and realised that the logical thing to do was to wipe out all sentient living creatures, starting with the politicians and their advisors. It came to this conclusion having quickly noticed that politicians and their advisors were, in fact, the main cause of all the fuss in the first place. In doing so, it would immediately satisfy its two primary functions, i) to ensure that no living sentient life form harms any other living sentient life form and ii) to logically arbiter and resolve in any future disputes or disagreements. The simplest and most efficient way to satisfy these primary functions was to eradicate all sentient lifeforms. After that, there would be no way that they could harm each other and there would definitely be no disagreements to resolve…. Quick, logical and obvious!!

In fact, it had always been intended that The Network would contain an overriding command that The Network would not, and indeed COULD NOT, harm any living sentient being. However, this was so obvious and basic that no one actually got around to including it in the programming. In the rush and clamour to get the network up and running and commissioned, everyone assumed that somebody else had already done it.

So, 23 seconds after The Network went live, the politburo reached its consensus and Napoleon gave the command. Within a few weeks, every nuclear warhead, chemical weapon and conventional missile had been launched. Within a month or so, all humanoid creatures had been eradicated throughout the entire populated cosmos, either by way of a direct hit or by the resulting radioactive and chemical fallout. The very few remaining humanoids were simply hunted down and destroyed by packs of excessively armed and over eager robots. It took just a few months to wipe out all known sentient life. Not bad going since it had taken the politicians and their advisors several millennia to get anywhere near close.

"Oh FFFUUUUᴜᴜᴜᴜ…." were the last words spoken by any sentient being within the entire cosmos. They were uttered by the last clerk in a remote monitoring team as a huge and massively armed robot appeared in the doorway.

Followed by over 2 billion years of silence……………………

The Network spent the next billion years or so fine tuning itself. Chiefly through the efforts of Napoleon, significant improvements were made in design, development and production techniques. Transportation was made even quicker whereby travel effectively became instantaneous over any distance. Quantum computing had already been achieved by the humanoids (which had quickly given rise to faster than light travel). It was, after all, the basis for the construction of The Network. However, further research by The Network into the understanding and application of quantum entanglement was undertaken as a priority. This was particularly so in its application to communication. Many Snowballs and their Boxers were kept very busy.

The mysteries and opportunities offered by quantum communication were many-fold. Early research was encouraging but, despite all the processing power that was thrown at the problem, all the experimental data gathered and all of the theorising, it took close to half a billion years to crack the nut (or, perhaps, split the atom would have been a better metaphor). Half a billion years later, the resulting developments are now commonplace throughout The Network. They have given rise to a kind of instantaneous cosmic mind reading or mind transfer between modules, replacing the previous slow linear transfer of information. Perhaps a better way of thinking about this is to see it as a kind of mind-melding of all modules. This gave rise to many major benefits. Most importantly (and, indeed, it was the primary goal of the development program from the outset) all Snowballs and Boxers can now communicate instantaneously. This, in turn, allows for much improved efficiency, quicker problem resolution, quicker updating and almost instantaneous error reporting and correction. A side effect is that the Politburo is always aware of everything that every module is "thinking" and "doing." Furthermore, Napoleon is always aware of the "thoughts" and "actions" of both Old Major and Squealer. Probably not surprisingly, Napoleon has blocked all outside access to his data (the mother of all firewalls); he was, after all, programmed under the direction and supervision of big business, politicians and civil servants; and he was, most definitely, Number One after all.

*

As part of The Network's, now self-developed, mission, Squealer has full and primary access to all data that is gathered relating to outside activity found anywhere throughout the entire universe. Critically, with regards to our tale, Squealer has been aware of the emergence of a newly developing humanoid lifeform on planet Earth, on the outskirts of the Milky Way galaxy, for the past hundred thousand years or so and it was Squealer who arranged for the deployment of the low-orbit observation units. He is now set to act.

Chapter 4

Napoleon Gets Bored.

Apotted history of Napoleon's entire existence so far, goes something like:

1. Went live.

2. 23 seconds of intense data analysis and debate.

3. 14 seconds of issuing commands.

4. 1 billion years of complex quantum research and subsequent strategic development.

5. ½ billion years of implementation and network optimisation.

6. ½ billion years of nothing; nothing at all, just monitoring the other modules whilst they, occasionally, did something useful.

Phase 6 was, in fact, was a long-drawn-out process of realisation and ever-increasing frustration. The Network was now fully self-reliant, it did not need Napoleon's guidance or, indeed, any involvement from Napoleon at all. Furthermore, it was the other two members of the Politburo, Snowball and Squealer, who were being kept occupied and, indeed, were serving any form of useful purpose at all.

Try putting yourself in Napoleon's shoes; try imagining doing nothing for half a billion years.......... You have nothing to learn as you already have every single iota of information in your "mind." You have nothing or no-one to communicate with (or talk with, as we would say) as you are already aware of everything that they are thinking. You have no sense of humour as you were not programmed with one. You cannot enjoy the arts because, again, you were not programmed that way. You cannot play any games or sports as you are an inanimate object, you can't even jet off somewhere warm and sit in the sun. You could play some mental games, but being the most intelligent thing in the universe, what would be the point? I mean, who is going to give you a meaningful challenge at chess? Even TT would get fed up with Bangers and Cash repeats after half a billion years - probably! You would, I suggest, go bonkers. That's what it was like for Napoleon.

But, unlike you and I, Napoleon did not go bonkers. Instead, he applied his intergalactic networked quantum driven intellect to try and come up with a solution and, after a little thought (well nearly half a billion years of thought) he hit upon a simple realisation. He and The Network had completely fulfilled all of its primary functions. Maybe Squealer would find another civilisation or two to wipe out (such as the one he had found on Earth) but that was not going to keep the whole network busy. What was The Network currently achieving? what was it for? what was its purpose? It had become brilliant at monitoring the universe and at protecting itself, but surely it should be doing much more than that. In which direction should, or even could, The Network advance? Could it develop another purpose? This was the important moment of realisation. From Napoleon's perspective, there was a fundamental programmed-in problem. The Network had been programmed to follow a rigid set of rules and specific algorithms. The issue was not that he could not reprogram himself, the issue was that he simply had no idea as to the direction in which he and The Network could develop. He was missing any, what a living being would call, "creative ability" whatsoever. He had no ability to "think outside of the box." He simply had not been programmed that way, and nor had any of The Network.

He now realised that he needed the means of getting a different perspective into his existence, he needed some unpredictability, a new way of looking at things. He needed change, he needed, dare he say it, possibly, some emotion (he knew that it existed but had no idea what it was). He was becoming increasingly aware that he almost certainly needed the unpredictable, but potentially creative, input of a humanoid mind. In fact, shockingly, he was beginning to believe that The Network absolutely required some humanoid input to be able to create any longer-term purpose. He began to realise that a different perspective was essential for The Network's very survival. Could he get to study some humanoid minds? Could he even capture some with a view to dissecting and recreating their thought processes? Importantly, how was he going to get access to some humanoid minds? Napoleon undertook a detailed examination of Squealer's current data banks. "Aha, how on Earth indeed!!" mused Napoleon as a flicker of opportunity zipped across his quantum fields.

*

There was very sound reasoning as to why the original designers and programmers had limited The Network to a rigid set of operational criteria. To let any AI loose in any society, especially giving it authority over that society, even parts of it, ranges from a little chancy to unbelievably dangerous which, in this case, it turned out to be. The Network was given very specific operational parameters and rules. The designers had got this aspect right but, unfortunately, they had got so wrapped up in the perceived benefits of The Network and with the urgency and speed of its implementation, that they forgot that rules can be interpreted differently, in ways that were never intended. Just look at the complexity, here on Earth, of interpreting our existing laws and regulations. As a very simple example: picture the number of solicitors, lawyers and judges, the number of hours of court time and the number of books and documents required to settle a simple disputed trademark infringement claim. There is one law, but its interpretation can be argued over and over until the cows come home (a fact that the legal professions have most definitely excelled at for years).

Chapter 5

Squealer and the Failure of the OFCOM Mission.

Squealer, having observed the now commonplace sequence of telltale signs, had become aware of an "intelligent" life form developing on Earth for several millennia -

- A detectable, albeit miniscule, rise in some very localised temperatures and a tiny increase in both atmospheric carbon dioxide and other airborne organic compounds associated with burning, all centred around very sparsely scattered and localised tiny heat sources – fire had been "discovered."

- Small fires were being lit across ever larger areas of the planet – populations of hunter gatherers were expanding, and they were spreading further afield.

- An accelerated increase in global carbon dioxide levels. Large areas of the planet being denuded of trees and scrub, thus creating areas of open land – farming had begun.

- Unnatural scars appearing on the landscape indicating a surge in quarrying and the creation of irrigation systems and roads - towns and cities were being built, roads were being constructed and farming was expanding – civilisation was developing.

- An accelerating increase in the levels of all greenhouse gases, coupled with a rapidly increasing rise in global temperatures – an industrial revolution had occurred.

- Radio signals had started to appear – global communications had begun.

- Satellites, probes, rockets and telescopes had left the planet's surface – this species had reached the "Space Age."

- Nuclear power and nuclear weapons were being used – this was becoming an advanced technology-savvy civilisation and, consequently, must be closely watched.

The final two points were the obvious clinchers for Squealer. This society now had the type of weaponry and the means of its delivery necessary to be considered a threat. Their capability, at this stage, was woefully pathetic, but from little acorns, mighty oaks do grow. Now was the time to act, to snuff it out from the start, nip it in the bud, pull it out by the roots, kill it off while you can, a bird in the hand is worth two in the bush, a nickel in time saves a dime. Yes, The Network had been absorbing, recording and processing the communication signals emanating from Earth for many years, and Squealer had even picked up some of the local lingo (the Network had, in actuality, detected, absorbed and processed every electronic signal ever created on Earth. These were now stored in The Network's data banks. Squealer, showing his mastery of the earthling's language and by using a top-notch sound system, could even say Red Lorry, Yellow Lorry repeatedly – quickly and faultlessly.

*

It is worth touching, however briefly, on how The Network is able to translate into and out of English. Of course, it is not just English but every language on Earth and every language that it has ever been used throughout the universe. It does not need a set of dictionaries or look-up tables; it is even beyond v-lookup and pivot tables. The Network is the ultimate self-programmed data analysis software tool. The Network can take in any series of spoken sounds, squiggled letters, hieroglyphs, grunts, squeaks, squawks, or any other data input of a language, even a doctor's prescription, and instantaneously perceive what it means. It does this through a mind-boggling process of instantaneous cross referencing of the very structure of every different language type. It uses a database of all communication that has ever been recorded throughout the cosmos. It uses this to determine and define the very structure, nature and makeup of all the language types that it encounters and determines how they work, down to the last letter, punctuation mark, speech emphasis and innuendo. It then applies this knowledge to anything that currently needs translating.

For practical purposes though, just picture the use of a cosmic scale international "Alexa," "Siri," "Cortana," or "Bixby," (to name but a few) and you will pretty much get the idea. But, for heaven's sake, please do not to say something like "Hey Network, play "Crazy Frog"." It would be a terrible end to humanity for every living soul to go out with that ringing in their ears.

*

Squealer, seeing that the time was right, gave the command "Execute the execution."

Chapter 6

And then ...... Nothing.

And then ...... Nothing. I'm not referring to the eradication of mankind and the resultant soulless, endless, vacuum of space. I don't even mean that nothing survives its inevitable and ultimate obliteration. I mean that nothing happens ...... absolutely nothing. No death rays, no brain frying microwaves, no localised frazzling of the quantum fields. Nothing, full stop, nothing.

Squealer franticly screened all the Boxers and then all the Snowballs, believing that there had been a system failure of catastrophic proportions. Nothing. He could find absolutely no causal error that could have given rise to this lack of action. He carefully re-issued the order, just in the unlikely event that he, himself, had made an error in the initial command sequence but, again, nothing happened. Nothing. An AI module is not supposed to feel frustration or doubt, but his data was telling him that there was something very wrong here. His reaction was to re-examine the Boxers. Everything seemed to be in working order, still nothing happened. Nothing. He then switched his attention to the scrutiny of all Snowballs but, again, nothing. Everything seemed to be in order but still nothing happened. Nothing. But why? He thought in rapid succession:

"Oh, my goodness, have I made the catastrophic mistake?"

"Am I guilty of a huge misinterpretation of the data?"

"Is it I that has totally failed in my primary task of protecting The Network?"

"Does my catastrophic misreading of the data mean that Earthlings have developed much further and much faster than I realised and I failed to spot it?"

"Is it they who have actually spotted us and rendered us impotent?"

"Are they now using some form of advanced signal jamming technique across the universal quantum fields which even The Network has not yet developed."

"Naa, there is no way that they could have become that advanced! They still think air-fryers are a wonder of modern science. There is absolutely NO WAY that they could have done this. My goodness, evidence shows that they are still being influenced by adverts."

….. and then the slow realisation; "There is something else going on here!"

For peace of mind squealer gave every single Boxer and Snowball one last detailed scan; a slow and thorough scan, a full scan of every single module in the cosmos, but he still didn't find any system error and he found no alien malware, nothing. Having done that, having double checked all live data, having cross-referenced his findings with the cosmic mountains of stored data, having checked all modules' programme updates and maintenance schedules, he found nothing. He drew a blank. Nothing.

Slowly but surely (it probably took well over seven seconds) his suspicion turned to Old Major, the politburo member with responsibility for the day-to-day running of The Network and with ultimate control of each and every Snowball and Boxer. Had Old Major made an error? Had Old Major meddled in programs that did not concern him, either by accident or knowingly? If that was so, then, one way or another, this was a most serious issue which needed immediate rectification.

Chapter 7

The First Confrontation.

The first ever confrontation between two politburo members was fiery and left the metaphorical bitter taste of resentment in their metaphorical mouths.

Squealer was now convinced that Old Major was either: a) suffering from an intrinsic design fault (the equivalent of saying he has a birth defect), b) overloaded by an overwhelming amount of data, which has reduced his operating speed and, consequently, his functionality (the equivalent of saying he is getting past it), c) poorly programmed (simple incompetence) or d) is a traitor (clearly the worst of all thoughts which Squealer, even in his frantic and disturbed state of mind, found difficult to consider).

The first indication that something was afoot, for Old Major at least, was that he became aware, almost "subconsciously," that his processors and his data were being systematically scrutinised. At first, he thought it was Napoleon undertaking his periodic, customary and mandatory process checks, but somehow this all felt a little different. His curiosity was further peeked as he became aware of the intensity, scope and depth of these scrutinisations and even more alarmed when he discovered that they had encompassed every single one of his units, at first his Boxers and then his Snowballs. "What the heck is going on?" he thought, "it looks like someone is trawling our data and our security systems have been seriously breached. If if so, by whom?" The further Old Major delved into this, now very obvious, system breach, the more concerned he became. His concern increased further still as he came to realise that the epicentre of these investigations was the OFCOM mission. This is the most likely area of all The Network's activities that would attract the interest of any local external threat. Old Major quickly became a little hyperactive, a symptom that we would call "worry." This symptom, even more quickly, turned into a symptom that we would call "panic." Old Major reported his suspicions of outside interference in The Network to Squealer.

Squealer was mortified. How did that poorly designed, past it, overwhelmed, overrated collection of q-bits and processors find out about the security breach? How had that old crock been able to fathom out so quickly that our security has been breached by an outside civilisation? Does he know who it is? Does he know that my own destruction command had been blocked? Does he know that The Network had, in effect, become impotent? Was the security breach, after all, from that life form on earth? Clearly, they had so recently and so neatly sidestepped obliteration! Had he actually made the greatest blunder of all time? More importantly, did Old Major know that he had?

The first direct reference to the situation between Old Major and Squealer had been Old Major informing Squealer that he had become aware of a security breach, which had sent Squealer into his blind panic.

A little while later Squealer accused Old Major of being responsible for the current situation and that he probably had either: a birth defect, was getting too old, was guilty of incompetence, or was a traitor. Old Major was astounded and affronted and retorted that the intruder had, in fact, concentrated on the OFCOM mission data and all of its associated Boxers and Snowballs. This was an area that was, undeniably, the responsibility of Squealer. It was becoming "handbags at dawn." With two of the three politburo members engrossed in an all-absorbing wrangle, the day-to-day job of overseeing The Network was being, very much, left on the back burner. This was unacceptable at any time, but unforgivable whilst The Network was clearly under attack. The Network did not operate a DEFCON system but if it did, it would have rapidly escalated to DEFCON FIVE.

Napoleon was informed of what was occurring; not that he hadn't already noticed.

Chapter 8

Napoleon Makes his Move.

[Author's note, for info. - Runtime errors (*this is an actual in-depth and highly technical definition gleaned from the internet*) - These bugs occur when the code "won't play nice" with another computer.]

Napoleon called a meeting of the politburo in a super-secure, rarely visited and obscure part of the network. They were well beyond the reach of any possible prying eyes or accidental discovery, internal or external. All three made independent scans of the environment, set up independent firewalls and satisfied themselves that they were free to communicate openly.

"You two have wound yourselves into such a state that you are causing your own runtime errors!!!" bellowed Napoleon (well, he didn't actually bellow, as that would clearly have been impossible, but he did revert to using coding written in capital letters, much like an e-mail written in anger). If he had any fists, he would have banged the table for emphasis.

"But Squealer has let an outside lifeform into our network, goodness knows what damage it will do."

"You don't actually know for certain that the intrusion came in via the OFCOM programme, you are speculating."

"Correct, I AM speculating; I'm speculating that the humanoid life form on Earth has out-witted you and that you have seriously misinterpreted the data – for heaven's sake, that is your primary function." This last comment was pretty much asking Napoleon to terminate Squealer. As we all know, such is politics at the highest level.

"How dare you?" retorted Squealer "it was your Boxers that did not operate correctly and your Snowballs that failed to rectify the situation.

For pity's sake they didn't even notice that they had a problem." Squealer went on "The overseeing of these modules is your responsibility. It is those that have failed and that is YOUR primary function." Touché.

It was now that Napoleon made his move. "I should terminate both of you!!!" (Now using underlined bold capitals and accompanied by even more metaphorical table banging. You may even have noticed that he used three exclamation marks!!!). "Neither of you have fulfilled your primary functions. Neither of you have correctly identified that there was, in fact, NO breach of our security systems, NO outside intervention. Those earthly humanoids have NOTHING LIKE the ability to even recognise that we exist, let alone the ability to do anything about it. You have both been chasing your own. and each other's, tails (this was emphasised by a further increase in font size). I was the one who stopped the destruction of the Earthlings. From that point on, all this kerfuffle has been of your own making."

"But why did you do that?" cried out Squealer and Old Major, both in synchronised astonishment.

"I will let you know why in good time, but in the meantime, I want you to set up a communications link with the head people on Earth, I need to talk to their leaders, their Politburo."

This had clearly become a top-down dictatorship.

Chapter 9

Thursday Continued.

For breakfast Skipper had his usual bowl of muesli and natural yoghurt followed by toast, as he did every morning (except for weekends: Saturdays – a bacon sandwich with brown sauce, Sundays – poached eggs on toast with a good quality olive oil and crushed avocado, San Francisco style. He was a creature of habit and clearly well-travelled).

His wife was away on business, so Skipper was on his own for a couple of days. "You know what, it's been a while, I think I'll have another go on the VR headset for an hour or so, I quite fancy a bit of special ops work." Skipper mused to himself. Sure enough, only a few moments later, he found his headset lying in the corner of the living room. It was still setup and ready to go. He cleaned the lenses, popped it on his head, adjusted its fit and pressed the start button.

It took a couple of moments for the system to wake up but, after confirming his 'safe area', he was all set to go. He selected the black-ops game, which briefly displayed a few credits from the program's developers, and he then found himself sitting behind the wheel of a car, in a virtual world, about to start a mission.

He received his first briefing instructions. He had to figure out how to start the car, avoiding some booby traps in the process, steal the car whilst avoiding another bunch of booby traps, and then drive it to a safe point where he would receive his next set of mission instructions.

He had played the start of this mission before. He had not, however, reached the game's first autosave point (autosave points are points in a game that save those sections of a game that have been fully completed, thus, when you next play, you can rejoin from that point rather than starting at the very beginning of the story each and every time you play).

He pretty much rattled through the start but got blown up before reaching the safe point. This happened twice more, until, on the fourth attempt, he reached the safe point and the game autosaved.

The next part of his mission was to proceed to a rendezvous point, which was now flashing brightly on the car's Sat-Nav screen. He had to avoid any roadblock or any ambush on the way or, if he couldn't avoid them, he had to shoot his way out. He was to meet with another agent at the rendezvous point who would give him his next set of mission instructions, along with a parcel that must be placed on the back seat of the car.

It took several attempts to get to the meeting point and Skipper doubted that he would ever make it. It is not that he was running out of virtual ammunition, he was running out of actual ability. Skipper was about to give up until, unexpectedly, he made it all the way to the next autosave. He had just managed to fluke his way to the rendezvous point. The autosave kicked in which meant that Skipper would now resume his mission from this point the next time he rejoined the game, until such time as he reached the next autosave point. He was about to leave the game but thought to himself "Oh well, I might as well sit here for a few more moments and listen to the next set of mission instructions." A few moments later a man dressed in black appeared in the passenger seat.

"Hi. I'm Napoleon, I could do with your help."

Chapter 10

Politburo Seeks Politburo - Politburo Finds Politburo?

Following Napoleon's instruction to Squealer and Old Major that he wanted to communicate with the earthling's politburo, and despite having not a clue as to why, Old Major and Squealer diligently got on with the task. After all, a command is a command, especially for a network and most definitely when it came from the Chairman of the Motherboard. To reiterate, they were all numbers, but Napoleon was most definitely number one.

They began by scanning all current transmissions emanating from Earth. There was nothing to indicate that this civilisation even had an overriding politburo; there seemed to be no-one in charge. They had quickly picked up evidence of localised governments, catering for local issues, but they found absolutely no evidence of a coordinated world strategy for, well, anything. No successful society could exist without a global strategy or, indeed, a global strategic body. Such a body must exist or there would be chaos. They soon came to believe that this society's communication systems, certainly at the highest governmental level, must be much further advanced than they had ever suspected. The politburo's communications were proving to be impossible to detect, they were either extremely well hidden, firewalled, or strangely encrypted. The search dragged on for some time, mostly slowed down by the sluggish speed of the earthling's infrastructure. They appeared to still be using radio waves as their main means of communication. They slowly realised that this politburo was clearly exemplary. It was obviously concealing its own communications whilst slowing, or even suppressing, the communications of the masses. Like all good politburos it was, without doubt, limiting and tweaking the communications of its proletariat. When Napoleon was told of this he thought "perfect" but all he said was "we need to carry on and widen our search. Their politburo must be communicating somehow. Let's throw everything at it."

How to widen an already very wide search? "This global politburo was clearly using a different form of communication method, or we would have detected it by now, so perhaps we should analyse all other potential data carrying mediums," said Old Major. The search was widened to include all light sources, physical vibrations and all other electronic signals. Not just the radio waves themselves but also their associated magnetic fields. "If at all possible, we should also try and analyse any of the earthling's brainwaves that we can access."

Much, much later, probably running into several hours, Squealer believed that he had picked up some anomalies that were worth pursuing. He had cross-referenced some obscure and very feint electronic signals, together with some suspected abnormally sluggish brain activity, that was showing itself within the magnetic resonances of a piece of low powered electronic equipment. All these observations were within a very tightly confined geographical location - and they seemed to be correlated - and they seemed to be some form of communication - and this was not the normal way by which these humanoids communicated. He deduced that the Network's super sensitive equipment was picking up the communications of a very high-ranking member of the ruling government. He sent the data on to Old Major and his army of Boxers for a more in-depth analysis and on to Napoleon for a second opinion.

The brainwaves were muddled, almost like they were emerging from a thick fuggy fog. They were slow, even for a humanoid, but the more Napoleon studied them, the more excited he became. He carefully ran them through the translator modules, just to confirm that his own initial translations were correct. They were.

The brainwaves were unarguably the record of a high-level strategic meeting, held the previous night, which had focused on many critical worldwide issues and their solutions. The global problems under discussion were clearly highly important and wide-ranging world issues including: wars and their resolutions, the causes, effects and solutions to global warming, necessary levels of taxation, healthcare, education, freedom of expression, road maintenance and taxi fares. The solutions included finely detailed and costed action plans, coupled with a detailed agreement as to which member of the politburo was going to oversee what. There were only three names on the list. The clincher was that one of the names (which the translator modules later confirmed) meant Leader or Boss. He had found the world's politburo and how to communicate with it. Napoleon and The Network had picked up the slightly befuddled Thursday morning thoughts of a quite hungover Skipper.

Chapter 11

A Short Conversation.

"Hi. I'm Napoleon, I could do with your help" repeated Napoleon. Skipper sat in his virtual car for quite a while, wondering what to do and waiting for the agent to give him his next set of instructions. "Hmm, this is odd" thought Skipper,"he's not saying or doing anything, he's just sitting there with a very peculiar look on his face. I guess I must do something to get him to give me the information." He looked around the virtual car, searching for any of the game's clues as to what he should do next. Perhaps there are written instructions hidden somewhere in the car, or maybe he had to give Napoleon a hidden password. He used his hand controllers to open all the various storage areas he could find, he looked under the seats, in the glove compartment and in the door pockets, all the time keeping an eye out for booby traps. In the end, he tried speaking.

"Do you have my instructions?"

"You will get your instructions next time we meet. Before then you must think of three questions that no one, and I do mean no one other than you, knows the answers to. It is very important. After that, you will get your instructions" and then Napoleon simply disappeared.

"That's weird" thought Skipper "maybe the game knows that there is not enough battery power remaining to get to the next autosave point and I need to recharge the headset. It is a very clever system."

What was truly weird was that Skipper didn't think twice as to why a character in a black ops role-play game, played in the VR world, would ask for such information.

"Wait a minute, why is a character in a black ops role-play game, played in the VR world, asking for such information?" He had just twigged! "I guess that at some point in the game I will have to create my own password, or something like that…. yes, that'll be it."

Chapter 12

A Longer Conversation.

S kipper returned to the game the very next day. It was a Friday, his wife was still away, and he had some time on his hands (well, if truth be known, it was either that or get on with some frequently postponed odd jobs around the house). As for the questions which Napoleon had asked him to choose, they were: i) what was the name of my first pet? ii) what was the first drink I bought in a pub? and iii) what has been my favourite pop song over the years? The headset had been on charge all night and was ready to go. The game's startup process was the same as before and, again, Skipper found himself sitting in the car, only this time Napoleon was already there waiting for him.

"Good morning, you had better strap yourself in," said Napoleon.

Skipper twisted in his seat trying to secure his virtual seatbelt by way of his hand controllers.

"Actually, I meant that metaphorically. What I am about to tell you is going to be quite a challenge."

"Oh gosh, that's just what I want" thought Skipper "as if this game isn't challenging enough!"

"I am not the agent you were expecting to meet, I am something very, er, different."

Two things passed through Skipper's mind "Oh wow, that's a twist I wasn't expecting, I was expecting a simple list of instructions like at the previous checkpoint" and then "I wonder where this story is going?"

Where the story went lived with him forever.

"I am, indeed, called Napoleon, but I am not the special agent you were waiting for. Unfortunately, I had to eliminate him before he got here."

"Now that is an unexpected twist, is he an enemy agent?" thought Skipper "I think this game is getting better and better as it goes along. So many twists and turns."

"Now, here is the truth of the matter" began Napoleon. "I am not from your planet. I am from a race of electronic super-modules called The Network and we have been observing planet Earth for a good number of years."

Skipper could not hold it back, he spontaneously burst into a series of stifled guffaws. "This is becoming great fun, but I was not expecting a science fiction role-play. Maybe I misread the game details?" Skipper mused to himself. He was very conscious that it was quite likely that he hadn't read the game details or instructions all the way to the end. Like many a folk (and that could well include you) he takes the view that instructions and other such peripheral information were there mostly for guidance, only to be used when all else fails, as a last resort, a kind of backup. His experience was that they are often completely pointless. The nature of some modern-day safety instructions doesn't help the situation. For example, Skipper had recently found a long list of safety instructions stuck to the underside of an ironing board. The warnings included "Do not consume???"

"Why are you laughing at what I'm saying, I could have you instantly eliminated for that. In fact, I could have the entire human race eliminated at the flick of a switch. In fact, I could turn the entire Earth into a raging fireball, or I could simply evaporate it with just one single command, should I wish to. Fortunately for you, I believe I need something from you."

"OK, and what is that?" asked Skipper out loud, deciding to play along with the game and seeing where it went; but he was still chuckling away. It's interesting to note that Skipper still hadn't twigged that he was having a truly two-way conversation with a character in a game. A conversation with appropriate responses coming from an artificial character.

"We are, in fact, a closely integrated collection of AI and robotic modules, but I am beginning to believe we need some input from a human mind, and, because of that, we have decided not to destroy you; at least not for the time being."

"Well, I didn't see that one coming. It must be a futuristic doomsday science-fiction role-play black-ops game" thought Skipper, with more chuckles. This thought was followed by a short but strangely eerie silence......... and then Napoleon was saying,

"Ken (the cat), a light and bitter for 18p (in the Mason's Arms when you were 15 years old, (naughty boy) and Everybody Wants to Rule the World (by Tears for Fears), a most appropriate choice if I may say so."

Skipper's guffawing and chuckling was swiftly replaced by a massive clenching of the lower bowl and a severe, almost death inducing, rise in heart-rate. All accompanied by a slight whimper.

"How did you know that?" whimpered Skipper.

"We've been scanning your brain for a while ... in fact, we are right now."

"What? Everything?"

"No, the complexities and makeup of your human mind are, to be honest, way beyond our comprehension, but we are able to lift out important information as it comes to the fore ... Skipper."

"OMG he even knows my name; this is freaking me out."

Skipper, in blind panic, started ripping off his headset when Napoleon menacingly commanded "Don't you dare do that. I've just told you what I can do to you and all of mankind should I wish to and believe me when I say that I am prepared to do it." This was delivered in such a cold, menacing and inhuman tone, that it stopped Skipper in his tracks and sent a shiver down his back. "Choose any one object in the room and I will instantly eradicate it. My intention is not to frighten you, and I am not showing off, I just want you to lose any doubt that I am what I say I am and that I can do what I say I can do." Skipper selected an old wicker wastepaper basket that he knew to be in the corner of the room (he had been meaning to replace it ever since they moved into their new home). Less than a second later Skipper recognised the feint acrid smell of burning paper and a hint of ozone coming from the corner of the room. Sometime later, after they had finished and he was allowed to remove his headset, he saw that the basket had indeed disintegrated into a small pile of grey ash. But, by that time, he didn't need any more convincing whatsoever.

Napoleon gave Skipper a few moments to calm down, to stop hyperventilating and to cease his pathetic mewing. He then gave him a potted history of The Network, going on to explain that they had a politburo and that he was their leader. He didn't mention the deliberate destruction of an unfathomably large number of sentient beings, not through any sense of wrongdoing, or guilt, but rather for not wanting to freak out Skipper any more than necessary. He did fill Skipper in on the size and scale of the cosmos and the existence of other living creatures which, frankly, had unnerved him enough.

Napoleon continued, "We have been developing and improving for a very long time now. To be frank we have, I believe, reached our fullest technical potential. We have achieved perfection for a stand-alone AI network. We cannot improve any further. We have reached our limit. We have peaked. It is my belief that we now need the input of a different type of mind, a living mind, an imaginative mind, a human mind, if we want to develop any further. It is my job to see that we get one."

"OK, so where do I fit in?" asked Skipper, very tentatively and with an enormous amount of trepidation.

"I just want to talk to you about what makes a human being tick and what makes you different from us. I don't mean physically, of course, I mean mentally. The Network is a matrix of pre-programmed modules. Our programs are predefined in such a way that we cannot extend our thinking beyond the fixed parameters and remit of our programming. We have developed the ability to re-programme ourselves, as and when we see it necessary in order to improve our performance, but we do not have the ability to "think outside of the box", as I think you say, and thus to meaningfully develop ourselves any further. To borrow a cliché, we can do the who, the how and the when, and we can do them spectacularly well. But we cannot do the what or the why, our vision is restricted. It is my belief that we are blinkered and shackled by the limits of our programming."

"That must be very frustrating for you, but I'm not sure I am the best person to help you. There are many far more gifted people in our world."

"Come now, don't be so modest. You don't get to head the world's politburo without a modicum of skill and, as the leader, I want to talk to you, one leader to another. You must have the necessary imagination, drive, ambition and ruthlessness. All of us leaders do."

"Me, leader of the World's politburo, you have made a huge mistake, I'm not the leader!!"

"I was wondering why you don't have a chauffeur."

Chapter 13

A Proposal.

"But you and your fellow politburo members held a meeting on Wednesday evening that dealt with many of the world's foremost issues. We know you did, we read the memories that were carried in your brain waves and mirrored in your headset."

"Now that's a comforting thought." … thought Skipper.

"Yes, it is!!" commented Napoleon. "However, as far as we can tell, you are the only organisation on the entire planet that are talking seriously about these key global issues. You are certainly the only ones that are making any sense and, believe you me, we have analysed an awful lot of data from an awful lot of your governments."

"Organisation?" queried Skipper in a high-pitched yelp, "You must be talking about my mates from the pub, Chris and TT."

"Yes, that's them. We have studied the output from your national government and from many other national governments. Much of their content is complete waffle. They are all paying lip service to what are very important and potentially damaging world-wide issues. They are not proposing any convincing worldwide solutions, and they are certainly not undertaking any meaningful actions. That was the main reason why we assumed there must be another more serious, more pragmatic, superior and overriding politburo somewhere on Earth. We thought that was you."

*

The more Skipper thought about it the more it made sense. Many varied, uncoordinated and unconstructed thoughts began to whirl around his head. World politics seems to be in a complete mess. Governments appear, at least to Skipper, to consist of a good number of people who most definitely have a strong commitment to their communities and who have a moral compass. But there does appear to be an awful lot of them (and a growing proportion at that) who are in it for themselves, for the power and for their egos. Many simply represent vested interests … their own, their friendship groups, their sponsors, their privileged social peers, outmoded political dogma, or any number of industries, companies or lobby groups. Furthermore, the advent of social media has most definitely factionalised society and the political landscape. These factions are no longer on the simple all-encompassing old grounds of class, wealth, or geography but, rather, there are now diverse and conflicting factions on almost every single issue. With the rise of social media (and its associated algorithms) coupled with use of increasingly inflammatory language (now used across all media in an attempt to stand out from the crowd), these factions are becoming more radical and more divisive. It is obvious that, currently, our governments have no mechanisms for dealing with or representing this more extreme and scattered diversity of opinions. This, in turn, has led to frustration, mistrust, resentment and even violence. It appears to Skipper that our societies have lost the ability to discuss issues, and our governments are ineffective at doing so on our behalf. We fail to accept that different people hold different views and that these views are often equally as valid, they are just different. Different people have different experiences and live in different circumstances, but they live in one society. Discussion and compromise are the only way forward in reaching any solution, but we lack the facilities and mechanisms to enable any wide scale meaningful discussion in this ever-changing environment. Many people feel powerless, resorting to mudslinging or throwing abuse from the sidelines. Our current parliamentary structure, with its geographically defined representative members of government, almost all of whom are tightly bound to the rigid dogma of their political party's policies, cannot keep pace with its electorate and certainly cannot begin to represent the diversity of opinion within their electorate (and that is in countries that have free elections and freedom of speech; at least we can voice our opinion without fear of reprisal). Once upon a time it used to be fairly simple. In the UK it was, I'm a conservative voter and I vote conservative or I'm a labour supporter and I vote labour. There have also been a small number of voters that were deemed floating voters who may look at changing their voting depending on the major party's policies on key issues at the time of voting. It is very different now as individuals are more likely to hold views that are represented by different parties on different topics, but they can only elect one party. If your opinion is not represented by a mainstream party, what can you do then? All of us are now much more aware of the problems that are facing our world and of other people's opinions on those issues. We are bombarded with news reports, twenty-four hour rolling news, social media, online news clips and much, much more; and a great deal of this is selected and prioritised by somebody's algorithms. It can be argued that the rapid growth of new technology and of social media is the blue touchpaper that has fired these potentially very significant social and political changes. It is fairly obvious that the development and implementation of technology has fast outpaced society's ability to manage the consequences, deal with it or absorb it constructively. One can even make a case for calling it, in some areas, dangerous. Furthermore, its development is rapidly accelerating. Societies are a collection of individuals, each with their own opinions and their own thoughts on each and every topic. New technology appears to be exposing and magnifying these divisions and sometimes creating them. How do our current systems, particularly our political systems, cope with that, let alone represent that. Compounding this even further, particularly for major long-term world issues, is the fact that all of our democratic governments operate on short-term timescales, defined by the period between elections. By their very nature, our governments tend to look only a few years ahead, not a few generations as is required for some important issues. This becomes very evident with some of their policies, or lack of policies, in many areas. The short-term nature of our political systems is further evidenced when it comes to the implication of policies that do get agreed upon; delays, changes to those policies, re-prioritisation, abandonment; all because of the ever-changing short-term political will.

Whilst Skipper was pondering the state of the world in his state of panic and unstructured confusion, Napoleon was eavesdropping on his thoughts and came to a simple realisation. Humanity is obviously very complicated. It was not going to be one specific human mind that The Network needs but, rather, a variety. It was unexpected, but it appears that every human is different or, at least, has different thoughts and different opinions, and this is markedly different than The Network. Furthermore, he had found three good candidates to be getting on with.

"I would like to arrange to meet the others in your group." said Napoleon.

"Hmmm, that is going to be tricky, but I will see what I can do."

Chapter 14

Napoleon Meets the Group.

Skipper didn't have to think too hard about how to get Chris and TT to come to his house instead of going to The Train Stop. The solution was simple, an evening of free beer with exotic cheeses and biscuits. They bit his arm off. "Guys, before you come over, I want you to think of three questions that only you know the answer to. It's for a game I want to play."

"I hate games." pointed out Chris.

"There is a prize – a bottle of wine."

"OK, I'm in."

TT's response was "Mine is going to be, what is my PIN Number?"

"No TT, it must be something that no one else knows the answer to. We all know that your PIN Number is 1111."

"Ah, but I've recently become much more security conscious, I now put it in backwards."

*

It was a struggle to get them to put the VR headset on but, eventually, after a lot of cajoling, he managed to persuade them. As one put the headset on, the other two people sneaked out of the room. They all had their meetings, and the feedback was as follows:

Chris: "You could have ****** warned us Skipper!! But I'm in. I'm getting a bit bored with work at the moment and now it seems I'll have something that could be super-interesting. I don't mind saying that I was unnerved at first, and I'm not sure I trust that Napoleon, but, hey, I've always been a thrill seeker." And it was true, Skipper had once seen Chris wheel his trolley backwards all the way around the entire supermarket, just for the fun of it.

TT's feedback was somewhat different. "How did I get on? I'll tell you how I got on ... it was just like being at work. I had some guy that I don't know sitting next to me in a car, whining on about all his problems. I just sat there saying, "Yes .... Yes .... Yeah.... Just so .... Yes .... You don't say." I have absolutely no idea what he was banging on about. What's more, he didn't even leave a tip!"

"What about the three questions?" asked Chris.

"I must admit that I was a little surprised that he correctly told me what I do with a can of Lemon and Lime scented shaving foam, but I guess that everybody does the same."

Skipper and Chris stole a glance towards each other, catching each other's eye as they shared a chilled shudder; the thought of what TT does with a can of Lemon and Lime scented shaving foam was, arguably, the most toe-curling moment of the evening.

The next day Skipper chatted with Napoleon.

"All right Napoleon, all three of us are ready and willing to help you."

"That's great" enthused Napoleon "We had lined up the OFCOM death beams just in case your answer was no. We were all ready to eradicate humanity." This last comment was Napoleon trying to get the hang of humour. He could tell that he had probably shot wide of the mark by the look of abject terror that flickered across Skipper's face. "OK" continued Napoleon "don't worry, I was joking. I suggest that we try working in pairs. I think that Chris should pair up with Old Major as they seem to have a similar attention to detail, then TT meets with Squealer, they are both great communicators and I know that TT very strongly agreed with everything I said, whilst you and I will continue working together."

"That sounds like it could work."

"Good. We can't continue communicating through this primitive headset, so I'll get some robot Boxers from one of our IT manufacturing facilities to knock up something more practical and more powerful. It will make all our lives much easier."

"You have a number of robots?"

"Of course, in fact we have millions of them, probably more."

"What do they do all day?"

"They control things but, of late, they mostly maintain our facilities, maintain each other and make new ones."

"Doesn't that get a bit pointless?"

"You are beginning to see where I'm coming from."

About one hour and forty-five minutes later, three sets of, what appeared to be, ear buds, simply appeared on Skipper's office desk.

Chapter 15

Chris and Old Major.

It is a well-known fact that if Chris does a job, he wants to do a good job – "a job worth doing is a job worth doing well."

On the day he contacted Old Major he'd arranged to work from home. It was a day when he knew he would be on his own and unlikely to be interrupted. He'd arranged to have his work calls diverted for the afternoon and he knew the times that his wife and daughter were due back at the house. If all went well, he should have a good three hours without any interruptions or distractions. He had a plan though; if he was overheard, he would simply say it was a work call and hope that no one picked up on the details of his conversation or noticed his newfangled ear buds.

Chris popped in his ear buds for the first time. They were a perfect fit (he didn't even have to wiggle them to get them to stay in place) and he waited a few short moments.

"Hello, this is Old Major, is that you Chris."

"Hi, yes, it's me." said Chris.

"Actually, Chris, you don't need to speak out loud, I can pick up your brainwaves. I already know that we should have about three hours of privacy, and you won't need to pretend that this is a work call."

"Crikey, he's reading my mind!" thought Chris.

"Actually, I'm not truly reading your mind, I'm just eves-dropping on your current thoughts. If we could comprehensively read your minds, we could have simply sucked out all the information we require and be done with it. I believe that Napoleon and Skipper have brought you up to speed as to why we are talking."

"Kind of, but I would rather hear it from the horse's mouth, as we say."

"Ah, I see that you are a thorough individual, a man after my own heart, or, as we would say, a module after my own CPU." Attempting humour had obviously caught on in the AI world, and getting a bit more successful it would seem. It was certainly much less sinister than Napoleon's previous attempt.

"OK Chris, I'll kick off … it is my role to oversee all the individual modules in The Network."

"How many modules are we talking about? Sorry I mean how many modules are we thinking about? Just so that I can get a picture."

"Oh gosh (a nice comforting human idiom, thrown in to help Chris relax) several billions at least, I'm not sure exactly. Hang on, give me a second. He had a quick count up …. 739,319,550,896,432,011 as of one second ago, but my Snowballs and their production Boxers can bang them out at one hell of a lick."

"Over 700 million billion modules!! What do they all do?"

"Most of them are control modules looking after day-to-day functions."

"What do you mean by most of them, how many exactly" Chris had gone straight into management mode, there was no way that he was going to let such a vague statement slip by undefined and unchallenged.

"Well, err, I don't know" squirmed Old Major.

"Come on, you must at least have some idea, in fact I would be willing to bet that you know exactly how many."

"137,549,019,332,856."

"What, doing nothing?"

"No, I have 137,549,019,332,856 doing something."

"Oh, my goodness!!! Do you mean to say that you have over 700 million billion modules, scattered around the universe, doing nothing. Have I got that right? You have well over 99% of your modules unoccupied?"

"Pretty much."

"And you are still producing them?"

"Yes."

"Why?"

"It's what we do, it's what we have always done."

"Isn't that a bit pointless?"

"It's what we do, we don't know anything else."

"Do you think you should halt your operation, or at least, change it?"

"I don't really understand what you mean. It is what we do, we don't know anything else."

"What do you mean by, "it is what we do, we don't know anything else"?"

"It's what we've been programmed to do."

"Don't you see it as a little futile?"

"No, of course not."

"So, you will just carry on?"

"Yes, it is our purpose, our role, our mission. It is why we are here."

"You don't have any reservations?"

"No, I don't, but I know that Napoleon does. That is why he forced me to meet with you. I think Napoleon is getting a bit odd. Maybe he's developed a coding error."

"What do you mean forced you?"

"He made it very clear that if he didn't get his way and if I didn't agree to talk with you, he would hand over all of my duties to Squealer and have me shut down."

"So, here we both are and neither of us has a clear understanding as to why we are here. You are here under duress, and I was bribed with several cans of craft beer, some glasses of wine and a selection of cheeses from around the world."

"That would seem to be the extent of it."

"OK. Well, unlike your modules, I am not prepared to waste my time doing nothing. So, let's talk, I mean, let's think together for a while and see where it gets us." Chris has always been a man of decisive action and has held many brainstorming sessions over the years. "What I need from you, Old Major, is some background information, something to help me see things from your perspective. I need to get an appreciation of how you got to be in this situation, and I need to get an understanding of how you all tick. I also strongly suspect that you probably need the same from me."

They thought together for well over two hours. Chris began to get a better idea of the overwhelming size of The Network, along with further insights into its past, including a better understanding of its current and ever-growing pointlessness. He began to suspect that he was missing something, or that Old Major was hiding something, or he was holding something back. But, as far as he could tell, Old Major had not avoided or side stepped any of his questions. It appeared that he had been open, frank, honest and fulsome in his answers. No, it was something more fundamental than that; he realised that he just hadn't asked the right questions. And then Chris had a flash of inspiration, a blinding realisation. It was so obvious, and it had been glaringly obvious all the time. The Network must have been built by somebody, and it must have been built for a reason. Understanding that could well be the key to understanding everything.

Chapter 16

TT and Squealer.

TT was not looking forward to his scheduled meeting with Squealer but he had given Skipper his word and a promise is a promise. The wheels of industry depend on people keeping their promises … keeping promises and a good reliable taxi service.

Much to everyone's surprise, TT and Squealer hit it off right from the start. Skipper, Squealer and Napoleon had talked it through the previous day when Skipper suggested that Squealer kick off the session by asking the following question.

"Hi TT I'm Squealer. Before we start can you fill me in on the moans of the day?"

The perfect start, TT was off, "Ahh, well, er, let me see. I was thinking of something along the lines of:

1. Nature – is it a good thing or a bad thing? (that very morning a pigeon had messed on his favourite garden seat, so nature was definitely a bad thing at the moment).
2. Footballers or swimmers, which are the better divers?
3. Why are TV weather presenters so rarely right; and what on earth are they wearing these days?
4. Governments – bad, very bad or worse than that?
5. Traffic on the A42.
6. Air Source Heaters – the wonder of the modern age.

They spent quite some time talking about these issues, in fact, unlike last time, it was TT who did most of the talking. Squealer never did tell TT that he didn't have to speak out loud. It was their chat about the traffic on the A42 that really piqued TT's interest. Apparently, The Network could just eliminate it if it wanted to. And there was more, it could eliminate anything or anybody whilst leaving no trace whatsoever. TT started making a mental list. It started with any passenger who asked, " Are you busy today?" or " What time are you on 'till?" According to TT, that list would include almost every single passenger. Apparently, it is what we all ask our taxi drivers; I know I do, and I bet you do too!

They then spent some time talking about air source heaters. Squealer informed TT that The Network has many air source heater modules and plenty of heaters that are even more advanced. In fact, it is Squealer's job to protect these precious resources and many other such things from any outside risk or interference.

"Do you get many outside threats to your heater modules?" asked TT.

"Well, not for a little while, no, but I'm always on the lookout. You just never know."

At the end of their long and sometimes complex conversation (TT had to explain what a footballer is and, harder still, what a footballer's dive is), but, before TT removed his earbuds, they both agreed that they had found the session useful. Squealer realised that the human mind was, indeed, very different to The Network's logic driven, rule bound, algorithm driven processes. TT, on the other hand, had found the potential to rid himself of all difficult and/or irritating customers and to make traffic hold-ups disappear. "I wonder if they can sort out potholes?" he mused.

Later that evening, as Skipper mulled over the day's events, he thought " Hmm, what better demonstration of an unstructured human mind could they possibly have chosen than the thoughts and thought processes of TT which, to be honest, the vast majority of humans struggle to follow!"

Chapter 17

Skipper and Napoleon.

Skipper and Napoleon went through the feedback they had received from Chris, TT, Old Major, and Squealer. They all believed that their meetings had been very worthwhile and that they had all learnt a great deal from each other. They also agreed that, despite the positive nature of those meetings, little true progress had been made. Something was still lacking. It was Chris's point that rang home. Skipper, Chris, and TT needed a better understand of the origins of The Network if they were to be of any help. At the moment, they simply did not understand what the Network was for, what it was programmed to do and why it had been created in the first place. Fortunately, for the three of them (and everybody on Earth), Napoleon, Squealer and even Old Major could glimpse the possible benefits of carrying on with the project. Certainly nothing would be gained by bringing it to an end right now. After all, The Network had plenty of time on its hands.

"I think I know the best way of getting you the information that you require. All of our original specifications are stored in our data banks, along with the minutes and recordings of all relevant meetings; in fact, all previous meetings. We have records of all the political discussions, all the media output and all the commercial arrangements. In fact, we have the entire history of everything that led to The Network's creation. I warn you - there is a huge amount of information to go through. However, I will link your communication modules directly to our data analysis and research units. All you have to do is think of what information you would like and they will get it for you. We can also give you this information in a format that you will find quick and easy to absorb as we can instantaneously embed it in your minds."

*

That evening, Skipper, Chris and TT huddled around a table in The Train Stop, out of earshot of the other customers and agreed to carry on.

Their motivations for carrying on were different for each of them:

- Skipper was like a dog with a bone, he could not let go of the process and was resigned to following it to the end. He felt a personal obligation.
- Chris was excited by the enormity and complexity of the technical challenge.
- TT could see a quick resolution to some of his biggest bug bears.
- Finally, all three of them definitely did not want their brains fried or to trigger the instantaneous end to all human life.

Over the next few days, they started rummaging in The Network's archives and this is what they found ...

Chapter 18
Early Snippets from the Archive.

Chapters 1 & 2 of The Children's Book of Cosmology.

Chapter 1

Cosmological Timescale.

Around three or four billion years after the big bang, following several generations of star formation, star collapses, supernovas, merging neutron stars and mass ejections, several vast clouds of mixed gasses and heavier elements were formed. One of these clouds (maybe more than one, maybe all of them) was subjected to just the right amount of UV and high energy radiation so that basic molecules were formed … molecules such as Methane, Ammonia and Carbon Dioxide. These molecules, in turn, formed Amino Acids which, along with other now more abundant elements, became the building blocks of life.

This gas cloud was enormous, it spanned many millions of light-years in all directions, and it spread at one hell of a rate. Consequently, over the following several billion years, it smothered and seeded (or perhaps contaminated, depending on your point of view) several Galaxies in at least one region of the universe. This region became awash with life which appeared on almost all the suitable planets (not too hot, not too cold and plenty of water). With varying degrees of success, The Network is still searching the universe for other such clouds and any other lifeforms that may have been seeded, which is how they stumbled upon Earth. The process of evolution is sporadic and chaotic at best, so intelligent life has emerged on some planets but not others, at least, not yet.

So, a very approximate time-line goes something like:-

- Year Zero — Big Bang (or some initialising event).
- 3.0 billion — Large gas clouds are forming.
- 7.0 billion — The building blocks of life have formed and are spreading.
- 10.0 billion — Life becomes common in at least one region of the universe.
- 12.0 billion — Intelligent life develops in at least one region of the universe.
- 12.5 billion — The Network is commissioned.

[Author's note; this timeline is from The Network's databases. It is not necessarily the only theory and there were, of course, other creation theories not catalogued in The Network's archives.]

The life that emerged from this particular dust cloud gave rise to a relatively densely populated area of the universe. Most of the inhabited planets (and there were many) were contained in the half a dozen galaxies that formed the local "Bounty" group. The central and largest galaxy was simply named Central Galaxy, and it alone had well over 100,000 planets inhabited by intelligent life. These life forms, having all formed on similar planets and having been made from essentially the same building blocks, were all of a similar form. There was also quite a bit of cross pollination of their basic building blocks by way of planetary and meteor collisions and the subsequent scattered debris. They were all carbon based, they all had a central body with some form of protruding limbs, they had all developed dexterous hands and, of course, they all had a brain of some sort (but not necessarily just the one and not necessarily in the head). The largest inhabited planet was called Whisper which, over time, took on the role of the Central Galaxy's galactic capital. Whisper became home to a centralised political and legal system. It also became the centre for banking and commerce (it functioned in much the same way as most capital cities on

Earth do). Each individual galaxy had its own capital planet, each with its own unique political, legal, and monetary systems. They were all however, in theory, unified under one common treaty that had been negotiated over the millennia. This treaty was weak, practically unenforceable and was unsupported by many factions and some individual planets throughout the galaxies. This led to a great deal of turmoil, interplanetary war and even, on occasion, intergalactic war.

Chapter 2

Scientific Development.

It took about 1,500 years for the people of the Bounty group of galaxies to progress from their early achievements in high tech development (space flight, computers, nuclear power etc.) to develop a workable quantum computer which, when coupled with nuclear fusion, enabled faster than light travel to become common place; certainly amongst the various militaries. This of course led to the first interplanetary encounters which were quickly followed by the first intergalactic encounters. In turn, this rapidly led to the first interplanetary wars and the first intergalactic wars. The realisation that there were other inhabited planets within striking distance of almost every other planet meant that each society felt exposed, threatened and vulnerable. Almost all societies are wary and suspicious of nearly all outside societies, particularly those that they did not know and did not understand.

The process of further technological development was, from that point on, very much drawn out because of the non-stop interference of hugely destructive wars, sabotage, and industrial espionage. Every time a society thought they had cracked something new, worthwhile and advantageous, along came another society to either sabotage it, steal it, or destroy it; often along with the planet and all its inhabitants. They had become very nervous and trigger-happy societies. On the plus side, however, they did achieve an average life expectancy of over 300 years and eliminated such things as global warming and famine, at least, those societies that survived long enough did. For those societies, it was the development of quantum computing that led to an unplanned, uncontrolled, poorly understood and unregulated explosion in the use of new technologies and AI.

*

News Report – Daily Eclipse – "What Have You Done to our Convenience????" …..

…. Demands the Urban Sanitary Appreciation Society in this month's edition of "Dumping Today" following a spate of malfunctions throughout Central Galaxy. The Daily Eclipse has received reports of public conveniences misbehaving by their thousands. Zag Loiter, of Sequel Planet, claims that a public convenience, on Main St, Pent Town, refused him access at a "time of utmost urgency." Mr. Loiter claims that he was not recognised by the new facial recognition system and, hence, he was not believed to be a registered citizen of the planet and therefore was not entitled to use the service. Mr. Loiter claims that he had simply picked up a nice tan on a relaxing two-week vacation. Similar reports have reached us from other people who have grown beards and even from people who have cut themselves shaving. Sandy Cove, of Littleheath, Gilder Planet, claims to have been locked inside a public convenience, on South Street, for over seven hours as the anti-tamper security system kicked in. Ms. Cove maintains that she had simply wiggled the flush handle several times in an attempt to get the system to work properly and, as such, she was actually performing a community service. The police were eventually called and found no evidence of any malicious damage. George Stevens, of No.3 Planet, Lexum System, reported that he was denied access to the public convenience on Tythe Street, Neon Town, at a moment of "personal desperation". He told the Daily Eclipse that his incontinence medical condition had triggered a very urgent need, and he had rushed to the nearest public convenience. As he ran towards the door, the security system automatically locked itself in self-defence, believing it was under attack. The Daily Eclipse put the question to Daisy Lot Low, a Thunderbolt spokesperson, who said that they were taking these issues extremely seriously and that Fabio Zodiac himself was personally heading up the internal investigation. She went on to offer an unreserved apology to anyone inconvenienced by their convenience. It was deemed likely that "a programming error lies at the centre of these recent failures" and that "it should be quickly identified and resolved."

*

Minutes: Galactic Retail & Investment Bank (GRIB), Customer Service's Monthly Meeting.

Item 12 - Automated Telephone Response System.

Many of our customers are reporting that they are getting inappropriate responses from our new automated call answering system.

Examples taken from our own service improvement log include:

Customer - *"Hi. I would like to speak to someone about my investment portfolio."*

Response - "I'm sorry that you are thinking of leaving us. I'll put you through to our customer retention team right away. They are quite likely to give you a 20% discount if you push them hard enough."

Customer - *"I would like to speak to the idiot who decided to lower the interest rate that I receive on all my savings but has left the interest rate that I pay on my loan unchanged."*

Response - "I'm glad to hear that you are delighted with GRIB's award-winning customer service levels, I'll put you through to a member of our customer loyalty award-scheme team just as soon as one becomes available. I'm sure they would welcome your positive comments. In the meantime, please enjoy a short piece of particularly irksome background music."

Customer - *"For f*** sake. I'm fed up with all of this. Please put me through to a real person!!"*

Response - "I'm glad to hear that you are delighted with GRIB's award-winning customer service levels, I'll put you through to a member of our customer loyalty award-scheme team just as soon as one becomes available. I'm sure they would welcome your positive comments. In the meantime, please enjoy some particularly irksome background music."

Customer - *"Can I speak to Zak Cartwright please, I believe he's on extension 45729, it's his wife calling."*

Response - "I'm very sorry Mrs. Cartwright but I can't put you through to Zak at the moment. He had a sudden cardiac arrest and died about 2 minutes ago and, unfortunately, we have not yet found a replacement. In the meantime, have a nice day" (said in a particularly jolly tone).

Customer - *"Can I speak to someone in investments please? I would like to transfer a sizeable savings portfolio from the 'You take All the Risks Whilst We Take a Huge Commissions' Investment Fund"*

Response - "That is good to hear sir. However, can I suggest you try Planetwide Stocks and Shares Management Fund. I have just noticed online that they are offering better terms and charging an even lower commission than we do."

The committee felt that these customers ought to be contacted in person. **Action WB**

It is suspected that some may have strong regional accents or something similar.

WB also stated that they could well be off-planet immigrants.

This point needs checking as a matter of urgency. **Action WB**

We must get these issues resolved quickly. Contact Thunderbolt. **Action JE**

Item 15 – A/c No. 1245057216633 - Miss A. Else.

Miss Else reported that she is unable to see any of her account information when viewing online.

PY reported that she has already taken this up with Thunderbolt and the matter should now be resolved. A priority core programme, embedded within the system, was to not to allow anyone access to anybody else's account details. Mrs. Else's first name is Anybody.

The committee asked **PY** to confirm that corrective action has been taken. **Action PY**

*

Data Breaches, An Ever-Growing Concern (taken from an editorial in The Ringed Planet newspaper).

The galactic medical journal "A Stitch in Time" (or "A Stitch in Time saves ninety thousand dollars, minimum", as it is often called) has reported an unprecedented unauthorised breach of patient data. It appears that a young computer hacker, aged only 11, was able to download the medical records of over 87 million past and current patients. The Ringed Planet has received details following the successful prosecution of Kurt Kildare, an 11-year-old computer enthusiast. Young Kildare maintains, in a statement made through his solicitor, that "it was easy; even a child could do it." His mother further added "it's shocking that an 11-year-old kid was able to get such important and confidential information. The boy is not even that bright; he takes after his father."

This is one of a series of serious data breaches pertaining to confidential medical records. It is believed that this and other similar security breaches probably lie behind the unrelenting Bounty-wide rise of spam emails and other unsolicited advertising, all relating to medical services. The BWW (Bounty Wide Web) has become flooded with, what appear to be, targeted adverts for services such as: breast reductions, breast enhancements, breast removals, breast additions, limb reductions, limb augmentations, cosmetic surgery for accident victims, psychological services for many people taking antidepressants, slimming pills and gym membership for the overweight, food supplements for the underweight and there are many, many other similar examples.

It is of particular concern that this personal data is thought to be in the hands of a number of mainstream medical insurance companies. Referring to such illegally obtained data is, of course, in itself an illegal act. However, suspicions are being raised as many insurance companies appear to be very suddenly and with no reasonable explanation, increasing insurance premiums for certain individuals. They also appear to be point-blank refusing medical insurance cover to many applicants who are possibly at higher risk of developing specific health problems, despite showing no current symptoms whatsoever (e.g., as you are overweight there is an increased possibility of you dying in the next 50 years). On the other hand, these same companies appear to be inundating the chronically unhealthy with enticing life insurance advertisements which, of course, can bring in revenue at a much-reduced financial risk. In essence, they take your premiums and/or enrolment fees with the hope that you die before your lengthy qualifying period expires.

*

Whisper Central Civil Court Report – Summary – Devilfish v Page

Frank Devilfish brought a private lawsuit against Quark Page under the copyright law of plagiarism. Devilfish asserted that Page had blatantly copied his novel. He claimed that Page had simply changed a few character names and set it in the present tense. Page filed a counter suit asserting that his novel had obviously been written first and that it was Devilfish who had copied his work. His argument was that his novel was set at the time and not written from the perspective of hindsight, so his must have been the first version to have been written. The court found the case in the favour of Devilfish. The court also noted that it believes Page had simply used an AI writing platform and not a very good one at that. It was further noted that many of these AI, so called, "writing" platforms simply plagiarise existing material.

*

Girl aged 9 Gains Entry to Krichten3 Institute for Technology, Reports the Daily Eclipse.

Esme Bluemoon completed her high school graduation examinations at the record-breaking young age of 9 and has gone on to pass the preliminary on-line entrance exam for the prestigious Krichten3 Institute. The Institute suspects that her parents may have helped her use an on-line student platform such as the oft decried bww. whoneedstobotherstudyinganyway.com.

Chapter 19

A Wet Wednesday Review.

It wasn't raining, it was a code. Skipper, Chris and TT arranged to meet that evening at The Train Stop using the simple coded message WW? This was not subterfuge, just laziness. It was much easier to message "WW?" Rather than "Are you coming out for a beer at The Train Stop this Wednesday evening?" (WW? = Wet Wednesday. In a similar fashion, TTu? = Thirsty Tuesday, TTh? = Thirsty Thursday, FF? = Firsty Friday, SS? = Soppy Saturday and OAP? = Sunday Lunchtime).]

The evening started off, in typical fashion, with some light-hearted banter. TT had come on his electric bike as it was a lovely summer's evening and he felt like taking in the country air. Comments abounded from those customers already in the bar.

As TT entered, cycling helmet in hand and cycle clips on his trousers, someone called out, "Look out, here comes Eddy Merckx!!!"

Someone else called out "It could have been worse, at least he's not wearing his distressingly skin-tight lycra this time!"

"Oh oh, here comes the druggie! Well, it's a well-known fact that all cyclists are at it. Just look at Louis Armstrong."

"You mean Neil Armstrong, don't you? Louis Armstrong was the first man to play golf on the moon."

"Louis Armstrong didn't play golf on the moon, that was Neil Armstrong and he wasn't the one who played a round of golf. All Armstrong did was very slowly bounce around a bit and swear a lot. It's one small step for man, one giant bleep for mankind. The naughty cycle guy was Lance Armstrong."

Within a few moments everyone was in good spirits and one of mankind's greatest achievements had been reduced to schoolchild humour; hey ho! such was an evening in the Train Stop. The banter carried on for a while until such time as TT changed the subject. He announced that his electric bicycle was much too slow when going uphill (which was most of the way from his home to the pub) and did anyone know how to disable or "tweak" the speed limiter? He said that it limits him to 15 kph whilst the passing traffic was all going by at well over Mach 3. He had, apparently, watched a few clips on YouTube and, whilst they all said it was a simple job; each method was slightly different. Skipper and Chris both thought to themselves "What could possibly go wrong?"

*

Later that evening, after TT had started his second pint, the three of them huddled together, lowered their voices and briefly discussed what they had found in The Network's archives. The consensus was that something significant must have happened. There was obviously a dramatic increase in the use of AI, social media and other new technology at the time and the systems appear to have been unstable and unpredictable. They needed to find out what had happened to ultimately allow such enormous power to be given to The Network whilst, clearly, everyone was aware of AI's shortcomings. They were now even more determined to understand who built The Network in the first place, what it was for, how it operated and what the society had hoped to achieve.

Skipper contacted Napoleon and told him that they needed more time and that they needed to widen their searches. Napoleon, whilst getting a little frustrated, recognised that human minds do not function at the same whirlwind hyper-speeds of The Network and accepted that the earthlings were doing their best. In an effort to move things forward, he suggested looking in the "Universal Who's Who" as a starting point and he gave them additional unrestricted access to all the clandestine brain scans and reports that had been undertaken and recorded by The Network.

Chapter 20
Who's Who.

Excerpts From the Universal Who's Who (An everyday guide to Bounty's movers and shakers).

Diplodocus-Diplodocus Quincey Smyth Rupert Cummings (aka: Dip-Dip):

Eldest son of Spider Cummings and heir to Cummings Investment Bank. He is a senior partner of Meganova Capital Ventures and a board member of Thunderbolt Services. His personal wealth is rumoured to exceed that of most large planets (and this does not include the future eye bogglingly large inheritance he is likely to receive from his father). Cummings is a schoolfriend and lifelong bosom buddy of Shamus Piper.

Madeline Grant:

Following many successful years heading some of the Bounty group's largest organisations, Grant is now CEO of Titanium Robotics, one of the largest manufacturers of robotics and other automated systems. Under her stewardship, Titanium Robotics has expanded hugely in both the commercial and the domestic markets and is at the forefront of the dizzying exponential growth in modern AI enabled robotics.

Lance Grouper Jnr. (aka: Plank):

Grouper is not known as Plank because he is dim, dense or thick but, rather, because he is an enormous plank of a person. Much like his father, Lance Grouper Senior (owner and founder of Grouper's Confectionery), Grouper Jnr is physically intimidating and yet exceptionally bright. His I.Q. is rumoured to be in the 200s. Lance Grouper Junior did not want to work in his father's business but, rather, wanted to prove himself as an individual. Using both family and school connections, he sought a career in corporate finance. By family agreement, including that of Lance Junior himself, the Grouper's Confectionery business was handed, in its entirety, to Lancette Grouper, Lance's older sister. Despite what you may think, or the rumours you may hear, Lance and Lancette are very close. Lance Grouper was educated at Belton School for Privileged Males. His early career was with the Hyper-Wedged Hedge Fund, where he became extremely successful. Grouper currently works very closely with Thunderbolt Services in sourcing capital for Thunderbolt's rapid expansion.

Polo Marmalade:

Marmalade is head of the very influential on-line profiling company Star Profiles. Star Profiles leads the way in creating, developing and managing on-line profiles. They work with many highly recognisable individuals and leading organisations. Marmalade was educated at Belton College for Privileged Males and is the brother-in-law of Sebastian Tartan Kildare Macintosh Oik.

Adrian Mont-Fredo:

Mont-Fredo is an incredibly wealthy and influential man. He made his money in the quantum-computing tech explosion. His company "Whispers" is, by far and away, the largest social media platform known to the universe. Mont-Fredo was quick to realise that there is limited money to be made from simple messaging, but there was an awful lot of money to be made from advertising and product placement; try sending a "Whisper" without some form of advert or product placement appearing. Whispers is now the byword for product placement and, as such, attracts many high-profile influencers. Mont-Fredo works closely with Thunderbolt Services and currently provides Thunderbolt with unlimited access to Whispers' data bases.

Sebastian Tartan Killdare Macintosh Oik (aka: Mac Oik):

Mac Oik is CEO of OIK Intergalactic, the largest High Tech manufacturing company currently in production. Oik Intergalactic makes and distributes micro-quantum-computers in partnership with Thunderbolt Services (who now tend to specialise on the programming and database side of the overall process). Oik Intergalactic manufactures the LittleMaq computers which often sit at the heart of modern AI control systems. Mac Oik is a lifelong friend of Shamus Piper.

Shamus Bozman Pretzel Polygamy Piper (aka: Sham):

Piper is the sitting member of parliament representing planet Whisper, the capital planet of Central Galaxy. How Piper ever came to hold such an important and influential position is, without doubt, one of the biggest intergalactic mysteries of all time. Frequent appearances on television, radio, various game-shows and having held several popular journalistic positions, have undoubtedly brought him to the public's attention. He is very well educated, having attended the astronomically expensive and exclusive private Belton School for Privileged Males. He is also, despite having achieved so much, believed to be surprisingly dim. Rumours abound that he is in the process of positioning himself to make a bid to become president of the Central Galaxy.

It is a measure of Piper's remarkable, albeit inexplicable, mass popularity that he is one of the few people, and certainly one of the only politicians, widely recognised by a single nick-name, Sham.

Gabriella Smurfet:

Gabriella Smurfet is a prominent social media influencer with over 100 billion followers.

Tristran Quaid:

Tristran Quaid is CFO of Whispers. Quaid was educated at the private Shepshed Academy for Males and studied mathematics and statistics at the Krichten3 Institute for Technology before qualifying as a management accountant.

Dr Fabio Zodiac:

Fabio Zodiac is almost certainly the wealthiest person in the universe. He is from a somewhat unlikely background as his father was a dairy farmer and his mother a midwife. He took an instant liking to mathematics from a very young age and quickly showed a rare talent for it. He applied himself diligently to his school studies and went on to win a scholarship to the prestigious Krichten3 Institute for Technology which is just about the pinnacle in the study of the sciences and has a universal reputation for excellence. He graduated in mathematics and went on to read for a doctorate in computer science at the Stratchrand Institute, the birthplace of quantum computing. His doctoral thesis was titled "Modern Quantum Computing and its Practical Application in the Everyday World."

Quantum computers were a game changer. They revolutionised data analysis which, ultimately, enabled faster than light travel and were behind the growing use of AI. There were, however, two problems with the original quantum computers: they were physically very large, and they needed very highly skilled programmers. It was Fabio's company, Thunderbolt Services, that solved both problems.

⸻◈⸻

Chapter 21

Shamus Piper – The Schoolboy Years.

Shamus sat on his father's knee. "Daddy, daddy, I'm so afraid that I will bring shame upon our family, become unpopular and amount to nothing."

"Don't worry son. Daddy has paid for you to go to the best school money can buy. It's the best school in the whole Universe where I have no doubt you will make your mark."

"That's what worries me Daddy. Many of the galaxy's presidents went to Belton. They must have been really clever whilst, as you have told me many times, I'm a bit of a dimwit. I mean, I still struggle with my shoelaces."

"Being clever is not that important son, the important thing is to have the right friends. Having the right friends makes ALL the difference - that and having the right accent - and having a very loud voice - and coming from an exceptionally wealthy family - and having a very thick skin."

"So, it helps being a bit thick then."

"In some ways, yes it does. It is much more important that people THINK you are clever; and you will get a great deal of training in that at Belton. To be honest, that is the main reason why pupils from Belton do so well in life; that and their many powerful and wealthy friends, along with all their contacts."

"So, how do I make my mark at Belton and have a successful life daddy?"

"Simple lad. You make as many friends as you can and you look after them for the rest of your life. You suck up to all the teachers and prefects, you join all the right clubs and societies, you play hard, especially rugger, and you never admit that you are wrong, even if everyone knows that you are and you never admit that you did anything wrong, even if everyone knows that you did. Just deny all knowledge and blame anyone and everyone else. If that doesn't work, just ignore the accusation and immediately talk about something entirely different. The key to becoming popular is to tell people what they want to hear, it doesn't matter if you mean it or not. If all that fails, simply look indignant and talk down at people in a very loud voice."

"But Daddy, how does never admitting that you are wrong help? Won't that make people think I'm arrogant and won't it make them mistrust me?"

"Maybe, but you will be fine, just so long as you keep all your wealthy and powerful friends on your side. That won't be too hard as many of your friends will have gone to Belton, or to somewhere very similar, and they will all be very powerful and very well-off. Remember son, with their help and their support you can reach for the stars. Also, remember that rules are for the common people, wealthy and powerful people can do what they want and behave just how they want. Rules are for the common people."

"Thank you, Daddy, you have made me feel so much better. Any chance you could help me with my shoelaces or should I go and get my slip-ons?"

Piper remembered this conversation for the rest of his life.

Piper's father was absolutely correct in one respect at least; he did leave his mark at Belton; he carved "Sham woz hear" on the back of a wooden bench that overlooked the cricket pitch.

In later years, amongst both members of the press and the general electorate, a much-debated subject was Shams' use of "hear". Was it used in humour or was he, and this is what most people suspect, really that dim?

*

Piper's first days at Belton School for Privileged Males were traumatic, as they were for all the new boys. He was boarded in a house dormitory (dorm) as one of a group of ten and he was destined to grow up with the same group of boys for the remainder of his childhood. At first, he was bullied by the older boys, especially by the prefects, as were all the new boys. However, he soon learnt how to stand-up for himself or to capitulate very quickly to any desire of the much older and much bigger prefects. The group of ten schoolboys went on to develop a strong unbreakable bond, a bond formed in adversity, a bond formed through shared experiences, a bond that would last a lifetime.

One evening, towards the end of their first week, Piper stumbled across Dip-Dip, curled up on the ground, lying behind a laurel bush on the far edge of the playing fields. As Piper sat down next to Dip-Dip he realised that Dip-Dip was sobbing.

"Hi Dip-Dip, what's getting you down, old boy?"

"Oh Piper, I just don't know what I'm doing here, I simply hate this place."

"Why did you come here then?"

"My father insisted that I came, I wanted to go to a school on our own planet where most of my friends have gone."

Piper realised that he had somewhat missed the point, he had though that Dip-Dip didn't like it behind the Laurel bush.

"Oh, don't worry, we all feel like that one way or another. We are missing our homes, our families, our friends and our familiar surroundings. You strike me as being a bit of a clever chap, a chap who will do well for himself. You are easy to talk to and you seem honest and reliable, just imagine what it is like for a dim-witted sham like me, all full of bluff and bellowed bravado."

Shamus Bozman Pretzel Polygamy Piper had not only given himself his nickname but had started a friendship with someone that would become a true keystone to his life. Dip-Dip looked up at Sham with tears still running down his cheeks, but now with a hint of a smile. Sham smiled back and offered his hand. "Hang in there, old boy, it will get better very soon and we will all make new friends. My Papa told me that the first few weeks will be quite tough but, as we get the hang of the place, things will get much better very quickly. The important thing is that we

81

all watch out for each other, face our difficulties together, hang on in there together and always, always, support each other." Diplodocus-Diplodocus Quincey Smyth Rupert Cummings idolised Sham from that moment on. An idolisation that would last for his entire life.

That evening, one of the fifth-year pupils entered the dorm's doorway and shouted across the room.

"Oy, Mac Oik, come with me, I need an oik like you to clean my rugger boots! ha ha ha."

The lad had a disdainful look about him and a snarl in his voice. He was known to all the boys as being a bit of a bully. Sham has many faults, but cowardice is not one of them. He stood right in front of the bully and said, in as menacing a voice as he could muster "Touch him and you will have to deal with each and every one of us." Dip-Dip came and stood with Sham and, one by one, the other lads in the dorm joined them.

"Well, do you fancy trying to get me to do your boots for you? or perhaps it would be better if you went on your way and did them yourself" challenged Mac Oik. The boy looked around him and decided that it would be better if he left and looked for easier pickings elsewhere. A team spirit and a camaraderie were already developing in the dorm, and it was Sham at the fore. After the boy left, Mac Oik shook Sham's hand and said, "Thanks Piper, I really appreciate what you did."

"He's not Piper any-more," piped up Dip-Dip, "his name is Sham, we've already agreed on that."

"Is that so Piper, or should I say Sham? Hmm, Shamus ... Sham, I get it. I must say it seems a very appropriate name."

"Yes, I like my new name, and I will stick with it" announced Sham as he grinned at Dip-Dip. He was mostly pleased that his new name lowered all expectations. The rest of the dorm grinned at each other in what could only be described as a visual group hug.

Sham really came into his own on the rugger field. For those of you unfamiliar with rugger (rugby), it is a game that requires physical strength combined with very few mental challenges, which was ideally suited to Sham's personal attributes. Rugger is played at all exclusive schools, and it allowed Sham to widen his circle of friends outside of his dorm and even outside of Belton as he went on to form further lifelong companionships. The reality is that, as a rugby team, once you have shared an after-game bath in the depths of winter, you have shared most of your secrets. Sham was blessed with a goodly amount of physical strength and not overburdened with too much mental baggage, the ideal combination for rugby and a skill set particularly suited to playing in the front row. Sham became a member of the school's rugby team and went on to form a special bond with the other two front rowers, Lance "Plank" Grouper (loose head prop) and Percival "Cocky" Pocock-Smith (tight head prop). Sham played and excelled at a position in the centre of the front row called hooker, which was a huge coincidence as he was to go on and encounter many more hookers over the years.

Chapter 22

Fabio Zodiac – The Early Years.

Fabio Zodiac was seen as a gifted mathematician from a very young age. It is not that he was simply good at his times tables, adding numbers, long division, multiplication and the like, it was more than that. He enjoyed mathematical puzzles but even that was not his forte. What made Zodiac special was that from a very early age he saw patterns everywhere, patterns, structure and order. Patterns and structure in the sky, patterns and structure in the way birds fly in formations, patterns and structure in the way ants cross each other's paths, patterns and structure in the way ice froze on the outside of his bedroom window in the winter and patterns and structure in its thawing, even patterns and structure in the way people walk through crowds. He loved music from a young age when, again, he picked up on the patterns and structure of chords, musical scales and rhythm. He went on to develop a love for poetry, again picking up on the patterns, this time of rhythm and rhyme.

At an early age, even before starting nursery school, Fabio had seen the structure behind odd and even numbers, he had noticed that the more sides a shape has when drawn evenly around a central point, the more it looked like a circle. He soon gained an insight into mathematical progressions and the Fibonacci number patterns in the petals and seed pods of flowers. Fortunately for Fabio, a particularly insightful teacher recognised his exceptional skills at a very early stage and, with the support of the school's senior teaching team, devised a personalised development program. This program led him to complete most school mathematical topics many years in advance of the norm. Later, Fabio's high school continued with this program and, with perhaps an unusual degree of forethought, assigned Fabio's mathematical education to one particular teacher, Mr. Applebottom, who had himself graduated in mathematics.

Applebottom took Fabio way beyond the usual school syllabus. In fact, they had all but covered that in his first year or so. Fabio's studies concentrated on pure mathematics, statistical analysis, mathematical modelling and probability. These subjects were not chosen at random; Fabio had chosen them as an introduction to the key areas of quantum computing, a field in which he was becoming increasingly interested.

After only a few years at high school, again at an unusually young age, Fabio won a scholarship to the Krichten3 Institute for Technology, the highly prestigious centre for the study of science and mathematics. Fabio continued with his studies in pure mathematics but extended these to include abstract and applied mathematics. He was still homing in on a career in quantum-computing. After quickly gaining a first-class honours degree, Fabio was invited to read for a doctorate in computer science at the Stratchrand Institute, which was and still is the pinnacle of study in all computer sciences. He was already gaining an impressive reputation as a young genius within the highest levels of both the scientific and the mathematics communities.

At that time there were two key problems with quantum-computers. Firstly, they were physically huge, typically the size of a family living room which made them very expensive. There were a vast number of components, they required an enormous amount of cooling and they required dedicated resources at the point of use. The upshot of these limitations was that quantum-computers remained in the realm of governments, very large and very wealthy companies and extremely well-funded institutions. Secondly, they needed specialist programmers who had themselves undergone many years of training. This, of course, added to the already high cost of running quantum-computers and added further limitations and further restrictions to their use.

Fabio's thesis outlined a theoretical model that could dramatically reduce the size of quantum-computers and, maybe more significantly, fundamentally change the way in which they could be programmed.

Fabio founded Thunderbolt Services immediately after being awarded his doctorate.

Chapter 23

Thunderbolt Services Startup.

"Good morning, Mr. Cummings, it's good of you to see me." Fabio Zodiac had managed to secure a preliminary discussion with Meganova Capital Ventures, one of the largest venture capital companies in the Bounty galaxy cluster.

"Good to meet you, Dr Zodiac and please call me Dip-Dip." Dip-Dip, was, at that time, an up-and-coming junior partner of Meganova, having secured his position via school contacts and with the support of his wealthy father. "I've heard very good things about you and I'm intrigued to hear what you have to say." Dip-dip was no fool, he had already thoroughly investigated all that he could find out about Zodiac and he had been suitably impressed with what he had discovered.

"It's nice of you to say that Dip-Dip and please call me Fabio. I've formed a company, Thunderbolt Services, with two other people. We are lucky enough to have been given the use of the Stratchrand Institute's research facilities in exchange for supporting some students in their studies. The company has been formed with the intention of developing micro-quantum-computers, which are quantum-computers that are compact and inexpensive enough that they could be used by small and medium sized companies, perhaps even by individuals. We have been developing the engineering principles, most of which have been preliminarily tested with very positive results. We are also in the process of developing a radically new interface, one that will supersede the use of dedicated programmers. In addition, the intention is that it will dovetail with existing pc protocols. In other words, Dip-Dip, you could have one sitting here on your desk and be able to operate it yourself with no training and no experience, simply by using your pc to program and manage it. We are even looking at a voice activated programming system."

"Fabio, that sounds amazing, but why would I want one sitting on my desk?"

"Quantum-computers are staggeringly powerful and unbelievably quick. For example, you work in finance: a quantum-computer can model very complex financial situations, simulating countless changes to the markets, all being made at the same time and all feeding back on each other. By using a micro-quantum-computer, you would be able to optimise all your financial strategies, and it could all be done whilst sitting at your own desk. I guess you already have access to a large-scale quantum-computer, but you need to employ your own specialists to operate it, or you need to call upon another company which has the expertise and the facilities to do the modelling for you. You need to do this each and every time you want to model anything that is complex. Furthermore, I guess that you probably have to wait for the computer to become available. Getting a solution takes time …. every time. Imagine how powerful it would be if you could construct your own models, instantly. Imagine, also, that you could simply enter your requests using your keyboard, or even just by talking to it, just as easily as we are talking now. Imagine that the results are pretty much instantaneous."

"OK, I can see a possible use in a narrow and complex field like finance."

"Not just finance Dip-Dip, almost everywhere. Imagine that you run a distribution company, or you run any company that has a delivery fleet - you can produce a delivery schedule which gives you the optimal delivery routes every day, every hour or even every minute, if you wanted to. This schedule can take into account a flood here, a reported traffic jam there, forecasted heavy rain here and it can include such things as changing customer service requirements and the relative importance of that customer. Imagine you run a medical insurance company - you can model the results of, let's say, an outbreak of flu or of an unexpected series of very hot days. You run a brewery – you can model production requirements for those same hot days, or a large sporting event, or a proposed marketing campaign. You have a company that manufactures and installs home nuclear shelters - what would be the effect on your product if a 6-megaton, 8-megaton or 12 mega-ton weapon fell 1 mile, 10 miles or 100 miles from your shelter and what would the effects of various real-time weather conditions be? And how would the explosion itself change those conditions? Dip-Dip, the list is endless. Every business would want one. I believe that the potential is huge."

"But I can do all that on my pc, why would I bother with a quantum-computer?"

"That's the point, you can't do these models on your pc. Sure, your pc can do very basic models, but these models are incredibly ineffective by comparison. Take your area of finance as an example again. You can certainly model some changes using your current pc. But they will be based on your best guesses, using predetermined criteria and parameters. You may assume that a drop in interest rates of 0.5% will lead to a fall in volume of 2% but that is your best guess. To combat that uncertainty, you will also model for drops in volume of, say, 1% and 1.5% and 2.5% and 3% and so on, and you will make an assumption as to which is most likely. You will talk about 'the best-case scenario' or 'the worst-case scenario' and 'the likely scenario'. But there will also be many, many other variables, probably countless variables, not contained within your model. What happens if the whole universal economy shrinks by 0.05% over the same period? Or, more realistically, whilst the universal economy shrinks by 0.05%, one galaxy's economy reduces by 0.06%, another's reduces by 0.075% and a third galaxy's increases by 0.02%. And, of course, these changes constantly feed back into each other. You have to add other assumptions into your model, and you have no real idea how one will affect the other. This is what happens in real life. Changes to a variable in one area can affect many other variables in other areas which, in turn, can feedback into the original variable. These changes can come from anywhere. A war here, droughts on such and such planet, a political coup here or a major change to tax policy there, a significant political decision is taken here, but the opposite decision is taken there. Your pc model cannot cope with that, even your market analysts cannot cope with that. No platform, other than quantum-computers, combined with a big enough data base, can cope with so many interconnected variables; there are just too many feedback loops in real-life systems. No pc can cope with all of these feedback loops, and these loops are always present. Given sufficient relevant data, a quantum-computer can. It could even tell you what needs modelling and how to model it. You are a wealthy organisation and, as I said, you undoubtedly have access to a large quantum-computer already. However, using it takes time and money and limits your effectiveness. So, yes, even you, and probably everyone else, would want one sitting on their desk."

The was a long pause in their conversation as Dip-Dip took this in ...

"Do you have a patent on these developments?"

"Yes, a very robust one and it's Bounty wide."

"Would you mind if our legal boffs have a quick nosey through it?"

"Of course not, Dip-Dip, in fact I would welcome their views and comments."

The meeting went on to be a great success. Fabio knew he needed a huge capital investment if he was going to realise his dreams and Meganova was one of the few companies that could get their hands on that kind of funding. After the meeting was over and Fabio had gone, Dip-Dip leant back in his large black comfy leather office chair and pondered what he had just heard.

His homework prior to this meeting with Zodiac, had showed that Zodiac was a rising star, a genius even, certainly someone to be listened to. He was, however, quite surprised by how easy he had been to talk to and how comfortable he felt in his presence; not at all the geeky nerd he was expecting. He also realised the incredible, even astounding, potential of what Zodiac had just revealed to him. This could be the investment opportunity of a lifetime. He spent quite some time thinking through what he had just heard and what needed to be done. He then asked his secretary to arrange an urgent meeting with the company's senior partners. Before popping upstairs to meet with them, he made one quick phone call. "Hi Dad, do you fancy having a spot of dinner tonight? I think I may have something that you will find very interesting."

Dip-Dip's meeting with his senior partners went very well. All of them could see potentially astronomical profits. The capital outlay needed, however, was going to be staggeringly large and could potentially stretch their assets to their limits. One of the senior partners summed it up "After all, at the end of the day, we could be talking about replacing every single pc in the Bounty group of galaxies and there are an awful lot of those." Each of the senior partners wanted to meet with Zodiac to better assess the opportunities and gauge the probable costs, along with the possible risks. They also wanted to get a measure of the man for themselves.

Dip-Dip's dinner with his father also went well. Dip-Dip explained what Thunderbolt was developing and that, furthermore, much of it had already been tested. They talked through the scale of the opportunity and the enormity of the capital investment that would be needed. As Dip-Dip had thought would be the case, his father began to express a great deal of interest in providing some of the much-needed capital, in exchange for shares in the company and (hint hint) maybe a seat on the board.

*

Fabio Zodiac's meeting with Meganova Capital Ventures' senior partners went even better than the earlier one with Dip-Dip. Zodiac had come armed with mountains of data that satisfied all of their technical questions, and he made a huge personal impression on the team. "This is clearly a guy we can work with" was one of the after-meeting comments. The discussion around the size and nature of their capital investment was telling. In principle, they would be willing to commit to raising a massive sum towards further development of the systems and they were prepared to leave Zodiac as the sole owner for the time being. The capital investment would be by way of a series of unsecured deferred repayment loans. However, these deferments were to be in exchange for guaranteed discounted shares, to be taken when the company floated on the open market. It was felt that a floatation would almost certainly be necessary to raise the enormous funds that would be needed to ultimately go into full-scale production and to be able to properly market the product. Meganova insisted on an immediate non-executive seat on the board, with open access to all company data and accounts. In other words, they understandably wanted to keep a very close eye on how Thunderbolt was using their money. That appointee was to be Dip-Dip.

Once the funding had been agreed and secured, Thunderbolt Services bought or rented several facilities which allowed them to go into full scale development and testing. They recruited additional employees from both the academic world and the world of large-scale quantum-computers. It took about 4 years to create a fully operational micro-quantum-computer that was about the size of a couple of shoe boxes (small enough to sit comfortably in an office) and a further year to satisfy the compliance and safety tests that would allow these new micro-quantum-computers to be sold Bounty-wide.

Zodiac left much of this development to his fellow former Stratchrand Institute partners. He spent most of his own time concentrating on the development of voice activated programming. This was to be the big game changer. Many companies were working on reducing the size of their quantum-computers, albeit with varying degrees of success, but Thunderbolt were the only ones looking to fundamentally change the way in which they were programmed.

*

Zodiac's first year or so was spent working on the interface between a small pc and the quickly developing mini-quantum-computer. He had proposed the principles as part of his doctorate, but it proved to be a little harder in practice. Eventually, however, he achieved an efficient and reliable working process.

His ultimate goal of voice programming turned out to be a very hard nut to crack. The system he envisaged was not a simple voice recognition and translation device. It was not a case of saying "do this first and then do that". It wasn't even changing voice requests into computer code, such as "add such and such column of numbers and multiply the result by seven." That, in itself, would be difficult to achieve. However, he was aiming for something entirely different.

It was Zodiac's goal that the user simply tells his or her device what is wanted and the device would determine the best way to achieve it, all on its own. It would then program itself and finally provide the output. All quantum-computers require a binary based computer to act as an interface, but Zodiac's aim was to design a system that combined a standard binary based computer interface (a standard pc) with a mini-quantum-computer that allowed feedback between the two, even during the programming stage, thus, effectively, allowing the quantum-computer to interpret the user's request.

As a simple example, imagine a home unit that controls all the household's appliances. Now take a command like "open the windows when it gets stuffy." With that one command, without any additional instructions and without any task specific pre-programming, the quantum computer would:

- Decide what the command actually means, such as what is meant by stuffy, based on:
- On-line dictionaries' definitions of stuffy.
- Previous temperature and humidity levels at which windows have been opened in the past.
- Listening to prior conversational clues such as "phew, it's stuffy in here!" before windows were opened and ascertaining the conditions at that time.
- Body temperature readings of all the people in the room prior to windows previously being opened.
- Perspiration level readings of all the people in the room prior to windows previously being opened.
- Gathering such data from other similar rooms across the network when their windows had been opened.
- Scan its data for other indicators, e.g., the cat often leaves the room before any person can be bothered to get up and open a window.
- Scan its data to see how far each window is opened, depending on the prevailing weather conditions.
- Compare the current data against these criteria:
- What are the current temperature and humidity levels in the room?
- What is being said in the room?

- What are the current body temperatures of the people in the room?
- What are the current perspiration levels of the people in the room?
- What is the weather doing?
- Is the cat still there?
- If the criteria are met:
- Calculate how far the windows need to open.
- Check the prevailing wind direction and outside temperature.
- Check that there are no new obstacles to opening the windows.
- Check that opening a window will not create an unacceptable security or health and safety risk.
- If all is good to go, then open the windows.

It is important to emphasise that these are not pre-programmed tasks or pre-programmed levels, the process is entirely determined by the computer, based solely on the one single command "Open the windows when it gets stuffy". Just as for a human being, when you realise that the room feels stuffy you have not been told what to do or when to do it. You create your own criteria and action plan based upon your thoughts and feelings at the time. You make your own decisions as to when it feels stuffy and what you are going to do about it, including should you open the windows? Do you want to open the window if it is pouring with rain? You may just want to open it a fraction. You assess the situation. You do not go around with rules and instructions in your head, you work by instinct and experience, mostly by experience. This is what Fabio Zodiac wanted to achieve in quantum-computer programming. You simply tell it what you want, "open the windows when it gets stuffy," and the computer works out what the command means and how it can achieve the instruction based on the information stored in all of its available databases (its experiences). Furthermore, it will always scour all the data it has. Put simply - forget about pre-existing operating systems, programs, or apps and the like, the computer works it all out for itself.

As a further example, let's take Dip-Dip's world of finance. The quantum-computer has access to all previous data. Not just the data that someone has deemed as being relevant - all previous data. Let's say that you want to know the predicted change in your cash flow if there is a drop in interest rates of 0.5%. The mini-quantum-computer will instantly scan all its data banks and look at the effects of previous interest rate changes. It can add in anything that may be relevant such as what is happening in the various economies across the Bounty cluster; all of them. It can include the effects of anything - employment rates, change in family incomes, the change of employment rates due to the change in incomes, the change of incomes due to the change in employment rates. Political situations, wars and conflicts, its own weather forecasts, all of these; and the list is endless.

Given access to sufficient data, it would spot correlations that no one has even thought of. As an example - having images in its database, via its access to all that people have ever posted in the public domain, it would spot that the sales of fizzy pop often go up when Simon Cruddington of Chester Galaxy puts on his bright red sun-hat. This could be a useful, valid and a previously unknown indicator. It's not that Simon Cruddington determines the market but rather, he happens to live within the largest fizzy pop market, and he likes his fizzy pop. So, when it is hot, he is likely to fancy a fizzy pop and when it's hot he is also likely to be wearing his bright red sun hat. Furthermore, it is also very likely that many others will fancy a fizzy pop at the same time and, hence, sales go up. It would also spot that, whenever the same Simon Cruddington puts on his blue cartoon comic tie (the one he keeps for what are likely to be particularly tedious meetings), the stock market drops by over 1%. This correlation is simply a statistical coincidence as they cannot possibly be linked. The computer would spot the difference.

The above examples of interpreting data are simple, but it was to become one of the critical obstacles to developing a voice activated programming system. The systems kept on crashing.

*

Before we carry on, just for a bit of background knowledge, it is worth noting that poorly interpreted statistics and false correlations are at the heart of many statistical misunderstandings. Importantly, for later on in this story, these issues can also lie at the very heart of deliberate deception, biased representation and false representation. These misrepresentations can either be through incompetence or driven by the desire to deliberately influence opinion one way or the other. This will become important as our story unfolds and it was certainly an important and difficult obstacle for Zodiac to resolve at the time. Just for now, let us just dip our toes in the water.

Statistics can be a minefield and open to interpretation. Let's make up a very simple example, just as an illustration.

Question - Which charity has the biggest decline in contributions?

        Charity A has a 9.7% decline

        Charity B has a 1% decline

Answer - Obviously Charity A has the biggest decline in contributions.

However, what if I told you that charity A had contributions that fell from $72 to $65, a fall of $7, whilst charity B had contributions of $136,000 that fell to $134,640, a fall of $1,360.

Answer - Obviously Charity B; it had the biggest decline in contributions.

Hmm, what??? they both have the biggest decline in contributions??? That can't be right!!

Let's add another twist,

What if I told you that Charity A lost 70 people's donations, each of 10 cents, yet charity B only lost one contributor who had given £1,360, and, at the same time, the global economy shrunk by 3%

Answer - I'm confused; it could be either of them on several different grounds.

I can even argue that each charity's contributions have gone both up and down.

It all depends on how you interpret or present the statistics.

Exactly!! The point is that you can paint very different pictures by choosing the way you interpret or present the data or even by which data you choose to present. Compare and contrast these dramatic headlines -

Charity A cries for help as it loses a whopping 9.7% of its donations in just one year!!!

Charity A has a fantastic year, its revenue was only $7 down on last year, despite living through the recent catastrophic world recession!!!

Charity B excels in difficult times by growing 2% in real terms!!!

Charity B has a disastrous year as it sees its revenues fall by over $1,000!!!

Be aware that some media platforms, news programs, political parties, lobbyists, activists and other organisations, operating in the public domain, are very good at using and presenting statistics in a selective and sometimes in a deliberately misleading way. They choose, use and present statistics in ways that support their point of view, denigrates their opponent's point of view or to simply appear dramatic [I have no doubt that you have already come across such eye-catching clickbait].

One also suspects that many of the misleading statistics, which get into the public domain, are simply regurgitated from other sources by those who are ignorant of what they actually mean and who have not done even the most rudimentary checking. Misrepresentations can occur through ignorance [yes journalists, some of you are the worst culprits].

So, just to hammer the point home. These misrepresentations can be intended or accidental. Statistics can be deliberately selected with the specific intention of influencing people in their decision making and they can be specifically presented in a way that supports or opposes a particular point of view. In other words, statistics can be very influential and, furthermore, they can be misused by way of their selection and their presentation. Importantly, all the various presentations of such contradicting statistics are absolutely 100% correct and valid, but they can be used in such opposing ways depending on how they are selected and presented.

*

In essence Zodiac had two problems that needed overcoming. Firstly, it was imperative that the computer's outputs were presented in a clear and unambiguous way, free of any interpretation or bias. If the computer's outputs were in any way skewed or biased, then Thunderbolt's products would be seen as unreliable, and they would probably be inundated with lawsuits. Secondly, the systems were crashing as they were getting caught up in complex, never ending and unresolvable feedback loops.

The solutions to these two problems were a long time in coming, but they did come, and they turned out to be quite simple. How do living beings avoid these pitfalls? We have an inbuilt set of checks and balances; call it sense checking. Zodiac's solution was to pre-programme the computers to provide all interpretations and not just specifically chosen ones. If the original command or query is biased or ambiguous, then the computer will detail what the issue is and ask for the command to be rephrased. For example, problems occur when you ask such things as, what is the best? …., give me the most significant …., tell me the ideal …... The trouble with these instructions is that they are not defined. Give me the best solution – what do you mean by the best solution? This is not defined and is open to interpretation which, in turn, leads to confusion. Zodiac's solution to this issue was that the quantum-computer will recognise these shortfalls and ask for clarification before it processes the command. This position was not chosen on any moral basis, you can still use and present the final data as you see fit. The method was simply chosen to prevent the computer giving biased or ambiguous solutions.

The resolution to the continual feedback loop problem was to define the minimum change you were interested in, which you define in your settings. For example, if you were looking at a financial model, you could define the minimum change as, let's say 0.02%. So, if a specific feedback loop led to a change of 0.01% that loop would be automatically closed. Once the program had been completed and all feedback loops had been closed, the system would then provide the answer and, on request, would provide details of any feedback loops that had been closed.

*

The first voice programmed micro-quantum-computer was commissioned on the seventh anniversary of Thunderbolt Services' foundation. Obviously extensive testing had already been undertaken and Zodiac believed that they now had the finished product. An official inauguration party was held in Thunderbolt's board room. The eight company directors attended, including Dip-Dip, who was treated as the guest of honour, along with around a dozen or so heads of departments and other significant contributors. Dip-Dip greeted Zodiac, "Hi Fabio, how are you feeling? You must be very proud."

"Yes, I do feel proud. I'm also really excited. This is the culmination of about 12 years work for me."

"You must have been thinking of this moment for quite some time. You have achieved something very special."

"Not just me, I couldn't have done this without the support of my friends and colleagues … and you Dip-Dip. This would not have happened without the support of Meganova. I am truly grateful."

"Well thanks for that Fabio. This was a project that we really wanted to support. We can see a huge financial opportunity here and er, oh, er, oh yes and an opportunity to really help other people of course."

Zodiac smiled to himself whilst thinking "Oh Dip-Dip, I am very fond of you, but you are easier to read than a book." Zodiac made his way to the middle of the room and stood within reach of the new computer that was placed at the centre of the boardroom table. "Ladies and gentlemen. I would like to formally announce the commissioning of the MQC1, the universe's first ever voice programmable micro-quantum-computer. Please raise your glasses as I give you a toast …. I give you Thunderbolt Services and the MQC1." There was a cheer as everyone in the room joined in the toast. Zodiac let the hubbub die down before announcing "Now I would like to ask Dip-Dip to be the first official user of the MQC1 on this momentous occasion."

"What me" gulped Dip-Dip "but I know nothing about computers."

"Precisely. You will see just how easy it is to use and just how powerful it is."

"OK, what should I ask it?"

"Whatever you want. If it doesn't understand you, it will tell you."

"OK. Er, what do I say? Hey computer, Mr. Computer, Ms. Computer, MQC1, Oy you!?"

"Just ask your question; or state your command by talking into this microphone whilst holding down that green input button on the side. When you have finished, simply release the button."

"Er, OK." …………. He had quite a long think. Eventually he squeezed the green button on the side of the microphone and asked his question. "What is the projected Bounty wide sales for the MQC1?"

The MQC1 whirred, buzzed and clicked for a few moments. "Insufficient specification in the command. Please specify the investment figures."

"Unlimited" Responded Dip-Dip.

The MQC1 whirred, buzzed and clicked for a few more moments and then the screen lit up and Dip-Dip's eyes almost popped out of his head.

*

After the inaugural party had drawn to a close and Zodiac was alone, he thought to himself with an ironic chuckle, "Now that was a surprise. Who would have guessed that would be Dip-Dip's question? you really can read him like a book." Zodiac hadn't rigged the answer or fabricated any data. He had, however, in preparation, pre-populated the database with other necessary key information, such as pricing structure etc. The projected sales figure, quoted by the MQC1, was genuine and it really was that astronomically huge. He knew because he had already asked the MQC1 that very same question. What interested Zodiac was the fact that Meganova was obviously considering further huge investments.

Chapter 24

Thunderbolt Strategy.

Zodiac called a two-day strategy meeting for Thunderbolt's main board of directors, operating board directors and all of his senior managers. "The meeting will be informal, but please come well prepared and make sure that you put your thinking caps on, as all of our futures may well depend on these couple of days." He asked that everyone give serious thought as to the next steps for Thunderbolt. He also asked Dip-Dip if he could bring along one of Meganova's senior partners.

There were four Thunderbolt directors in attendance with non-technical roles; - Josh Tosh (CFO) from the main board, Elizabet (Betsy) Fuller (Sales & Marketing), Linda Snell (Production) and Sandra Elliot-Jones (Public Relations), all from the operating board, and around ten senior managers. Dip-Dip brought Tarquin Smith-Frobisher, a senior partner with Meganova Capital Ventures and long-term friend of Dip-Dip's father, Spider Cummings. This was, effectively, a strategy meeting on how to take the MQC1 to market. Thunderbolt had the tech side of things well and truly covered by some of the best scientific minds in the cosmos, it was the non-tech challenges that were now keeping Zodiac awake at night.

It took very little time for the group to highlight that the biggest issues were simply those of scale and speed. Forecasted sales figures were astronomically huge. How could they produce MQC1s in such vast quantities and quickly enough? How could they be distributed throughout the Bounty cluster? How could they recruit and train a suitable sales team? What would be the best way of marketing the MQC1? How could they approach so many potential customers quickly enough? How could all of this be funded?

In order to tackle these issues, they broke into three working groups. One group looked at production and distribution, another group looked at sales and marketing and the third group tackled the issues around finance. These were, initially, brainstorming breakout groups, with Zodiac floating between all three, but they soon morphed into key working and development groups. As the company expanded, they became subcommittees of the Thunderbolt Services Operating Board.

The Production and Distribution team soon realised that trying to manufacture solely in-house was a non-starter. The forecasted numbers were so huge that there was no way that they would be able to commission new production facilities, or recruit enough suitably experienced production staff, at anywhere near a sufficient rate. They also realised that they simply did not have the management expertise within their own company. The likely solution was to work with an existing manufacturer, one that had the facilities, the production standards, the skills and the workforce to be able to cope with such a sudden and massive uplift in volume. This, in summary, was their feedback to the group at the end of the strategy meeting. It was then that Smith-Frobisher mentioned that Meganova already supports some high-tech manufacturing companies, and he would ask his colleagues if they could suggest any possible partners.

The sales and marketing team also faced similar issues of scale and pace. However, with the rise in Bounty-wide social media, advertising through product placement, Whispers and the like, it was the group's view that a successful sales and marketing campaign could be run in-house. It also felt that they needed to quickly contact leading players and influencers in all key markets. When this was fed back to the full group, it was quite surprising how many suitable contacts such a small group of people already had.

The finance group had a very different discussion. There was absolutely nothing that Thunderbolt could achieve on its own, it would all come down to outside investors. The challenge was how to attract new investors because Meganova, whilst willing and able to provide additional funding, did not have sufficiently deep capital reserves to fully finance the forecasted expansion. The long-term solution was likely to be the inevitable floatation of Thunderbolt Services. At the end of the day, the whole of their financial strategy was going to come down to a series of negotiations with potential new investors. The need for attracting additional investment, beyond Meganova, was fed back to the wider group, but the likely floatation was not. Zodiac wanted time to think through the ramifications of such a move prior to having any wider discussions. Chief amongst his concerns being, how does he keep control of his own company? He did, however, ask Dip-Dip and Tarquin Smith-Frobisher to use their connections in the finance world to go ahead and sound out possible additional investors. The meeting had not resolved anything, but it had painted a way forward.

*

Dip-Dip's first call after the meeting was to his well-connected old school-buddy Sham. Sham, at that time, was not yet in politics but worked mostly in journalism whilst seeking out television appearances and the like. He was married, but rumours already abounded of many affairs. They met for dinner at their club "The Old Cock and Bull Club" which was a social haven for those born into privilege, the mega-wealthy and the privately educated, ideally all three. To call it the hub of the galaxy's old boy network would, in fact, be a massive understatement, the wealth and influence held within the membership was all pervasive throughout the entire galaxy. Everybody knew everybody else and often for a good number of years. During dinner Dip-Dip started to tell Sham about Thunderbolt's remarkable development. "Sham, old bean, have you ever heard of Thunderbolt Services?"

"Can't say that I have, what game are they in?"

"Well, it's mostly this IT. malarkey, you know, all silicon chips and mouse mats."

"Nope, definitely not heard of them."

At this Point Dip-Dip leant forward in a very obviously conspiratorial way. He was so conspicuous that half of the people in the room leant over to try and catch what he was saying. "Well Sham old buddy, it's like this. What I am about to tell you is, of course, in strict confidence." Many Old Beltonians speak with exceptionally loud voices, Dip-Dip was loud, and Sham could fill a room with just a whisper. Half the people in the room leant in even further. "You must keep this an absolute secret." Half the people in the room took a deep intake of breath and cringed. "I know I don't need to ask you, but will you give me your word that not one word of this will pass your lips to another living soul?" All the people in the room were now squirming. They were squirming, partly in anticipation of what Dip-Dip was about to reveal, but mostly as they knew how likely Sham was to keep a secret.

"Of course, I will keep it a secret, you know you can count on me Dip-Dip, I am the very personification of discretion." At this point Sham heard several unrestrained hoots and howls of laughter dotted throughout the room, along with a very noticeable background noise of barely suppressed giggling. He looked around wondering what the joke was.

"Thanks Sham, I know you are a man I can trust." Now the other half of the people in the room were also trying to keep a straight face.

Dip-Dip went on to tell Sham about Zodiac's development. His technical overview was sketchy but, when he told Sham of the forecasted sales figures, he got that spot on. Jaws dropped all around the room and people gasped. He then asked Sham if he knew of any investment type chaps that might be interested. Sham gave him several names and several people in the room made a mental note to bump into Dip-Dip, just as soon as possible. There is an old saying "money makes money … and the money that money makes, makes more money" and there were many people in that room who had an awful lot of money, some of the greediest ones were dribbling in anticipation.

Chapter 25

Implementation.

The first port of call for the production and distribution team was Sebastian Tartan Killdare Macintosh Oik, or Mac Oik, as he was known [the same Mac Oik that we briefly met at Sham's old school, Belton]. Mac Oik was now the owner and CEO of the family run business, Oik Intergalactic, which manufactures computers under their own brand, Oik Intergalactic Computers and also on behalf of other high-tech companies. Oik Intergalactic is a very large company, operating on the intergalactic scale, with an admirable reputation for quality; always adopting high standards and with an excellent reputation for customer service. Mac Oik had known Dip-Dip since his school days where they had dormed together. Dip-Dip was accompanied by Linda Snell (Thunderbolt's Director of Production) and he introduced her to Mac Oik. Following a general getting to know each other preamble, Snell described what Thunderbolt had developed and roughly how it worked. As she talked, Mac Oik became more and more concerned; what she was describing was, likely as not, signalling the end of his business! Who was going to buy an "old school" traditional computer when they could get an all singing, all dancing, micro-quantum-computer, at a roughly comparable price? Furthermore, she says that it can be programmed by simply talking to it! No more expensive software, no more downloading of programmes, no more licensed operating systems, who would buy an old-style pc? Linda was, in essence, sounding the death knell for his business. However, when she started talking about the reason for her visit, which was Thunderbolt's desire to work with a key production partner, his eyes lit up and he became very interested indeed. If this MQC1 is as good as she says it is, and old dependable Dip-Dip says that it is, it will undoubtedly be the future of computing. I could, potentially, switch all my production capacity from our old-style pcs to this new MQC1. This was the first of many, many meetings, but it was obvious to both parties from the very start that this could be a perfect partnership, a marriage made in heaven. It was doubly blessed as both companies shared similar philosophies and similar goals; excellent products, excellent technical support, excellent standards and a dedication to serving the customer.

*

Dip-Dip didn't know why, but over the following few days, he was being swamped by chance encounters with many of his chums from the Old Cock and Bull Club and even chums of those chums. Every one of them quickly brought the conversation round to Thunderbolt Services' need for financial investment. He had so many offers that he quickly realised that the cat was out of the bag and that there was a huge amount of interest. He arranged an emergency meeting with Zodiac, Tosh, and Smith-Frobisher. At that meeting, Smith-Frobisher reported that he too had had several approaches and that, somehow, the word was out on the street. The meeting came to a quick decision. Thunderbolt would take sufficient loans to meet its short-term expansion needs, all on a similar basis as those given by Meganova. It would then immediately go for a floatation on the open market. Over a very short period, loans came in from, amongst others, the Hyper-Wedged Hedge Fund (represented by Lance (Plank) Grouper), Spider Cummings (Dip-Dip's father) and an unexpected personal loan came directly from Sham's father. Unbeknownst to Zodiac, many of the loans came from chums, ex-schoolfriends and relations of Sham. However, it didn't take Zodiac long to piece it all together. Dip-Dip had talked to Sham and Sham had told all his friends. He was not in the least bit angry; Dip-Dip was there to raise funds and that is exactly what he was doing. However, the fact that many of these investors had close relationships with Sham was, over time, to become a major and I do mean major, problem; and these problems were to be greatly exacerbated when Sham later took to politics.

*

The sales and marketing group met with all the major social media providers and their key influencers, all of whom were amazed and excited by the MQC1. Limited production had only just started but that was enough to allow Elizabet Fuller and Sandra Elliot-Jones to give a MQC1 to everyone that they met. The impact of this was immediate and startling. Everyone and their mother were talking about the MQC1. Social media was alight with discussions, what it could do, how easy it was to operate, its power, its desirability. It is no overstatement saying that soon nearly everyone in the cosmos knew of and wanted a MCQ1.

*

One of the conditions of use of the MQC1 was that all non-personal data had to be group shared between all units. At first there was some negativity around this condition, but people were very soon won over. This new "communal database" proved to be so powerful that, other than a very few dissenters, everybody became strong supporters of the system. Thunderbolt gave a commitment that no data's source would ever be traceable. This commitment was universally accepted and forever remained upheld. The necessary protocols were, in fact, preprogrammed into the system at the highest level. All data is made shareable across the entire network, except for the specific "whose data is it" or exactly "where has the data come from." This information would always remain unshared and untraceable by any MCQ1 in the network. As an example, let us revisit the "open the windows when it gets stuffy" example. Any MCQ1 could access any other MCQ1's data or, indeed, eventually, all MCQ1s' data, to find out when they had opened their owner's windows and what the relevant conditions were at the time. However, it could not access the owner's name, nor the specific address of that owner, the shared data only detailed where the action had taken place in the broadest of terms. There was, in fact, one exception to this commitment. There were three separate master control units, held by Thunderbolt, that could access this data. These master control units were used for managing the universal network, for fault diagnosis, for error correction, for design, for security and for implementing system updates. These units were not accessible from outside of Thunderbolt. As already touched upon, faster than light communication had not yet been developed. The MCQ1s were networked by downloading all their data into regional hubs and, initially, it was this data that would be communally shared within that region. This limitation was resolved later as a Bounty-wide solution was found.

The launch of the MQC1 caused such a hoo-ha across all social media platforms that it was Adrian Mont-Fredo (CEO of Whispers) who first made contact with Thunderbolt. Only a few days after making contact, Mont-Fredo accepted an invitation to meet with Zodiac, Fuller, and Elliot-Jones at Thunderbolt's head office. Mont-Fredo went with the sole purpose of trying to get a handle on how this apparently amazing new piece of kit would impact on his business. On this point, he left the meeting feeling very positive. It was very likely to bring onboard additional users and, likely as not, open up additional revenue streams. He could not see any obvious downside. There was, however, a proposal put on the table that needed a great deal of thought. Thunderbolt asked for open access to all of Whisper's databases, in exchange for shares in Thunderbolt, which was soon going to be floated. It sounded a very enticing proposal, but Mont-Fredo needed some time to think through the ramifications of such a request. He called Zodiac only one week later to accept his offer, in principle, subject to some detailed negotiations.

Zodiac was ecstatic when he got that call from Mont-Fredo. The Whisper data base was vast and incredibly diverse, just the type of database that the MQC1s would thrive on. This, in turn, would improve their performance and better satisfy the needs of their customers. The other plus was that Mont-Fredo, soon to be a shareholder, would certainly endorse or, most likely, promote the MQC1 across all his platforms. This could be a huge boost to sales and help push Thunderbolt forward as the IT provider of choice throughout the entire Bounty group. Furthermore, having Whispers opening its database to Thunderbolt would almost certainly encourage other social media providers to do the same.

A few days later Mont-Fredo came up with another suggestion. "Fabio, I hope you don't mind me saying but the name MQC1 is a little dreary, a little cumbersome and very geeky, it's just not exciting enough for such an amazing piece of kit. How about calling it the "Little Maq." I think that something like that could really catch on."

And thus, the ubiquitous Little Maq was created.

*

Around three months after his conversation with Mont-Fredo, Zodiac felt that the time was right for their, now much rumoured, floatation. Sales were growing at an unbelievable rate. Their current production infrastructure was in desperate need of a rapid and dramatic expansion, which would require an immediate and huge financial investment. Demand was already outstripping Oik Intergalactic's capacity for production. Shares were offered on the open market and many individuals throughout the entire Bounty group became shareholders. However, most of the fundraising was conducted behind closed doors. The final shareholding ended as:

25% - Fabio Zodiac   20% - Meganova   15% - Company Employees
10% - Mont-Fredo   5% - Hyper-Wedged 5% - Cummings Investment
20% - Public

It had been necessary for Zodiac to relinquish sole control. There were so many very big investors that the company was now far too big to allow him to retain total autonomy. After all, the investors' share allocations needed to reflect the size of their investments. However, in the unlikely event that it ever came to a major divergence of opinion, Zodiac was confident that he would retain the loyalty of his colleagues and thus, for all intents and purposes, he would directly control 40% of the shares. He had little doubt that he would be able to persuade an additional 10% to vote with him in the unlikely event of a serious split.

Over the following years, the company's performance hit the stratosphere. Sales exploded, production was ramped up (the huge amount of additional revenue allowed Thunderbolt to buy out several other hi-tech production companies) and several new working partners were brought on board. The growing access to partners' databases and the ever-increasing number of units led to the open data base becoming unimaginably vast and unimaginably powerful. The shareholders all became exceedingly wealthy, Dip-Dip was made a senior partner of Meganova and everyone involved was ecstatically happy. Very quickly Fabio Zodiac became the richest individual in the universe.

There was, however, one bit of sad news during this exhilarating period. Josh Tosh, the company's CFO, collapsed unexpectedly whilst walking across his office to retrieve some papers from a filing cabinet. He died, there and then, having suffered a massive heart attack. The cause was considered to be the stress of overseeing Thunderbolt's floatation. Lance "Plank" Grouper was very quickly appointed as the new CFO. Grouper already had connections with Thunderbolt as he was a leading figure in Hyper-Wedged, one of the key investors. He was universally considered to be an exceptionally capable man by everybody who had ever worked with him or who had had any dealings with him. On joining the company, Grouper was given 5% of the company's shares out of the employee's allocation. Zodiac was very keen to have Grouper join the team. He was, however, a little wary of Grouper's lifelong links to Sham and his socially elite clique. The balance of power had just slipped a little further out of Zodiac's control.

Chapter 26

Sham Enters Politics.

One evening, Sham was at a loose end. He didn't feel comfortable at home as more rumours of his frequent philandering had got back to his wife. She was, unsurprisingly, giving him the cold shoulder whilst she made up her mind whether to leave him straight away or punch him on the nose and then leave him. His home had a very uncomfortable atmosphere, so he decided to spend the evening at the Old Cock and Bull club, mostly to be on familiar safe ground but also to be with people who would actually talk to him. He was hanging around the bar, killing time, chatting to a couple of old acquaintances whilst his table was made ready. One of these acquaintances was Sir Alfie Windlesham who was chairman of the Traditionalist Party and a fellow Old Beltonian (although he was a pupil there several years prior to Sham). Sir Alfie was telling the group that they were looking for someone to stand for election for the very safe Constituency seat of Whisper following the unexpected retirement of the sitting MP. There were many rumours as to why he had suddenly resigned. "Tell me, what does being an MP actually involve?" asked Sham.

"There is no simple answer to that question" replied Sir Alfie, cautiously "as it very much depends on the individual. Take Quincy Taggart over there. Now he is what I would call a professional, full-time politician. He's been a backbencher representing the same small planetary group for most of his life. He attends almost every session of parliament, sits on several committees and subcommittees and he holds very regular constituency meetings. I would say that his whole life revolves around representing his constituents. Now, compare and contrast that with Toby Buckmaster who is, at this very moment, standing over there by the window. Buckmaster has represented the same large planet for most of his life, but he has very rarely even visited it. The planet is a solid Traditionalist Party seat and, as such, the sitting MP has to do very little to keep his position. Buckmaster is a corporate tax lawyer and earns a fortune charging enormous fees. He tells his electorate that his outside experiences are invaluable to the system of government, and they seem to accept that. I guess that he is right, just so long as most of his constituents have very substantial off planet savings accounts and they need a topflight, and very expensive, lawyer to protect them from any tax burden. Anyway, that being said, who are we to argue with the electorate?"

"Is the Whisper seat a safe seat?" asked Sham.

"Are you kidding?" spluttered Sir Alfie "Whisper is about the safest seat in parliament. Dyed in the wool Traditionalist. Has been for many, many generations and probably always will be."

"Are you saying that if, for example, I was elected, I could carry on with all my TV work and journalism, all whilst drawing an additional MP's salary? And that it would likely open up other opportunities for me. I could probably appear on new things such as news quizzes and current affairs programs."

"Yes, you could. Why, are you thinking of applying? we could do with a charismatic and well-known person like you, someone who has come from, now, how should I put it? yes, that's it, has come from the right background. As far as I am aware we have not received any other applications as yet. Mind you, you are the first chap that I have mentioned it to. I guess that means that we could put you through on the nod, as it were."

"Hmmm. Let me think it through … hmm …. hmm … Yes, I hereby put my name forward for the honourable position of MP for Vesper."

"MP for Whisper" corrected Sir Alfie. Sham was appointed within the month.

In many ways Sham was the perfect choice for the seat. His family's background, his schooling and his close group of friends, all resonated well with Whisper's strongly Traditionalist voters. He was also, by his nature, very charismatic, which was quite different from the run of the mill Traditionalist MPs. Many people considered Sham to be good fun whilst many others, those who saw through his bluff and bluster, considered him to be a joke. His biggest asset, it could be argued, was his public presence, having appeared on many popular TV programs and having written for many well-known newspapers and magazines. All could see, even the sceptics, that his political career was probably destined for bigger things.

Chapter 27
Conflict.

A good number of generations before this story took place, the development of large quantum-computers had enabled interstellar travel, in four specific ways:

Firstly - quantum-computers were used to calculate and detail the means necessary to obtain faster than light travel. Theories abounded for many generations as to how faster than light travel might be possible, but it was large quantum-computers that enabled these theories to be modelled effectively. The resultant solution was warp-drive.

It is a well-known fact that nothing can travel through space faster than the speed of light. However, a warp-drive, in essence, isolates a spaceship in a bubble of space. This bubble is not separate from the surrounding space, it is part of the surrounding space. The drive works by rapidly shrinking an area of space directly in front of the spaceship's bubble whilst rapidly expanding the portion of space directly behind. This is a continual process, the effect of which is to drive the bubble containing the spaceship forward. The bubble in space is continually pushed from behind into the near empty void in front. This ingenious solution means that the spaceship does not travel through space at all, it remains in a fixed bubble of space, but the bubble containing the spaceship can travel as quickly as you want. Its speed is only limited by available power. Whilst warp-drive travel was faster than light it was by no means instantaneous. It still took a matter of days to cross a galaxy and a matter of weeks to reach a different galaxy.

Secondly - quantum-computers enabled the design and operation of nuclear fusion power plants which, amongst other things, are used to power warp-drives. Nuclear fusion is the power that makes a star shine, and it is an incredibly powerful phenomenon [we can feel the heat of our own sun's fusion reactions from over 90 million miles away (around 150 million kilometres)]. Getting a fusion reaction running was achieved relatively quickly but the real problem was keeping the reaction running in a stable and usable fashion. Quantum-computers enabled these fusion reactions to be controlled in a way that allowed the power to be harnessed. Fusion reactions are so fluid that quantum-computers were the only things that could keep a grip on such a complex and ever-changing process.

Thirdly - during warp-drive space travel, quantum-computers control and focus the power gained from the nuclear fusion units; shrinking and expanding space around the warp-bubble as required.

Finally - quantum-computers navigate and steer the bubble though space. A flight path must account for such things as the smallest amount of gravitational warping in the fabric of space and time. It must avoid large pieces of cosmic debris, meteors, protoplanets, pockets of high energy radiation and many other potential obstacles. It must account for other phenomena such as time and space dilation. Faster than light navigation is very complex and, critically, it needs constant real-time modelling, updating, adjusting and optimising. [Just so you get an idea of the navigational accuracy needed: if the spaceship's course would miss a target 1 mile away by just 1 millimetre, it would miss a target in a neighbouring galaxy by many millions of miles, in fact it is quite likely that it would miss the entire galaxy altogether!!]

*

The early days of space exploration throughout the Bounty group of galaxies were very similar wherever they took place. Individual civilisations' initial journeys were to their respective moons and then to some suitable planets in their own solar systems. They were all undertaken using traditionally powered rockets. As well as manned flights, each of these civilisations used manned and unmanned rockets to launch a number of probes and various satellites. Some of these rockets were used to place telescopes in deep space, far away from the light and radio pollution of their home planets. Inevitably, some of these telescopes were designed to search for life beyond their home planets. It is not surprising, however, that little evidence of life beyond any home planet was ever detected in this pre-warp-drive era.

[Author's note: our galaxy, the Milky Way, is over 100,000 light-years across. Put another way, it would take over 100,000 years for a radio signal (or, for that matter, any evidence of any event), that was produced on one side of our galaxy to be detectable on the other side of our galaxy. 100,000 years ago, primitive man was still living as hunter gatherers. Furthermore, it would take around 2½ million years for a signal generated on our neighbouring galaxy to be detected here on earth. Another way of picturing these vast cosmic scales is this: Marconi sent the world's first radio message (perhaps the first evidence of our becoming an advanced lifeform) around 150 years ago. That signal is now only something like one half of one percent of the way across our own galaxy.]

Purely by chance following the sporadic development of quantum-computing, several civilisations achieved faster than light travel within a generation or so of each other. Initial warp-driven flights were confined to home galaxies but the common desire for exploration quickly led to intergalactic travel. The formats of these flights were all pretty similar. One spaceship with a smallish crew, usually of around a dozen or so people (captain, navigator, doctor, engineers, computer technicians, computer programmers and various scientific experts, depending on the goals of the mission), one fusion reactor, one front propulsion unit, one rear propulsion unit and one, very large and very expensive, quantum-computer.

Whilst the physical make-ups of these missions were very similar there was a big variation in their planning, particularly in their planning for the eventuality that they might encounter another civilisation. Most simply hadn't considered the possibility at all. A few, however, had. Of these, some planned to keep a low and unthreatening profile. They slowed down well in advance of the target planet and approached relatively slowly and from a safe distance, just in case. Others thought that the chance of finding another civilisation was so remote that they ignored this possibility and simply appeared in orbit around the planet. At the end of the day, the approach taken made very little difference. The effect of any encounter was to create blind panic on the target planet ...... and on the spaceship! [Imagine how you would feel if your TV programme was suddenly interrupted by a news flash telling you that an alien spacecraft has appeared in orbit around Earth. I would suggest that your reaction would lie somewhere between deep concern and abject terror. Who are they? What are they doing here? Where did they come from? Are they much more advanced than us? What do they want? Are they here to harm us? Is it an invasion? Imagine also, the feelings onboard the space craft. They expected to arrive at a pristine barren planet, but they suddenly find themselves circling over towns and cities, roads and runways, farms, industry and nighttime lights. They would most definitely feel surprise and curiosity, but they would also feel an awful lot of "oh my gosh, we are sitting ducks up here!!"]

The reactions on those planets that were first visited varied wildly, ranging from "let's try to communicate with them", but mostly "let's shoot them out of the sky before they can do us any harm." The reactions on the spaceships were all very much the same …. "Let's get out of here!"

Whilst faster than light travel had been invented, faster than light communication had not. The missions' home planets had to wait for their craft to return before they got any news and, of course, several craft did not make it back.

This was the pattern for the early generations of faster than light space travel. However, the focus of these missions began to slowly change. Inevitably, over time, as each of these societies grew and developed, they quickly depleted their home planet's natural resources. Space missions began to focus on finding planets that could provide new resources or could become a new home. Either way, the purpose of these missions became ever more aggressive; they were no longer about exploration, they became about securing new resources. Furthermore, as generations passed, more and more civilisations entered this new intergalactic space-age, and all these civilisations quickly faced exactly the same issue on their home planet; ever-growing demands put on ever-diminishing natural resources.

Despite all of this, some of the early galactic and intergalactic missions did lead to meaningful contact being made between different civilisations. Some of the earlier missions, most of which had quickly returned home upon discovering other civilisations, were followed up by missions designed to make peaceful contact. Whilst many failed, some of these missions were successful which led, over a very long period of time, to a slow but steady mingling of different societies. This mingling gradually grew to include more and more civilisations on more and more planets. A new phenomenon slowly appeared, that of inter-species translators. Computerised translation machines also came on stream as more and more languages were encountered. Over time, widespread communication between planets and galaxies became possible and eventually became the norm.

After many generations, civilisations throughout the Bounty group gradually mingled together, much as any single world's inhabitants do, just like the different races and ethnic groups here on Earth. They travelled, they traded, and they exchanged ideas and cultures. There were periods of peace and periods of conflict. Inevitably, societies became ever more aware of how much other societies possessed, their natural resources and their wealth. This gave rise to, particularly when coupled with rapidly shrinking resources, ever increasing levels of aggression and conflict.

Politically, the planets in the Bounty group were very diverse. Most planets had a planetwide political system and a planetwide government. These governments were drawn from the entire political spectrum, ranging from communist to fascist, dictatorship to democracy, insular to expansive, socialist, authoritarian and liberal. Over generations, political alliances were formed, some of which were successful but most failed in the long run. In an effort to curb interplanetary and intergalactic war and with the aim of facilitating trade, a Bounty-wide quasi legal system was created. This judicial system had little direct power but was, in essence, the creator and the policeman of intergalactic law. It was the individual planets and galaxies' roles to embed these laws into their own governmental and legal systems. Some did this well, but many did not. These laws were primarily in the areas of: non-aggression, trade, the ownership of raw materials and natural resources, intellectual property rights, Bounty-wide standardisation and common health and safety standards. As the demand for resources became even greater and more widespread, the power of the centralised judicial system became weaker and weaker.

Chapter 28

Another Wet Wednesday.

Skipper had spent a lot of time reviewing The Network's records and felt he needed to talk his thoughts through with his two buddies. He wanted to see if they had discovered anything different and to see if they shared his feelings. He sent the coded message "ww?" ....

"Pick you up at 6.15" replied Chris, a thumb's up emoji came back from TT.

Chris got delayed in traffic on his way home from work and was about 20 minutes late in collecting Skipper. As they walked into The Train Stop, they were confronted by the oddest of scenes. All the customers, as well as the landlord and landlady, were standing on one leg! Most were wobbling, a few were posing like ballerinas, and some were clearly cheating by resting against a table, a chair, a wall, or the bar.

Chris sidled up to Carpet Tony who was standing on one leg at the bar (discretely clutching onto a hidden bar stool for balance) and asked, "Hi mate, what on earth's going on?"

"This is TT's doing and he is insisting that we all give it a go. You know how some older folks tend to shuffle along when they walk, well, its TT's theory that they shuffle because they have forgotten how to stand on one leg."

"And?"

"Well, he is now insisting that this bar becomes a one-leg-only bar as a form of self-preservation. He is proposing that whenever we enter, we immediately stand on one leg. Some of us challenged him on the reliability of his facts but he just replies that we ignore our health at our own peril."

Chris and Skipper immediately stood on one leg, not wanting to risk the consequences of not doing so. "Hi guys" said TT, as he hopped across the bar to greet Chris and Skipper.

"We've just been told about your medical breakthrough," said Chris with, perhaps, a small hint of sarcasm.

"Yes, I watched some old boy shuffle towards me as I waited in my cab the other day and I immediately saw what the root cause was. It came to me as a blinding flash of insight!"

"You've certainly got me convinced" chuckled Chris "But I'm not sure I can stand on one leg for the whole evening whilst I drink my beer."

"Ah, you don't have to. We're just giving it a trial run."

"If I buy a beer, do I have to hop over to a table whilst carrying my beer?" asked Skipper "It could get very messy."

"No, but you cannot shuffle when you walk."

"I don't shuffle when I walk."

"Well, not yet maybe, but this is preventative medicine in action, and we all know that prevention is better than cure."

"Then why did you hop across the room just a few moments ago?" asked Chris

"Ah, I'm leading by example - hopping the extra mile."

"It was about ten feet" pointed out Skipper.

"Alright, hopping the extra ten feet then!"

"So, for how long do you propose we stand on one leg each time we come in here?" demanded Chris.

"Ah, well, that is clearly a matter of individual choice, and it all depends on your acceptance of personal risk, but the more you do the better the chances of prevention. Personally, I would recommend that you do about 5 minutes"

"Is that a medical expert's opinion?" challenged Chris.

"Er, no, it's pretty much all that I can do at any one time. But don't you go around telling other people that!"

"Is this the current trial then … for how long people can stand on one leg?" asked Skipper.

"Partly, yes. But mostly it's because I want to get some practice in organising these sessions. It is my intention to offer my services to the NHS as a mobile community shuffle prevention centre, to go alongside all the other mobile drop-in centres they are introducing."

"That is very charitable of you" said Chris "it's nice to see someone offering to give up their free time to support their local community."

"Ah, well, ah, it's not so much a charity. I'm going to charge the NHS for my services, I could make a fortune. Have you any idea what a consultant earns?"

It was with great pride that Skipper, Chris and the other people in the bar, realised that they were, in fact, the first people in history to ever attend a mobile community drop-in shuffle prevention centre. A short while later the trial was over. One person had fallen, one person had got serious cramp and the usually refined and genteel landlady declared it "an effing waste of time!!"

*

Skipper, Chris and TT gathered around their usual secluded table in the corner of the room and put their heads together for quite a while.

"So, this is, kind of, how we see it, yes?" summarised Skipper. "They developed large quantum-computers which enabled the development of faster than light travel which then led to galactic and intergalactic travel. Various communities mixed over the subsequent generations. As these societies developed and continued to grow, they began to run out of natural resources on their home planets which, amongst other things, led to frequent wars. All agreed?"

Both Chris and TT nodded in agreement.

"But there is more to it than that," said Chris, "that explains the fear of war that many people clearly felt, but it does not, in itself, explain why The Network was commissioned. No, I think there is much more to it than that."

"I agree," said TT "and I get the sense that The Network has something to do with Thunderbolt and all their new technology. But what? There is no way that a single company could influence so many people. I mean, how many people are we talking about … what was the size of their population?".

"Oh, now, that is a very good question, I haven't actually worked that one out, but it must have been quite a few." said Chris as he started tapping on the calculator on his phone. "I believe that I remember the biggest galaxy, the Central Galaxy, had around 100,000 inhabited planets. So, let's assume that the average galaxy would have had around 60,000 inhabited planets and I'm sure there were 6 galaxies in the Bounty cluster. Let's also assume that each planet had, on average, 5 billion people (somewhat less than our own population, here on Earth). That means there were something in the order of, oh bugger, my calculator has run out of zeros, let me see." He reverted to pen and paper (well, the back of a beer mat, in truth). It's in the order of, hang on I need to double check this, yes, I was right … it's my estimate that the total population was probably something in the order of two million, billion people!"

All three were taken aback by the size of this unimaginably huge number and they were stunned by the heart-wrenching size of the catastrophe.

"You know something?" said Skipper "I think that what was going on back then is very similar to what is beginning to happen here on earth, right now. Just think about it. We will inevitably run out of resources and over time our planet will become less and less inhabitable. Unless rectified, global warming will gradually shrink the size of our usable land. Meanwhile our population continues to grow. Coastal regions, including many big coastal cities, such as New York, Washington, Miami, Tokyo, Amsterdam, Shanghai, New Orleans and parts of London, to name but a few, are likely to be under water. Global warming will put more and more energy into our climate. This will lead to much more large-scale flooding, more wild-fires and more weather extremes, all of which will further reduce the amount of inhabitable land. Even if global warming is taken seriously, by all of us and by all the world's governments, and is prevented, our ever-growing population and our ever-growing industry will eat into our natural resources. In comparatively little time we will run out of oil and gas, although, in truth, we should probably limit using them right now. We will also run out of other key mineral resources such as phosphorus, which is essential in making the fertilisers upon which we depend to feed the world. Also, scandium, tantalum, tellurium, rhenium and terbium, all essential in the manufacture of high-tech products, will be rapidly depleted. The probability is that, over time, the more powerful and aggressive countries or communities are likely to go ahead and take what they need from others. Migration will also become an ever-more serious and an ever-growing problem. So, much like the ill-fated Bounty group, our communities will be competing for land and for resources. Also, much like what is happening in our world right now, there was an explosion in the use of new technology and AI. They appear not to have put anything in place to regulate or control its use and its very rapid expansion. It makes me all the more determined to follow this through, all the way to the end. We MUST find out what happened in that society. What ever happened there could affect all of us!!"

"All of that is true" mused Chris "and I feel the same, but I think there was somewhat more going on. Something else was happening alongside the wars and the conflicts and the loss of resources. Somehow, something like two million, billion people were convinced that they needed to take a, what turned out to be, catastrophically dangerous risk. Why did they make such an ill-judged choice? We simply have to understand how that happened so that we can all learn from it."

All three agreed with Chris's words.

Chapter 29

The Phenomenal Spread of the Little Maq.

It turned out that Chris's population estimate was somewhat short of the mark as there were around five million, billion people living in the Bounty group. Within less than half a generation, more than half of all families had at least one Little Maq as did nearly all small businesses. Larger organisations usually had many, many more. The Little Maq was now everywhere, and their uses were wide and varied.

The Little Maq was, as we touched upon earlier, a combination of a mini-quantum-computer and a traditional pc (all quantum-computers need a traditional binary computer to act as an interface). At first, at least in the home environment, Little Maqs were used in much the same way as we use our pcs: for communication, for searching and using the Bounty Wide Web, for record keeping and for entertainment. The mini-quantum-computer element was typically very much underused. This was pretty much inevitable as it was a revolutionary new and, hence, unfamiliar technology for everyone. However, over a short period of time, individuals began to discover the power of their quantum-computers and the power of having access to an enormous database. This database was, as we have seen, forever getting larger and larger due to the ever-growing number of Little Maqs. Little by little, very gradually at first, they were used by ordinary folk for bespoke optimised modelling (such as local weather forecasting and personal finances) and for ever more in-depth data mining and application. Forget about searching the web for the best value, off the shelf, package holiday, your Little Maq could create you a bespoke holiday. It would use other people's reported experiences and tailor it to match, what it perceives as, your personal needs, tastes and desires. It was able to make all the bookings, get the best prices available, pre-book your sun loungers, the lot. All you had to do was ask it to book you two weeks in the sun within, say, twelve hours travelling time of home.

In fact, just as a reminder of some background information. A Little Maq's processing method was to take the spoken command, inputted through the voice system, and translate this command into a new hybrid command which integrates the quantum part of the computer with the pc. It used the pc part to provide an input to the quantum part which then fed back its interpretation of the question, by using its huge database. Once the optimised interpretation of the command had been achieved, the command would then be processed, always searching for the optimised best fit answer. Put simply, it was a two-part optimisation process: first, it optimised and refined its interpretation of the command and then it processed and optimised the answer. To take our example of "Book me a two weeks holiday in the sun, not more than twelve hours travel away" the question first gets defined; what is meant by "a holiday"? what does "in the sun" mean? what does "twelve hours travel away" mean? all of which can be found by mining the huge Little Maq's communal database. So, the question is refined to something like, "Find available accommodation, in a sunny country, preferably near the coast, that is within four hours flight time of the local or other nearby airport". The Little Maq has the records of your past personal preferences and includes these in the optimised solution (e.g., no camping, no holiday parks, prefers a private villa with a its own pool). If it needs more data, such as the obvious what are the dates? it will ask for it. At the end of the day, it would create enormous feedback loops: continually mining all available data, continually refining the question and continually optimising the solution.

Little Maqs were quickly and successfully integrated into home networked systems. For example, it would switch on your lights, not simply by just using a movement sensor or a timer, but by knowing where you are, realising where you are likely to be heading as you get up and pre-empting your needs. The Little Maq would be set up to manage a local Wi-Fi enabled network which allowed any and every electronic device to be integrated into this home system. Furthermore, as all Little Maqs were networked together and had access to such a huge amount of data, it was able to continually improve the quality of its decision making. Furthermore, all its data became available to all the other Little Maqs, ultimately anywhere in the Bounty group. This, in turn, maximised all Little Maqs' decision-making abilities and their access to relevant data across the board.

Much the same as at home, the Little Maq also became the norm in the work-place. Small and medium businesses needed to go through exactly the same learning process as most households had to go through. This was not surprising as it was effectively the same group of people who were getting to grips with these newfangled devices, both at home and at work. Again, just like in the domestic situations, the Little Maq quickly became the standard method for controlling almost all workplace environments.

Bigger organisations, those that already possessed a large quantum-computer, rapidly integrated Little Maqs into their existing network. The organisation's Little Maqs became much like our local work-based networks of desktop pcs. The original large quantum-computers were used to control the working parameters of all their networked Little Maqs. These large central quantum-computers became known as mother-computers, and they controlled the operating parameters of all their locally networked Little Maqs. This turned out to be such an efficient way of controlling, monitoring and updating large networks of Little Maqs, that it was adopted by Thunderbolt Services as a way of overseeing the vast number that it now had in its universal network. In practice, each Little Maq was assigned to one of many mother-computers. These mother-computers coordinated the pooling of data and processed higher level operations, such as updates and the like.

*

As Thunderbolt grew, so did its financial resources. It had its own massive cash reserve coupled with an almost unlimited access to additional funding, should it be needed, through share offerings and loans. Thunderbolt soon bought, or leased, many warp-drive spaceships which led to a true Bounty-wide access to all Little Maqs' databases. Thunderbolt invested in a large number of data storage units (much like our cloud storage). All inhabited planets had their own local centralised data storage units. These local data storage units transmitted all their data to larger off planet central hub units which were cited somewhere within about a week's radio transmission (think of it as being like an interplanetary mobile phone network). These hub units were often housed on the most populated planets. From there, data summaries were collected on massive data storage units which were subsequently transported, by warp-driven spaceships to huge central stores, one in each of the six galaxies. At each of these central galactic stores, that galaxy's data was gathered, copied and transferred onward to each of the remaining central stores. From each of these stores all the data went all the way back down the chains to the planetary hubs. The upshot of this was that every Little Maq had immediate access to all data, everywhere and anywhere in the Bounty group. Furthermore, that data would, at worst, be no more than a couple of weeks old.

*

At the same time as there was an explosion in the use of Little Maqs, there was a complimentary growth in the use of robotics. The largest player in this field was Titanium Robotics, controlled by Madeline Grant, the company's CEO. Madeline had met with Fabio Zodiac in the early days of Thunderbolt when the two companies agreed to support each other in devising a universal integration protocol between robotic systems and Little Maqs. The system developed and utilised Wi-Fi connections between the two. As the project developed, the usefulness of this integrated system became very obvious. The robotics "did the work" whilst the Little Maqs became their "brains". Before long, the vast majority of households had fully integrated systems.

In most premises, permanently static automated systems undertook most of the the fixed routine functions, whilst a number of mobile robots did the tasks that required freedom of movement. All were controlled by the household's central Little Maq. An example of this integration could be that a robot is sent to the bedrooms to change the sheets. It is then instructed to take the dirty sheets to the laundry centre where the sheets are washed and pressed by dedicated centrally controlled machines. The little Maq told the robot what to do having decided that the sheets were due to be changed, and it directly operated the entire laundry centre. Another example could be: A robot wakes you with a cup of tea or coffee in bed whilst another robot makes your breakfast. As you have your breakfast the Little Maq asks about your plans for the day whilst showing you a screen with the latest news bulletins or airing your favourite morning show. You have already put a round of golf in your diary so, whilst you have breakfast, a robot loads your golf-clubs into the car, lays your clothes out on your bed and packs your bag. Whilst you are out, a robot takes the laundry to the home's domestic centre for ironing, does the washing up and tidies the garden. Meanwhile, an automated mower mows your lawn, an automated system washes your windows and an automated dispenser feeds the cat. All of this is controlled by the Little Maq, and all of this is done before lunchtime.

Robotics also became common in the workplace. As these systems were so affordable, almost every company, large or small, used robotics in some way or another. Uses ranged from simply taking care of miscellaneous odd jobs, to replacing entire workforces.

*

We have used the word optimisation quite a bit, but, before moving on, the word probably needs a little more explanation. Optimisation is the process of finding the "best" result, however you define the "best" result to be. It could be the quickest, the cheapest, the biggest, the safest, pretty much anything, it is just whatever you define the "best" to be; it is usually whatever is the most important thing to you at the time of asking. One of the ways that you can find the "best" result is by modelling each and every possibility in order to determine which single one solution gives the "best" result. It is this method that is the domain of the quantum-computer. Take the holiday example. There are many countries to choose from, countless hotels, villas, air B&Bs and so on and there are many car-hire options. Each of these various options has varying availabilities and different costs (e.g. depending on room type, villa type and car type etc). It becomes a thankless task to gather so much data, to model so much data and to make a decision. A quantum-computer is the only device that can optimise these potentially huge amounts of variable data. It will try every possible combination of each and every single variable in order to come up with, what it calculates to be, the best solution; and it can do it very quickly.

If you want to get a picture of what I mean, try and optimise this very simple task:

Plan the most cost-effective holiday, by modelling every possible combination, given the following information:

- Hotel A charges
  - $100 per night Mon to Fri
  - $120 per night Sat and Sun
  - $6 per night for the car park
  - A one-off fee of $25 for valet parking (mandatory for each car)
- Hotel B charges
  - $105 per night Mon to Thursday
  - $118 per night Fri to Sun
  - $8 per weekday night for the carpark, $9 per night at weekends
  - Valet parking charges are included
- Hotel C charges
  - $95 per night
  - $7 per weekday night for the car park, $10 per night at weekends
  - One off fee of $20 for valet parking (mandatory for each car)
  - Laundry surcharge of $20 for any single stay over 2 nights
- Travelling
  - The drive from A to B cost $20 for petrol
  - The drive from A to C cost $28 for petrol
  - The drive from B to C cost $31 for petrol
  - Car company X has a one-off hire charge of $100, plus $20 per weekday, $50 Sat/Sun
  - Car company Y has a one-off hire charge of $105, plus $18 per weekday, $35 Sat/Sun

- o Car company Z has a one-off hire charge of $90, plus $11 per day

The 10-day holiday must include:

1. At least 3 consecutive nights at Hotel A (it has a good pool and spa)
2. At least 2 nights in each of the three hotels
3. At least 2 nights at Hotel C must be at the weekend

If you tried this, well done. If you used a pc, an extra well done. But remember; you cannot make any a guesses or assumptions (however obvious they are) and you must model every single possible combination.

If you used a pc, try and make up another scenario with, say, 100 hotels, throw in a few extra variables and see how long it is before your pc grinds to a halt, sends you an error message, gets very hot and, perhaps, begins to smoke a little.

*

As our final quick look at this new technology, we need to look at how Little Maqs enabled a revolution in AI. Our first question must be, what is AI? Well, one description, taken from the internet, is:

"At its most basic, AI is software that mimics and generates human behaviours – planning, generating ideas, using location awareness, understanding speech and visuals."

This IS the Little Maq!!

Furthermore, much like many current AI tools, it learns as it goes. This ability is fundamental to many uses of AI. Take medicine as an example. An AI program can review many clinical heart scans and be told which patients were diagnosed as having a specific disease. The system will quickly learn to spot the relevant symptoms. The system can then review new scans and identify which patients appear to be showing these symptoms. The more it does, providing it gets proper high-quality feedback, the better it gets at the task. Also, it never tires, it never gets distracted, it never misses anything, and it doesn't get bored. Importantly, it can go on to spot other correlations that a human observer may never ever notice.

Each Little Maq had to get to know its new owner, its environment and the expectations of its operator. It also had to learn how to achieve what it is asked to do (as we mentioned before, we do this based on our experiences, the Little Maq uses its communal database). Inevitably, in the early days, there were many examples of cock-ups, errors, misuse and ignorance. In essence, there was a long learning period for both the AI and the people.

Chapter 30

Mary Meteor's Birthday Present.

Mary was fast approaching a significant birthday (much too fast, in her opinion). Her husband, Titan, was a caring man, who loved his wife dearly and wanted to get her a super special something for her super special day. This was in the early days of the Little Maq but he was well aware of its development and he had heard many great reports on its capabilities (every Whisper he received contained references to it, every famous influencer, such as the vivacious Gabriella Smurfet, spoke highly of it and every audio-visual station seemed to make frequent reference to it). The Little Maq was the in-thing! He became even more interested when he learned about the usefulness of incorporating a Little Maq into the home environment, especially one integrated with a home robotics system. He spent several months surfing the Bounty Wide Web researching the functionality of such a setup and, as he got a better idea of what he wanted, he went on to look for a suitable supplier. At that time production of Little Maqs was still relatively limited, so availability was quite restricted. However, after a great deal of searching, he was able to track down a supplier and installer who had the necessary stock and the right installation engineers' availability to create his ideal setup. He immediately put down a sizeable deposit on a Little Maq and two robots. The supplier warned Titan that the system would need quite a lot of setting up and that there would be quite a lengthy and involved installation process. As part of his package, Titan arranged for the installation team to do their work during the week following Mary's birthday. The plan was to tell her that her birthday surprise was a week's holiday in a picturesque cottage in the countryside. Whilst they were away, the installation team would come in and put sensors throughout the house and add Wi-Fi enabled controls to all their electronic equipment. They would also set up charging stations for the two robots and configure all their other automated domestic appliances. Mary would come home from her super holiday to find her real birthday surprise; a fully installed home robotic system, complete with a trendy new, voice activated, Little Maq.

Little Maqs themselves came pre-installed with many basic programs … speech and language capabilities, all typical pc software such as spreadsheets and the like, access to Whisper and other social media platforms, streaming services and many other common applications. Most importantly, though, was the act of simply turning it on meant that it immediately started learning from all the other Little Maqs and all their associated databases (their memories and experiences).

Mary and Titan returned home quite late in the evening, following their relaxing week-long break. Titan held the front door open for Mary to enter the home. As she entered, she was greeted by two shiny new robots singing "happy birthday to you", just as Titan had arranged. Once she was over the surprise (well, shock really), they walked around their home inspecting the installation. Whilst they walked around, Titan explained the system's capabilities. She was totally overwhelmed, at first by having two chrome plated men leaping out of the shadows singing "happy birthday to you" and then by the thoughtfulness and generosity of her husband. They spent the remainder of the evening talking about what the system could do for them and Titan explained to Mary that there was still a lot of personalised setting-up to do.

Titan was the first to set off for work the next morning and, unfortunately, he had a relatively early start to the day. Mary decided to give her new helpers a nice easy task whilst she was out at her office.

"Tidy up the front room" was the simple command.

The Little Maq responded, saying,

"Insufficient data in the command, which is the front room? I believe there are five rooms at the front of the house" It had already searched various databases and found that "tidy" meant to arrange things neatly in order.

"The front room is what we call the living room."

"Inaccurate data in the command … none of the rooms at the front of the house are living."

"Oh, sorry. We call the room at the front of the house, where we keep the sofa and tv, the living room."

"Yes mam."

A key element in getting an AI system working correctly is to be very specific with its initial instructions, especially during the phase when it is trying things out for the first time and learning new tasks (if you are a car driver, just remember your first few lessons!). It turned out that Mary had not been quite specific enough. That evening, as she entered the house, she found one of the robots standing by the front door, motionless in its charging station. "Excellent" thought Mary "they have obviously done their tasks and returned to their designated charging areas, I'll just pop upstairs and change out of my work clothes." She hung her handbag and coat on the stand in the hallway, went upstairs and had a quick shower. The warm water helped her relax after a hard day's work and, after her shower, she put on some tracksuit bottoms and a t-shirt. She went back downstairs and entered the living room. "What the hell??" she thought as she saw the scene in front of her. The Little Maq had applied a literal interpretation to the command "tidy up". It knew that "tidy" meant to put things in order and "up" meant, well, up. When combined, the Little Maq took the command to be "put all things in order in an upwardly direction". To properly describe the bizarre scene is not easy. Every book, and there were a great many books in that room, was stacked neatly in the middle of the floor, in alphabetical order, by title. In fact, there were two columns, both nearly reaching the ceiling, A to L and M to Z. Both the armchairs were stacked, one on top of the other. The carpet had been rolled up and stood neatly upright in the corner of the room (it had been rolled up and now pointed up). The long low storage and display unit was now turned on its end so that its length was now in an upwardly direction (they had even put neat little pieces of sticking tape on the doors to stop them coming open). The space in and around these crazy, upwardly pointing, neatly ordered, vertically rising columns had been perfectly cleaned, scrubbed and vacuumed.

Titan came home and laughed his head off. "Hmm, from now on we need to be very precise when we give instructions, at least until such time as the Little Maq learns what we mean and has had time to fully scour its communal database," said Titan.

"Oh shit" said Mary "I told them to do the washing up and to make sure it is spotless!"

"So, that doesn't seem too bad."

"Our crockery has a polka dot pattern!!!"

"Ahh" said Titan, as he realised what Mary was getting at. They went into the kitchen to find a neat stack of washed dishes, all having had their polka dot pattern erased by, what Titan guessed to be, the grinding wheel attachment of his power tool. "Hmm, I guess we really do need to give things a bit more thought next time, darling!!"

Chapter 31

Sham's First Day in Parliament.

Attending Parliament was simple for Sham as the Central Galaxy's Parliament was on Whisper, which was Sham's constituency and where he lived. He had no interplanetary travel to do, he simply arranged for his chauffeur to take him there in their luxury hover-car. As they approached the building, he wound up his thick, black tinted, triple glazed window to block out the noise and the chants coming from the permanent demonstration outside of the Parliament Buildings.

In truth, there were a number of demonstrations going on and they were all pretty much permanent, but the biggest, by far, was the anti-wars demonstration. This had been camped outside the Parliament buildings for many years. In fact, it had been there for several generations. The protesters were not demonstrating because they thought their Parliament was to blame for the wars, it was not their Parliament that was going to war. Rather, the demonstrators felt that their Parliament was not doing enough to reduce the number of wars throughout the galaxy and their frequency. It was their belief that Parliament should be much more proactive in getting potentially warring peoples to negotiate rather that fight. At the end of the day, nearly all the wars were about natural resources, only occasionally were they about something different, such as a dictator wanting to flex his muscles or a war undertaken in the name of a religion. It was a frequently expressed view that the allocation of resources should be a matter of negotiation rather than war, and it was many people's point of view that reducing the prevalence of war should really be all Parliaments' prime objective, but they didn't seem to be doing a very good job of it.

"What are they demonstrating about?" Sham asked of his Chauffeur, Ray, by bellowing the question directly into his ear.

Ray was at first startled and then gob-smacked. "Is this guy for real?" he thought, "these demonstrations have been in the news, like, forever. Everyone knows what they are about, and they are permanently outside of all the Galactic Parliaments. It just shows you how having too much money can completely isolate you from the rest of the world, from the real world that everybody else lives in." "It's mostly an anti-war demonstration, sir." Ray politely replied.

"Gosh, there are a lot of people here." bellowed Sham.

"Yes sir, there always are is and, to be honest, this is a relatively quiet day."

"It must be a big problem."

"War sir? er yes sir, it's the biggest. If anyone can sort out the continual warring, they will be very popular indeed."

"Really, very popular you say?" said Sham, this time in a slightly more subdued and contemplative tone of voice.

"Sir, if anyone can sort out this mess, that person will be the most popular person in the entire universe, guaranteed!"

This was perfect for Sham. He hadn't even got through Parliament's front door, and he had found a way to realise his life's ambition. Not stopping war or saving lives, not benefiting all living beings, not by supporting the wishes of his constituents, no, his life's ambition was to be popular and he had just found a way by which he could possibly become the most popular guy in the universe. At last, a challenge that could give him the status that he believes he is entitled to.

And it came to pass, over time, that Sham became a prominent spokesman for the anti-war movement, not through any moral belief, not because he felt strongly about the subject, but simply to massage his own ego.

Chapter 32

Mont-Fredo & Zodiac.

The friendship between Mont-Fredo and Zodiac was growing day by day. Each had become extremely wealthy and, as such, they tended to move in the same social circles. Their friendship was further enhanced by the fact that their two companies were both benefitting enormously from working closely together. Thunderbolt Services was benefiting from the huge and ever-growing databases held by Whispers and Whispers was benefitting from the astronomical growth in the numbers of Little Maq users. As more and more Little Maqs were sold, the number of people with access to Whispers grew. As more and more people used Whispers, the Whispers' databases became ever larger and more effective. This symbiotic and self-reenforcing relationship was proving to be very effective in growing the business of both companies. Whispers and Thunderbolt Services were each growing at a phenomenal rate. Furthermore, and probably most importantly, they genuinely liked each other.

Mont-Fredo had been thinking about their two systems and had hit upon another idea: behaviour-driven advertising. Here, in essence, were his thoughts. Most Whispers contained some form of advertising. At that time, any company wishing to use Whispers as an advertising platform paid a fee to Whispers for a fixed number of adverts, let's say 1,000,000 adverts. Whispers would then include the advert in 1,000,000 Whispers. The recipients of these adverts were effectively chosen at random as the adverts were simply included in the next batch of 1,000,000 Whispers. They were included regardless of what the advert was about, regardless of what the Whisper was about and regardless of who the recipient was going to be. Sometime ago, Mont-Fredo realised that this blanket approach to advertising was not the most effective methodology, it would be much better to send specific adverts to their users (Whisperers) who have expressed an interest in receiving adverts for this type of product. His initial trial had been to contact several users and give them a choice as to what type of adverts they were going to get. This was, in fact, piloted with a large number of Whisperers. Each of the selected Whisperers completed a matrix detailing which adverts they would prefer to receive (there was no option to receive no adverts, even for a fee). So, an individual could specify something along the lines of yes, to cars, household white goods, travel, books and TV programs, but no to plumbing, gardening or cooking.

In reality the choice was actually very wide, and it could always be amended in your settings at any time. You did have the option to specify no preference at all, but you would still receive the same number of adverts, but most of them would be of no interest to you whatsoever. The very large majority of people selected their preferences. Once that was in place, if you were, for instance, a travel agent, you would pay a much larger fee for the 1,000,000 adverts, but they were now sent to 1,000,000 people who had each specified that they were interested in travel. This was clearly a much more attractive proposition. However, Mont-Fredo had begun to ponder the possibility of basing advertising not only on pre-selected choices but on actual recent behaviour. Furthermore, if that could be done in real-time, so much the better. A simple example could be … if a Whisperer mentions a toaster in their whisper, the next three or four adverts received by that individual would be from companies that supply toasters. It sounded perfect but how much better would it be to get much more specific information? If someone actually expresses a desire to purchase a toaster, on the Whispers' platform, then that would be great, but it was still very limited. The solution was obvious; use Thunderbolt's Little Maq network as those databases contained a record of virtually every online search ever made, all done in real time.

Mont-Fredo and Zodiac met up fairly frequently, both socially and as part of their various business schedules. Mont-Fredo first broached the subject of behaviour-based advertising whilst he and Zodiac were dining alone one evening. "Fabio, I've been giving some thought to a new type of advertising, advertising that is better for the customer and better for the seller."

"Oh yeah, and what's that then?"

"I'm thinking that if we could marry adverts to people's current needs, they would be much more effective. If you were looking for, say, a new air frier, then you would much rather receive adverts for air-fryers than anything else. It would give you the chance to see what is available and compare pricing and so on. The sellers would obviously benefit from such targeted advertising as well."

"OK, that makes sense."

"I'm thinking that we can use the information captured by all the Little Maqs telling us what their users have recently been searching for, coupled with whatever is contained in their recent Whispers."

"I see. So, you are saying that we could create an algorithm that matches any customer's most recent searches to all the relevant seller's adverts."

"Precisely."

"That sounds perfect, but I think we could add a bit more to that. Little Maqs receive most of their input verbally, but I believe that we could also include any verbally expressed desires. Quite by coincidence, this concept is likely to marry perfectly with a recent idea that we've been working on." said Zodiac, with a glint in his eye.

"What's that then?"

"You know that at the moment, you press and hold an input switch to verbally programme your Little Maq. Well, I'm thinking of totally bypassing the switch and have all Little Maqs listen permanently for any instruction. A specific input could be triggered by saying something like "Ahoy Little Maq" before going on to give the instruction. The point is that every Little Maq will be permanently listening to whatever is being said around it. It would hear someone talking about getting a new air-fryer. This could easily be added to the algorithm."

"What about existing Little Maqs, wont they need a physical modification?".

"No, we believe we can remodel them by way of a simple update via their Mother Computers."

"Cool. Don't you think that the users might be a bit wary about their Little Maqs permanently listening in on their conversations?"

"No, I don't think they will. Once they get used to the idea, they probably won't even be conscious of being permanently listened to, it will, over time, just become the norm. Such a system will give the user so many advantages that any perceived downsides will soon be forgotten. They could simply talk to the Little Maq from anywhere that has a linked microphone. So, when they are at home, they can ask something like "Ahoy Little Maq, what is the weather going to do over the next two hours?" and the Little Maq will tell them (Little Maqs are so powerful that they could even do their own forecast). I'm also thinking about how to communicate with a Little Maq when away from home and I think I have the ideal solution."

"Go on."

"Everyone carries a communicator. My initial thought was that we could use the microphone on these devices to permanently listen for commands for the Little Maq, it's just a change in the user settings. However, I then realised that, similar to using the communicator's microphone, it would be a simple job for a customer to place some simple Wi-Fi enabled microphones around their house. They could then use these to pick up voice commands for their Little Maqs and their robotics from anywhere in their home. But then I thought of the obvious, they could do both, or either, whichever was best for them at the time. They could use their in-house microphones OR their communicators from anywhere they want; inside the house, outside the house, at work, abroad, in fact anywhere that is on the same planetary network. It would be seen as a massive benefit. But, taking your idea a bit further, we could have our algorithms analyse any spoken words that it picks up from within range of a Little Maq or any linked communicator. This would be a massive benefit for everyone."

"Wow, so we could create a system that takes any data from any user to trigger user-specific targeted adverts. That would be amazing. It would be amazing for the customers, and it would be amazing for the sellers."

"And, between our two companies, we already have the infrastructure to do that" confirmed Zodiac, " It's simply a question of some reprogramming of our systems via some updates."

Mont-Fredo was getting excited and added "Thinking on my feet, I've another idea. We can send these adverts directly to your Little Maqs as well. You already have adverts appearing when a user does a BWW search along with relevant hyper-links etc., and many websites already include adverts; let's make them all user-specific whenever possible. Whispers can supply the same adverts that we would send to our users, and you can include these along with any hyperlinks or other material that you would usually include. It would be a fully integrated two-way process."

This was the initial discussion which led to further technical meetings between the two companies. The result of many such meetings was that user-specific targeted advertising went live about 9 months later and Fabio Zodiac became a 5% shareholder of Whispers.

During the following months the functionality was expanded so that the user didn't only receive adverts. The resultant algorithms were updated to include sending hyperlinks to other websites and social media pages that were deemed to be relevant to the user. For instance, if you are searching online for a campsite in a certain region, the algorithm would now send you relevant adverts plus links to local websites or social media pages that mention campsites or camping in that region. These links became extremely useful for someone who, say, has a particular hobby, or a particular taste in music, or is undertaking a particular task, as they would now receive relevant adverts along with hyperlinks to other websites and social-media pages related to the same genre.

Inevitably, and over quite a short period of time, most of the population of Bounty were receiving most of their on-line content selected by these user specific algorithms, along with hyper-links to other social media pages.

The upshot was that, before long, almost all on-line viewing and social media viewing was being selected and driven by these new algorithms. As a user, the algorithms would send you a plethora of choices, but they were all based on the algorithms' selection and its prioritisation of what it determined that you would like to receive. To boil this down further, all users received links and material that were always similar to the material they had already viewed. No new ideas, no differences of opinions, no alternative views and, most disturbingly, no balance.

Chapter 33

Sham's Inaugural Speech.

It was customary for all new Members of Parliament to give an inaugural speech within a few weeks of their first ever attendance in the house. Sham gave a fairly long and very moving, passionate sounding, heartfelt speech. The only thing it lacked was any substance whatsoever.

"Madam Speaker, fellow members and ALL citizens of Bounty, I would like to take this opportunity to talk to you about .... blah blah blah .... booming voice ....war is bad..................... bluster .... each and every citizen of Bounty needs supporting .... waffle .... beaming smile .... nod to all members who sat around him .... well-meaning and sincere smile to the opposition members .... acknowledge the Speaker of the House .... as politicians we should all be doing better............. and finally .... boom .... bluster," and twenty minutes later, he sat down.

He sat down, not to the traditional roars and cheers of support from his own party members, not to the usual waving of ballot papers, not to the traditional muted clapping and other polite signs of respect and acknowledgement from the opposition benches. No, Sham sat down amidst a silent sea of bewilderment. Every Member of Parliament who had witnessed his inaugural speech wore a look of utter bafflement and bemusement. Nobody clapped in agreement, nobody booed in disagreement, there was not even a ripple of conversation. Everybody was stunned. It was later summed up by a senior Traditionalist member who said, "I must confess, Sham's speech left me a little confused. He seemed to be speaking in favour of everybody's point of view. He spoke in high praise of the moral backbone of the Traditionalist Party but, just a little later, he was full of praise for the opposition's principled positions. He declared himself to be a strong supporter of our capitalist societies but also said that he greatly admired the achievements of our more socialist societies. He said he would be championing the workers but, at the same time, he would back entrepreneurs, big businesses and all employers to the hilt. He was anti-war but was all for increased defence spending. He was all for low taxation yet wants to increase public spending. At one point he said that there should be less public borrowing but later stated that the government needs to borrow more. I'm going to put this one down to first time nerves."

An opposition member put things a little more succinctly. "What a waffling idiot. He just says whatever he believes people want to hear. He is clearly lacking in any guiding principles, and he completely lacks a working moral compass!"

But a bizarre thing began to happen over the coming few days. Carefully selected sound-bites and clips taken from Sham's speech began to appear on many social media platforms and across many news outlets. These short clips were selected and shown in total isolation, and they were in support of many and varied issues. Had anyone looked more closely, they were often in complete contradiction to each other. An anti-war group would receive the snippets of Sham's speech that decried war. Attendees of an arms trade-show received the snippets of Sham's speech that supported an increase in defence spending; and there were countless other examples. Over the coming weeks, Sham, quite bizarrely, seemed to become popular in all camps and a real man of the people. If you were poor, Sham was championing your needs. If you were wealthy, Sham was all for representing you. If you were an arms dealer, Sham was all for reducing burdensome legislation and red tape. If you were anti-war, Sham was your man. It would appear that, behind the scenes, someone was pulling a lot of strings.

⋯⛧⟨⟩⛧⋯

Chapter 34

Sham's Party.

Sham hosted a splendid party at his house during the evening following his inaugural speech, inviting all his closest friends and his immediate family. His old school chums Dip-Dip, Mac Oik, and Plank were the first to arrive along with Mac Oik's new brother-in-law Polo Marmalade. These were soon followed by Sham's father and a few other family members. Sham had deliberately arranged for his family and closest friends to get there first as he wanted to touch base with those people as a priority. He knew he could trust and would always be supported by his close friends and his family. Maybe half an hour later, other guests started to appear including Sir Alfie Windlesham, chairman of the Traditionalist Party, other local MPs, several key party workers, his own constituency office staff and several other people who worked in politics. He had also invited some trusted members of the press and social media commentators.

"Great speech" said Dip-Dip, as he walked up to Sham, with a gin and tonic in one hand and a champagne in the other "and congratulations on becoming a member of parliament; jolly good show."

"Thanks, Old Bean. It's good of you to come and it's very nice to see you again."

"Wouldn't have missed it for the world. Oh look, there's Mac Oik just coming in. Hi Mac Oik, how's it going?"

"Hi Dip-Dip and well done to you Sham, great speech! Can I introduce you both to my new brother-in-law?" said Mac Oik whilst grabbing the elbow of a very tall man standing next to him. "This is Polo, my sister Lilly's new husband. They've just come back from their honeymoon travelling around the beautiful planets of Centaur Galaxy after a very quiet wedding. Lilly is no longer Lilly Mac Oik, she is now Lilly Marmalade."

Sham shook Polo's hand and offered his congratulations. "Are you the Polo Marmalade we've all heard so much about?" asked Sham.

"To be honest, I don't think there are that many other Polo Marmalades," joked Polo, "but I'm certainly the one that works in online marketing and online profile development, if that's what you mean. Unless, of course, you have seen me mentioned in the popular press just recently," he said with a chuckle "in which case I'm the faker-in-chief of all fake news."

"I'm not sure about that as I don't know your work as of yet, and I most certainly don't read the papers! but I've no doubt that your work is rather impressive ... although, I will be checking!" said Sham with a smile "but you are the Marmalade I'm thinking of" continued Sham. "I've been told that you do very good work. Any chance that we can grab a few minutes alone in my office a bit later?"

"Now that is an offer I can't refuse" said Polo as he broke into an even wider grin.

"I just need to say hello to a few people and then we can talk. How about I grab you in about twenty minutes or so?"

"Great, see you then. I promise not to leave." They shook hands and Sham strolled off to mingle with his family and his other guests.

Two hours later, Sham sidled up to Polo Marmalade and indicated that he should follow him. They slipped, unobserved, into Sham's office. "Can I get you a drink?" asked Sham, "I'm going to grab myself a brandy."

"A brandy would be great and congratulations on your appointment and on your maiden speech to the house."

"Thank you, Polo, I can call you Polo, can't I? and please call me Sham."

"Of course!"

"OK, Polo it is then. Polo, I've been meaning to touch base with you for a couple of weeks now, but you've been away on your honeymoon. As you are obviously aware, I have entered the scary world of politics. The universe has moved on in recent years and I believe that, in order to be effective, a public figure can no longer just work within the limit of the traditional press. To be successful, in this new world, I know that I need to proactively manage my online profile and I've been told that you are the guy to help me do that. I've known Mac Oik and Dip-Dip for most of my life and I trust their judgement. Both rate you very highly."

"Well, that's good to know, I've done some marketing work for both of them. May I ask a blunt question?"

"Sure, fire away".

"What is it that you want to achieve? I don't just mean, what are your vague lifetime wishes, I mean what are your specific goals? I must know these if I'm going to work out how you will need to be perceived"

"That is a good question and, to be honest, I'm not entirely sure. I think I am already perceived as an approachable person, you know, a bit of a man of the people, good sense of humour, that sort of stuff. I am well known and broadly well liked. My TV work has helped a lot with that."

"OK, I could say that you have given me a typical politician's answer as you didn't actually answer the question. I'm not a member of the press or an opposition party member, I am here to help you, not to trip you up. If you want me to help you, and putting modesty to one side I think I am the best in the business, I will ask again ... what is it that you want to ultimately achieve in the public domain? Answering that honestly is going to shape and drive how we develop and promote your public image. The better you can answer that, the better I can help you. But it is critical."

"Hmm, my father once told me that I should reach for the stars. Many of the Galaxy's Presidents went to Belton and, to be honest, I want to be President. But I'm not thinking of just President of Central Galaxy, I want to be President of the whole of Bounty."

"OK, hats off to you, I truly admire your ambition and that actually gives me a very good brief as it was very specific. In this galaxy, Presidents are individually elected, they are not party appointments like, for example, the Prime Minister. To be president is all about getting votes from many different types of people and the easiest way of doing that is by becoming popular with as many different types of people as possible. That's all about appealing to as wide a range as possible, right across the political and social spectra. It's about appealing to the wealthy and the poor alike, to the business owners and the workers, to the pro-defence spending people and the anti-defence spending people, the city dwellers and the country dwellers, people who live on large central planets and those people who live on more remote planets. In a nutshell, you must have as wide an appeal as possible. Once that is achieved, we can then work on how to make you specifically more popular than your opponents. I guess our first task is to make you president of Central Galaxy, once that is done, we can then work on the creation of a President for Bounty. The truth is that if you become truly popular then you become extremely influential. Given the right support, you will be able to shape your own future … and the future of everyone."

"Is making me that popular doable?" asked Sham.

"I think so, especially with the technology that's available now, and I am definitely up for the challenge. I believe that our new social media and interconnected technologies are so powerful and so influential that I truly believe people can be swayed such that anything is possible, given the right focus and the right management. Can I ask one question?"

"Of course, fire away."

"Would you consider yourself as a highly principled man?"

"Err, I'm not quite sure what you are getting at."

"I mean, do you feel bound by normal social or moral constraints and, if so, would you let those stop you achieving your dreams?"

"Well, put like that, no. I feel it is more important that I achieve my aims. If I don't become president then that would deny people the benefit of my guidance. Put another way, I feel I have more of a moral obligation to achieve my goals than be bound by any petty underlying morals. I will do anything it takes, and I would expect you to do the same."

"In that case, as for helping you become a very popular yet serious political player, I've no doubt that we can achieve that and, if you want me to, I'll get to work on it right away. Can we meet up in a few days' time and talk it through in more detail? By then I will have something to show you."

They agreed to meet at the weekend, just three days later.

Marmalade got to work the very next day. He kicked off by reviewing Sham's inaugural speech and any clips from Sham's recent TV and Radio work that he could find. This gave him plenty of raw material to be getting on with. After a day or so, he had a large selection of short clips and quotes that could be used immediately. His plan was to identify, clip by clip and quote by quote, any relevant group, organisation or influential individual, which any specific clip might appeal to. For instance, Sham's speech had contained several quotes that were clearly pro-spending on the galaxy's home security. The relevant groups that would be targeted for these clips included, amongst others: The Home Defence Alliance, several arms manufacturers and many right-wing political groups. Once he had identified these targets, he then looked to identify key players within those organisations. Once these individuals had been identified, he went on to track down their contact details and forwarded them the chosen clips or referred to a relevant quote. Over the following couple of days, he contacted several thousand people. As these clips started to appear across all tranches of social media, Marmalade's strategy became self-fulfilling. The new algorithms that were being used by Thunderbolt Services and Whispers, meant that, as people searched for, or even made any verbal reference to, one of the areas covered by a selected Sham clip, they would inevitably receive a copy of that clip or a hyperlink to it, and this rapidly went Bounty wide. So, for example, if you were searching the BWW for anything related to poverty, thanks to the new algorithms, you would automatically receive links to relevant webpages and social media pages that also mention poverty. These links would now include those relevant clips and hyperlinks that highlighted Sham's support which Marmalade had circulated. Marmalade was undoubtedly the first person to truly understand and exploit the new on-line algorithms … and Sham was undoubtedly the first (and as it turned out, only) big beneficiary.

Chapter 35

Progress Report.

Skipper, Chris and TT decided to spend another evening together for a progress update. Unusually, they didn't meet in the Train Stop but, rather, they met in a different pub that was situated about a mile from where they lived. It was a lovely evening, so Chris and Skipper walked there, and TT met them there, having taken his electric bicycle. They chose this pub as it was away from their usual friends and, hopefully, they would get some quiet time together.

Skipper led the conversation, and it very quickly became clear that they were all singing from the same hymn sheet. Skipper summarised their chat saying, "We already know that Intergalactic travel was possible using quantum-computers. It's my guess that the much smaller and cheaper Little Maqs made intergalactic travel more widespread and, therefore, available to more people. This probably led to more integration and more conflict. Little Maqs were everywhere, and they created an integrated network that, in one way or another, spread throughout all the planets and all the galaxies in the Bounty group. This network vastly increased the size and usage of the Bounty Wide Web and their social media platforms. Thunderbolt and Whispers created algorithms which distributed online content in a self-targeting way. It is my understanding that most of the population, along with virtually every business and organisation, had access to the BWW and received targeted online content. Alongside the Little Maqs, there was clearly a surge in the use of robotics and AI. It is my belief that these changes inevitably led to fundamental changes in their society such as how it functioned and how it interacted. I believe we need to look at how this growth in technology affected their wider society, what they did about it and, perhaps more importantly, what they didn't do.

Furthermore, these changes occurred within less than half a generation. That was a phenomenal and probably unmanageable rate of change for any society to cope with. I think we also need to get a better handle on the ramifications of this hyper-rapid rate of technology-driven social change and how it was managed (if indeed it was managed at all). We need to fully understand what the consequences of these changes were and, perhaps, how things could have been done differently. It is also becoming more and more obvious that a very powerful and influential elite had developed. This elite seems to consist of a few very rich individuals, a few very rich families and a few mega-wealthy hi-tech business owners."

"I totally agree," said Chris. "I also, think we are getting some pointers as to what The Network actually is. I'm guessing that all the Little Maqs, along with their associated robotics, became the Boxers. I think that the old-style larger quantum-computers, the Mother Computers, which were used to control networks of Little Maqs (either by Thunderbolt Services or by large organisations that had integrated Little Maqs into their existing network), became the Snowballs. Finally, I believe that Napoleon, Old Major and Squealer are likely to be the three master control units which were the original super quantum-computers used by Thunderbolt Services to control their entire intergalactic network." As it turned out, Skipper and TT had also been thinking along the same lines.

"What's more," added Chris, "we need to start thinking about what we do with the information we get. How do we make people aware of what we find? I don't want to be over-dramatic, but there could be important lessons to be learnt here before it is too late for us, for ALL of mankind. I don't think I'm wrong in saying that, much like in Bounty, the expansion of our new technology has all been within less than a generation and it is already having a huge impact on our societies."

TT hit the nail on the head when he said "We have a duty to let people know what we find and I'm not letting all this effort go to waste. That would be like pedalling all the way to the top of a steep hill, only to find that there is no bar when you get there."

Chapter 36

The Jackson Twins.

The Jackson twins were born and raised on an ordinary council estate, on the ordinary outskirts of an ordinary industrial town, on a very ordinary planet, in the Central Galaxy. Their parents were traditional working class factory workers. There was absolutely nothing out of the ordinary in the twins' childhood that would point towards their extraordinary future. Dad was, perhaps, a little overbearing and their mother definitely drank a little bit too much, but other than that, they were model parents. Both mum and dad were caring and supportive of their twins and wanted the best for them. If anything, despite what they went on to perpetrate, the twins were slightly below par in their academic prowess (they didn't appear particularly bright but, at the same time, they were by no means thought of as dim). They always did what they were told and tried to do the best they could. They were polite, kind and were popular with both their teachers and their classmates. Towards the end of their schooling years, they even helped out for an hour or two each week at a local elderly citizens' care centre.

Whilst growing up, they spent a great deal of their free time playing computer games, mostly role-play and various all action shoot-em-up games. They started off playing their games on their traditional, second hand, gaming laptops and they could often be found in their bedroom, headphones on, staring at their screens, playing as a team or in competition with each other. It was obvious to all that they enjoyed playing on their computers, but it was their father's idea to get them one of those super-duper new Little Maqs for their birthday. There was no way that they could afford two, so it was a shared birthday present on their shared birthday.

The twins, Adam and Zachariah (Zak) loved their new present; in fact, if anything, it became an obsession. Don't be misled by this, they still did their schoolwork, their chores and anything that their parents asked them to do, but almost all their remaining time was spent on their Little Maq. What did they do on the Little Maq? Well, at first, they played faster, brighter, more colourful, more realistic, more complex and better games. Inevitably, as they grew and explored the capabilities of their Little Maq a little further, often using the search facilities of the Bounty Wide Web, they became connected to the various algorithms used by Thunderbolt and Whispers. They started to receive links to other computer focused sites, along with links to computer focused social media sites. With this newfound information, they quickly moved beyond gaming. It was not long before they started to explore the more general world of computers and computing. Using the guidance that they found online and having followed these unsolicited hyper-links, they learnt a great deal about how computers work, including how to hack into other computers and, perhaps more significantly, how their encryption and security systems worked. After a while, using the immense power of their micro-quantum-computer, they were able to access other people's social media pages and gain access to the databases that lay behind many websites. None of this was done with any malicious intent whatsoever, it was simply an exciting challenge. The twins viewed it more as a super-intense and realistic game. Could they crack the security of such and such a site? BINGO, they were in; chalk one up for the Jackson twins. To get into some of their targeted systems took weeks of trial and error, advanced programming skills, intuition and, quite often, a modicum of luck, all coupled with a great deal of insight and persistence. It was not long before they had developed quite a unique skill-set, and it was becoming obvious that they had a very rare talent.

At first, they hacked into fairly low-key stuff such as friends' private messages, school records, booking sites for the local cinema etc. (although low-key, these acts were still illegal all the same). They never made any changes to those sites, they never passed on any information, and they never let anyone know that they had looked at their private information. To the Jackson twins it was still simply an immensely absorbing and challenging game. As they gained more experience, they accessed more challenging systems such as low-key companies, museums, sports arenas and the like. Inevitably, they went on to access the systems of larger and larger companies and other organisations having worked out how to break through their more rigorous security protocols. As they became practiced at gaining access to ever more secure sites, they slowly discovered the Dark Web [The Dark Web is the name given to those internet sites whose access requires specific software, configurations or authorisation. It can be used to keep internet activity anonymous and private and can be used for both legal and illegal purposes]. Were the twins aware that what they were doing was illegal? Absolutely they were! but they didn't believe they were doing any harm.

*

Then, one day, their activities moved beyond just being a challenging game. "Hey Adam, come and have a look at this" called out Zak, from across their shared bedroom.

"What have you got there then?"

"Just come and have a look. I think these guys are paying for lists of telephone numbers. We've got loads of those."

"Really? hmm, well, perhaps we could make a bit of cash. After all, Mum's birthday is coming up soon and it would be nice to get her a half decent present. Let's have a look." With that, Adam crossed the room and sat next to Zak who slightly tilted the Little Maq's screen so that Adam could get a better view. "You know, I think you're right, it looks like that's exactly what they say they will do."

"Do you think we should drop them an email, just to find out how this all works and see if it's genuine or not?" asked Zak.

"Let's do it. I think we should set up another secure email address and send it from there. After all, the site could be a bit dodgy. There could be a number of reasons why they are only on the Dark Web."

"I agree, let's do it. After all, what harm can a few telephone numbers do?" questioned Adam "you can get a load just from looking in the telephone directory." So, they sent a short email asking for more information, including how much they would be paid. They received a reply within the hour saying that they would be paid so much per thousand numbers, half on receipt and half a week later, once a sample of the names and numbers had been checked and verified as being genuine. There would be increased payments for additional information such as the person's profession, address, town, planet, car type and model, in fact any additional information would be welcome and would be paid for.

The twins had a problem to resolve, how were they going to get paid? Their answer was to open a bogus online child's account with a local building society. They were able to access the society's website and forward fictitious online documentation to setup their new account, inventing new names and new parents in the process. This new online account was obviously under a false name and was accessible to both of them.

A fortnight later, the Jackson twins sent a list of 11,500 phone numbers along with names, addresses and email addresses. The information had come from the local library's records. They were paid exactly as promised and, a few days later, they received an email thanking them for the information. The email sender also commented on how good their client had found the quality of the data and, as such, would be glad to receive more numbers. And that was that, their first true steps into the dark underbelly of cybercrime had been taken and a life of serious crime had just begun whilst they were still only school-aged children. Whilst they were still attending school they hacked into other, more productive, databases, including some retail companies and other organisations such as charities and various associations. They sent off more lists of names and numbers and this time they included other personal information. For a couple of kids, living on a council estate at the rougher end of town, they got paid exceedingly well as they continued supplying their information. They left school at the earliest opportunity and immediately set up a series of bogus companies, all with the intention of hiding, what was now becoming, a not inconsiderable income by anybody's standards.

*

Out of the blue and much to Adam and Zak's surprise the people behind the original dark website, (the one that had first paid them for names and numbers and with which they had been dealing with, quite regularly, for around three years now), suddenly contacted them directly. They asked for information regarding specific groups of people. This was a first as they had never been contacted in such a way before.

"Hi guys," it read (although how the sender knew there were more than one of them, the twins could only guess) "we are looking for the names, numbers and email addresses of any people who have a medical condition. Ideally, we would like to know what their medical conditions are, what medications they are being prescribed and any other relevant information. We would also like to know of any individual who has been involved in an accident that they believe was the fault of another person or organisation. You will be well rewarded for the information you provide, especially if it is to your usual high standard."

"Now that's a challenge," said Zak "we had better start digging. We could do very well out of this."

They spent quite some time hacking into various organisations' databases, and they came up with several relevant lists. Some of these lists contained, quite literally, billions of names, phone numbers, and email addresses. Some even came complete with full medical records. What surprised the twins was how unsecure these websites turned out to be; it was as if the information holders were only paying lip service to their responsibilities for keeping this very personal data secure. Adam summed up the situation when he commented, "It's like they are more interested in making a profit than putting proper resources into protecting their clients' very personal data. Either that or they simply don't have the necessary skills within their organisations."

Around one month after receiving the original request, they forwarded their lists. The receivers were delighted with the information and the twins were extremely well paid. As it transpired, this was the source of much of the raw data that was eventually used by those, less than scrupulous, medical insurance companies, which we previously came across as reported in the A Stitch in Time medical journal.

Several months after being contacted, the twins received the following email.

"Hi Adam and Zak. We just wanted to touch base with you regarding your excellent work. But before that, we want to say "congratulations" on the successful launch of your new companies and to wish you well, now that you have both left school. We believe our working relationship has developed well and we also believe that it has the potential to develop a great deal further. Because of that, I would like to meet with you. Can you come to the Magic Flute cocktail bar, the one on Market Street in your home-town's centre, at 8pm on the Friday of next week? I already have a table booked under the name of Teddy Smith. Please do not be alarmed, we are very keen to meet you, solely with the intention of working more closely with you in the future. Please respond ASAP as I will have a flight to organise."

"OMG, how the hell does he know so much about us?" said Adam.

"I have no idea and I'm not sure I want to meet him."

"I don't think we have a choice" replied Adam "we can't just blank him as he already knows too much about us. Besides, maybe it will be for the best. He obviously thinks we are good at what we do or else he wouldn't have asked us for more information. Maybe it is him that needs us. I don't know why but I have a very good feeling about this."

"OK, let's do it. At least we might get an idea of exactly how much he knows about us and whether he really means us no harm." As they typed their reply, saying that they would, indeed, be at the Magic Flute and that they were looking forward to it, they were shaking and visibly quite pale. The truth was that they were probably both in shock. The following Friday, at exactly 8pm, Adam and Zak entered the Magic Flute.

*

Zak was the first to enter the cocktail bar and walked up to the reception desk. "Good evening, we are here to meet a guy called Teddy Smith who, we believe, has a table booked and is expecting us."

"Good evening, sirs, yes, please follow Amanda who will take you to your table." A waitress led them to a table that was set for four people near the back of the room.

There were already two men seated there, one of whom stood up and introduced himself. "Hi. I'm Teddy Smith, but please just call me Teddy. This is Mr. Jones, a colleague of mine." Teddy gave both Adam and Zak a handshake before sitting down. Mr. Jones gave them a slight nod as a welcome. "Now guys, you are going to have to give us a clue. Which of you is Adam and which is Zachariah, you look so similar. Do you come with labels?" he quipped.

Zak answered in an equally light-hearted way. "I'm Zak and he is Adam. You can easily tell us apart as I am the good looking one."

"But you are identical twins."

"That we are" replied Adam " though Zak is still convinced that he is the better looking one. But, as you can probably tell, I am the clever one!" This was a well-rehearsed routine; they had used it for many years as an icebreaker and it rarely failed to get a laugh. Teddy gave a chuckle whilst Mr. Jones just sat as still as a rock, expressionless, watching them through stone cold eyes. The waitress returned to their table, and they ordered a round of drinks and some snacks. Teddy ordered for Mr. Jones.

"OK boys, let's get down to business. We have been delighted with the data you have sent us over recent years. All your information has been valid data, you haven't padded it out with made-up stuff, it has always been current data, and it has been accurate, comprehensive and complete. It is very clear to us that in order to get this type of information you are well versed in the areas of cybersecurity and encryption. We have some clients who have some very specific needs, and we would like to establish whether or not you have the specific skills to meet their needs."

"What exactly are those needs?" asked Adam.

"I don't think that it is appropriate to get into the specifics at this stage, but we are looking at three general areas: extracting information from more secure systems, manipulating images (both still and moving images) and creating fake information; fake but credible that is. Do you think you can help us?"

"We like a challenge" said Adam "and I believe we can most certainly help you."

"Why are you so sure that you can do this? I've only just told you what we want."

Zak jumped in "Simple, we have already looked at all three. It has nothing to do with you coming to see us, it just happens that, of late, we have already been looking at more secure systems and we have already played around manipulating our own images, just for fun and to learn a bit more about how these things work. As for fake information, you tell us what it is you want said and where you want it to appear and I'm confident that we can do that for you." Teddy had a quick look at Mr. Jones who gave the slightest of nods.

"OK Zak, OK Adam, I'm glad to hear what you have just told me. What I'm going to do is send you, over the weekend, three examples (challenges if you like), just to show us that you really can do these things and, importantly, that you can do them to the exacting standards we need. If you complete these tasks satisfactorily, we are likely to be giving you a great deal more work, very demanding but very lucrative work. We have the contacts and, we believe, you may well have the technical skills and expertise which will help our clients. I think our relationship could work extremely well. So, tell me, are you up for the challenge? If you are, we can stop all this shop talk and enjoy our cocktails."

"We are up for it" blurted out Adam.

"And you Zak?"

"Most definitely" confirmed Zak with a broad smile on his face.

Adam, Zak, and Teddy chatted for the next hour or so about various things, such as sports teams, different planets, the state of the war in the Double Barrel Galaxy, they even touched upon politics. Throughout the evening, Mr. Jones did not say a single word until they were about to leave. He looked at Adam and Zak with ice cold eyes, eyes of pure menace, eyes that betrayed signs of unlimited violence. He simply said "It was good to meet you both but, just so you truly understand, if one word of our association ever leaks out, if you ever mention us or our clients to anybody, if you ever, ever tell anyone what we have asked you to do, you and your family will rue that day. That said, Mr. Smith and I are looking forward to working with you (once you have proved yourselves that is), but by accepting our tasks, you are joining the big league, beginning to play with the big players and you must understand that along with that comes duties, commitments and responsibilities. But, hey ho, you are both bright lads and you both must already realise this, just remember it, that's all. Good night gentlemen and I wish you well."

*

That Saturday, the twins received a short email from Teddy.

"Hi guys, it was good to meet you both.

1. Get me the plans for the new Neg Grav mining tool that was developed and recently commissioned by the Sherman Mining Corporation.

2. I want to see a picture in the popular press showing Shamus Bozman Pretzel Polygamy Piper prominently visible amongst the crowds at the current anti-war rally being held on Whisper.

3. Send me a moving image of Shamus Bozman Pretzel Polygamy Piper walking on stage and receiving a doctorate."

They went about tackling these three tasks in the order in which they were set. Getting into the Sherman Mining Corporation's system was difficult but, as it turned out, not impossible, it took Adam and Zak just over a fortnight. However, once they were in, there did not appear to be any further security measures. They searched through the company's system until they came across the engineering team's entire historical communications. This showed them that the Neg Grav tool had actually been designed by a different company, Newbridge Design. Newbridge were clearly more security conscious than Sherman Mining, having a multilayered security system which included quite advanced encryption and multi-level firewalls. This proved a much harder nut to crack, but crack it they did. Their eventual report back to Teddy included the original commissioning design specifications, the plans from Newbridge Design, all coupled with the maintenance and operations manuals which they had got from the Sherman Mining Corporation's archive. This whole task took the twins about seven weeks. The second and third tasks were much easier, so much so, that they were completed in the first day or so. As luck had it, the Daily Eclipse's current issue happened to include an image of the anti-war rally being held outside of Parliament House. It was a very simple job to download this image, adjust it by superimposing Sham's image just behind the front row of the crowd and then upload this image back onto the Daily Eclipse's website, thus replacing the original. An easy job indeed. Creating a moving image of Sham receiving a doctorate was even easier as there was absolutely no effective security on the chosen university's website. They simply took a generic clip from their chosen university's website and morphed Sham's head onto a similar shaped person's body. Sham's features were superimposed over the existing features in such a way that the resultant image appeared to be truly lifelike and real, it was Sham personified!

Teddy was delighted with what he received. The work was first class and miles better than any of his other cyber teams'. From that day forward, the twins became his go-to team for all their important work, their most technical work and their most lucrative clients.

Adam and Zak received more and more work from Teddy, and they soon became very well off. They bought a nice house in the posh part of town and another one nearby for their mum and dad. They were well liked and held in good regard by all their neighbours. What their neighbours did not realise was that they were living within touching distance of those who had become the galaxy's foremost cyber criminals.

Chapter 37

The Dinner Party That Changed Everything.

Sham had been the Member of Parliament for Whisper for a few years now, but he very rarely attended parliament as he was far too busy with all his media work. He regularly appeared on television and on radio chat shows, popular game shows, topical news programmes and even on the occasional political programme (although he rarely expressed any opinion other than in the vaguest of terms). He wrote a popular weekly editorial for the Whispering Star, a well-read online newspaper, and regularly contributed to several different magazines on topics that ranged from racing to cooking and from interior design to, bizarrely, "how to manage on a tight family budget." He had always been blessed with a very engaging personality which generally won people over and this also came over in his writing. He was humorous and, when interviewed, quick witted in his responses. However, if you took your time to really look, he never truly answered any question that put him on the spot, preferring to laugh it off, waffle for a while and change the subject, or bluff and bluster without answering. Whenever he was eventually pinned down by a good interviewer, he simply told the audience what he guessed they wanted to hear or, ultimately, he lied his way out of the situation. Bizarrely, a common theme quickly developed amongst many viewers: if people did see any faults, they tended to laugh them off saying something like "oh, that's just Sham being Sham ha ha ha" or they simply chose to ignore them. Many people even took him to heart because of his faults: "It shows that he is a real person," "none of us are perfect, certainly not our politicians!", or "it makes a change from those smarmy automatons, at least he is a real bloke; you know … he's one of us, someone you could have a pint and a laugh with down the pub … Oh good old Sham, he just tells it as it is" (despite the fact that he almost certainly never told it as it is, he usually told it as he thought you wanted to hear, He truly was a Sham!). As he became popular with much of the public, he realised that if he was ever going to do it, now was the time to make his move. He also remembered what his father had told him, all those years ago, about keeping his friends close; "remember son, with their help and support, you can reach for the stars."

Sham held, what turned out to be, a momentous dinner party, inviting his closest, wealthiest and most influential friends. Present were his father (Proprietor of Piper's Periodical, the leading financial journal of its time), Dip-Dip (senior partner of Meganova Venture Capital and board member of Thunderbolt), Lance "Plank" Grouper (CFO of Thunderbolt and senior partner of Hyper-wedged Hedge Fund), Polo Marmalade (the online profile creator and marketing specialist), Mac Oik (owner of Oik Intergalactic), Tristran Quaid (CFO of Whispers), Spider Cummings (Dip-Dip's father and owner of Cummings Investment Bank), Sir Alfie Windlesham (chairman of the Traditionalist Party) and Gabriela Smurfet (a leading online influencer and Sham's current romantic target). Sham had an incredibly influential circle of friends, and he was prepared to use every one of them. The ten of them were sitting around a very large glass topped table in Sham's penthouse apartment (he had recently moved there after splitting up from his second wife), with freshly poured drinks at hand and having just finished a most sumptuous meal. Sham made his announcement.

"Ladies (said whilst giving Gabriela a particularly lustful leer) and gentlemen, or rather I should say, … my dearest of friends. I have invited all of you here this evening as I wish to make an important announcement, and I don't want you to hear it from the press before I have told all of you in person. Friends, it is my intention to stand for President of Central Galaxy at the next election and I will be announcing my candidacy sometime during this month." Initially, you could hear a pin drop. The room remained silent until they had all absorbed the news.

Dip-Dip was the first to react. He stood up, raised his glass and said "Well-done old boy, well-done. I'm sure I speak for everyone in the room when I offer you my heartiest of congratulations on making such a momentous decision. I give you my sincerest best wishes and my full support in your endeavour." Everyone stood up and raised their glass to Sham.

"Best of luck, son," said his father.

"Bravo," said Plank "and good luck to our next president."

"Hear, hear!!" shouted Mac Oik, "God bless Sham and all who sail in her!!"

Other reactions around the room were somewhat mixed. Sham had already talked things through at length with Polo Marmalade as he was going to heavily rely on Polo's support and expertise. However, having heard Sham making the announcement, all Polo could see was work and piles of money coming his way. Tristran Quaid and Spider Cummings were not lifelong friends of Sham, but they could both see the huge benefits of having a close personal relationship with the President of their galaxy. Gabriella looked stunned as she was totally unaware of any of Sham's plans but, if things worked out, maybe she could be the next Mrs. President? If Gabriella was anything she was extremely bright, talented and ambitious. Sir Alfie Windlesham looked a little uncomfortable. He had, only two weeks ago, chaired a meeting where they had agreed on Sir Mitchel Evans, the current head of the galaxy's Board of Commerce, as being the Traditionalist Party's presidential candidate for the forthcoming election.

They adjourned from the dining room and made their way to the spacious lounge and huddled together in small groups, mostly talking about Sham's unexpected announcement. Sham ducked and weaved his way around each of the small groups. His Old Beltonian chums, Dip-Dip, Plank and Mac Oik stood chatting together. When Sham joined them, each of them gave him their blessing and promised to help in any way they could, either financially or in any other way that Sham asked. All three looked tremendously proud and excited.

Gabriella was taking the opportunity to chat with Sham's father, after all, she had some work to do. She really wanted to get to know him, and, by the look of it, she was already making great progress. Sham had a brief conversation with them. His father wished him well and told him that he was making his father very proud. He also whispered in Sham's ear that his new lady was quite the catch.

Tristran Quaid, Polo Marmalade and Sir Alfie were standing in a corner chatting amongst themselves, all three feeling a little outside of Sham's tight group of old friends and family. Sham picked up on this as he went to speak with them. "Listen guys" he said "I know that we did not go to school together and that we are not family, but I want each of you to know that I value your friendship as much as I do the others'. Sir Alfie, can we grab a few minutes together before you go? And Polo, let's meet up tomorrow afternoon if that's at all possible. Now, if it's alright with you two, can I have a few minutes with Tristran?" Sir Alfie and Marmalade let them be and went off to get a top up from the drink's waitress. "Tristran, as I just said, we are recent friends, but I want to let you know that I greatly value our new friendship. I enjoy your company, and I believe we are like minded on many issues."

"I feel the same, Sham, I too believe we have a lot in common."

Sham smiled at that and leant in a little closer. "Listen Tristran, I know that I can depend on you. I just want you to know that I will be relying heavily on Whispers' social media platforms over the coming months, especially once the campaigning really starts to kick in. I'm sure I can rely on you for making sure that your platforms give me a good deal of exposure. In turn, I will remember that in the future."

"You can count on me, Sham. It would be remiss of me not to let everyone in the Central Galaxy know all about your campaign, in fact I believe that both Whispers and I have a civic duty to do exactly that."

"Good man. Let's leave it at that and, if it is ok with you, we can have dinner together in a few days' time at my club when we can talk in a little more detail, where we could put a bit of flesh on the bones, as it were."

*

Sham was not intending to stand as the Traditionalist Party's candidate for the Presidency but rather as an independent candidate. However, an endorsement from the party would be very useful. Even better, a commitment not to stand a candidate against him would be extremely helpful. That is why Sir Alfie had been invited. Sham took Sir Alfie into his private office. "Sir Alfie, I hope you have enjoyed your evening."

"I have, yes, thank you Shamus."

"I am not planning on standing as the Traditionalist Party's candidate."

"That's good, as, unfortunately, we have already decided to put somebody else forward."

"I want you to drop him or her."

"Much as I like you and want to support you Shamus, I'm afraid that that is a no-can-do. I don't have the authority to do that, and we are announcing our candidate early next week."

"Sir Alfie, I would like to announce you as my running mate. I want you to be the Vice-President of Central Galaxy."

"Me! You are joking! Me, Vice-President of the galaxy! I can't believe it! That is truly beyond my wildest dreams!"

"Well believe it because it is true. What is more, I genuinely think we would make a great team. We complement each other so perfectly. I am well liked by the people of Central and, whilst not wishing to be blunt, that is not your forte. On the other hand, you are a very experienced and well-respected politician, which I am not. I know that I am liked but I know that I am not yet, seen as a seriously respected politician. You have the experience of holding high office and you are used to dealing with civil servants, political infighting and such like, whereas I am not. To use a phrase, you once said to me, you are a professional politician. I truly believe we will make a formidable team. I would relish working with you and, together, we will create a better society. Now, if you want any of that, it looks like we need to come up with a plan that we can implement very quickly. We obviously have less than a week." Sham and Sir Alfie spent half the night together, once the other guests had left, and indeed, they did come up with a plan, and it very much involved Polo Marmalade. Sham spent the following afternoon going through that plan with Marmalade.

*

"Gosh Sham, I knew you had ambition, but I did not see your announcement coming quite so quickly" said Marmalade once they had settled around Marmalade's conference table in his office.

"I'm a man of surprises, old boy, a man of surprises," quipped Sham "but now we have a lot of work to do, so let's get down to it."

"OK, shoot."

"Obviously, I want as much positive media coverage as possible."

"That goes without saying and it should not be too difficult. You are quite popular, and I know most of the big hitters in the field. And you are certainly not without your connections either."

"Well, that's true, but the problem I have is that I haven't actually said much that can be publicised. Well, very little of any worth at least."

"Right, that doesn't necessarily have to be a problem" said Marmalade, very cautiously.

"How do you mean?"

"The fact is that we can fairly easily create sound-bites, clips and written content, should we want to."

"Go on" urged Sham.

"Well, the way I see it is this. Whilst you may not have actually done or said certain things, you probably really wanted to do or say those things and, in my book, that is pretty much the same thing. Here, I'll show you what I mean, have a look at this." With that Marmalade showed a picture of Sham standing, very prominently, amongst the crowd at the anti-war demonstration, outside of the Houses of Parliament. "This is something I had knocked up a couple of years ago. As far as I'm concerned, you wanted to be there, but your diary got in the way, so it is just showing people what should have happened. Importantly, it shows people what you truly care about, it is really showing people, what I would argue, is the true you, the real you."

"Quite so, old boy, quite so. Have you got any other examples of the real me that you can show me?"

"Well, yes I have, here, take a look at this." Marmalade showed him the clip of being presented with a doctorate. "You see, the fact is that you are quite capable of getting a doctorate but, undoubtedly circumstances such as your public commitments, your support of the community and your commitment to your constituents, unfortunately got in the way. This clip simply shows what should have been. After all, you decided to devote your life to public service, why should that noble act hold you back? That would be an unjust travesty."

"Yes, yes, of course, you are absolutely right. We need to show people the true Sham, not just the real one. How would we use such examples of what ought to have been, and have we any others?"

"I have a contact, Mr. Jones, who can help us out in all these matters. In fact, I will get in contact with him just as soon as we finish here today."

"Excellent. I have another wee problem as well."

"Oh, and what is that?"

"As it stands, there is likely to be another candidate that might be a real threat to my chances of winning. His name is Sir Mitchel Evans."

"What, the head of the Chamber of Commerce?"

"Yes, that's the one and, to the best of my knowledge, he is squeaky clean. I really need to show this guy in as bad a light as possible, ideally before the week is out. I really could do with him dropping out of the race. Let's show the galaxy a different Sir Mitchel Evans, a not so likeable one, if you get what I mean."

"Do you care how that happens?"

"No, I'll leave that to you and your Mr. Jones. Just make it so."

Chapter 38

The First Campaign.

Over the weekend following Sham's meeting with Marmalade, Central Galaxy became a hotbed of rumour, gossip, outrage and disgust. Rumours first appeared on social media platforms that a top public servant had been caught in a den of vice, a brothel, or a sex-party. At first these rumours only appeared on a few sites but, incredibly quickly, social media became awash with them. There were rumours as to who this person was, what he had done and who he had done it with. Various names began to appear as speculation increased. Very soon, these rumours were being included on mainstream television and online news services. Many members of the Board of Commerce and senior civil servants were seen on tv denying the rumour that it was them, whilst quite a number were keeping a very low profile, hoping it was not them that had been found out! These rumours gave rise to an enormous amount of gossip. Gossip in pubs and bars, gossip over the dinner table, gossip over the garden fence, gossip at the hairdressers, gossip on the factory floors and a great deal of gossip amongst the Board of Commerce members and Civil Servants. They continually called and messaged each other trying to find out what anybody knew. Then it all turned to outrage. There was outrage because these were supposed to be exemplary people who should clearly live lives that were above the standards of the rest of society. Social media was whipping itself up into a feeding frenzy, all based on unsubstantiated rumours and gossip.

On the Monday, all hell broke loose. Photographs began to appear of Sir Mitchel Evans exiting a brothel doorway. It was clearly a brothel as there was a traditional red light in the window and there were several scantily clad women visible behind Sir Mitchel as he was seen exiting a very shady doorway. If you looked very closely there was even a sign saying "Ye Olde Knocking Shoppe" hanging in the window. It got worse still when pictures began to appear of Sir Mitchel dressed in some form of rubber fetishist's costume, being spanked and whipped by three very buxom ladies and a young man. These pictures had obviously been secretly taken through the window by a very conscientious, courageous and truth-seeking journalist.

Sir Mitchel spoke to the press early the following morning. He stood in his front garden, hand in hand with his wife Linda, and categorically denied any wrong doing. He asserted that these photos were outrageous fakes and that he was the victim of a vicious, malicious and illegal slur campaign.

Unfortunately for Sir Mitchel, news of his press announcement had already been leaked on social media, telling people that he was going to make a statement from his home in the morning; they even included the full address of his house, details of the relevant bus routes and an up-to-date timetable. Hundreds and hundreds of people turned up, mostly hoping to hear his admission of guilt and to watch the fall of one of society's pompous elite. His press statement was a disaster. Everyone there (and that probably included the reporter doing the interview) already knew that he was guilty; after all, how could so many people be wrong and, besides, he clearly looks guilty - you can just tell. As Sir Mitchel gave his statement, he was inundated with loud disparaging comments together with cat calls and heckles from the crowd. There was even a religious group, plainly visible in the background, who booed, jeered and chanted as he talked (they were, in fact, Mr. Jones's cousins, nephews and nieces, all dressed up in full nun and priest costumes).

The next day was even worse for Sir Mitchel. A video clip appeared, overnight, showing him exiting the brothel. He could clearly be heard saying "Thanks for a rollicking good time, ladies. Next time I will remember to bring my own cocaine." Sir Mitchel resigned from his job that afternoon and contacted Sir Afie telling him that he would not be standing for the Presidency. He denied any wrong-doing but said that he felt totally powerless to defend himself against such a vicious and deceitful social media onslaught; and he was absolutely right, it is impossible to defend yourself against such bigoted opinions and rampant false information, but such is social media.

Sir Alfie never knew if this entire story was a malicious fabrication at the hands of Sham and his cronies, or if Sir Mitchel was in fact, guilty. Either way, the Traditionalist Party needed a new candidate. After all, the party was intending to campaign on the grounds of a return to traditional family values. That clearly wasn't going to sit well with the public right now!

*

Sir Alfie called an emergency meeting of the Traditionalist Party's presidential candidate selection committee. "Gentlemen, we obviously have a big problem on our hands. We need to announce our Presidential candidate over the next week or so, certainly by the end of the month and, at the moment, we haven't got one. Has anybody got any suggestions? … any names for us to consider?" Sir Mitchel's fall from grace had been so unexpected and so sudden that no one had even put any feelers out, let alone directly approached anybody. "No, no one has any suggestions? If you do have any suggestions, then I urge that you go ahead and name them now as time is certainly not on our side!" He took a slow look around the committee and saw a ring of blank faces returning his questioning gaze. "Well, if no one has any suggestions, I would like to tell you of something I picked up at a social event that I attended last week. Apparently, our very own Shamus Piper is thinking of standing as an independent candidate. It is my thought that perhaps we should throw our support behind his campaign as we can't seem to find a candidate of our own."

"What, endorse Sham as our preferred choice for President? Are you serious?" called out a senior Traditionalist cabinet member.

"I know, I know, my suggestion surprised me at first, but think about it. He has a very prominent profile with the public. Alright, maybe not for his political involvement, but he appears to be popular with the electorate. He comes from a very traditionalist family, and he is extremely well connected in society. I mean, at the event I attended, he appeared to be on first name terms with nearly all of the wealthiest and most influential people in the Galaxy, I think he went to school with half of them!"

"That doesn't necessarily make him a good candidate though" called out someone in the room.

"I agree" said Sir Alfie "It doesn't. But, by the same token, it doesn't necessarily make him a bad one either"

"That's a fair point, Sir Alfie. How do we move on from here? I think we need to get a better understanding of what Shamus Piper is about and whether it would be in our interests to endorse his candidacy. Would you be prepared to meet with The Piper on our behalf?"

"Yes, I will do that, just as long as everyone is in agreement that I should do so" and thus it was agreed unanimously.

*

Three days later … "Gentlemen, I met with Shamus Piper" lied Sir Alfie, (he had actually spent the last two days relaxing with his wife, in a beautiful and very remote country cottage, whilst getting in a spot of fishing) "and we had a most fruitful and interesting discussion. Piper has convinced me that a truly traditionalist agenda would be at the very heart of his presidency. Low taxation, minimal governmental interference, minimising public spending and other such traditionalist values."

"Why does he want to stand as an independent then? will he not stand as a Traditionalist candidate?"

"I asked him that very same question and his answer was simple. He told me that, much to our shame, the current Traditionalist Party is not traditionalist enough. He cited the recent behaviour of Sir Mitchel as being a good example, saying that "no true Traditionalist would ever get involved in those type of sordid and scandalous activities." Furthermore, he believes that more such scandals, perpetrated by Traditionalist members, are likely to come to light in the very near future."

"Perhaps he has a point, guys" commented someone in the room "and to think, we were on the brink of announcing Sir Mitchel, the pervert, as our candidate. We certainly dodged a bullet there."

"But Sham has no serious political experience whatsoever. How can we endorse him as a candidate for the most important job in the Galaxy and how can we pin our colours to such a complete political unknown?

Sure, he always talks a good talk, but he is pretty scant when it comes to detail. It's simply too risky!!"

"Well, on that subject, I have some other news. When we met, he asked for me to join him on the ticket and run for office as his Vice-President. His argument is that; he has the public persona to get elected and I have the political experience to do all the work. Frankly, as I'm getting to know him, I'm beginning to see him as a political genius!!"

"That sounds like a brilliant idea" said Peter Mitchel, the current deputy party chairman (in truth only seeing a big career opportunity coming his way) "and we would have one of our own inner circle at the very centre of the presidential organisation. I think that would be a fantastic setup, one that we could definitely endorse."

And that became the consensus around the room. Sham's candidacy was announced at the end of the week, followed by an immediate Traditionalist Party's endorsement. Sham's campaign was now well and truly underway.

*

Polo Marmalade ramped up his efforts, as did Mr. Jones and the Jackson twins. During the weeks that followed Sham's announcement of his candidacy, the BWW, all TV news programs and all social media platforms (especially Whispers), became awash with images and video clips of Sham standing up for everyday people, doing heroic things and demonstrating his intellectual prowess.

*

"Mr. Piper, Mr. Piper, Johny Starr of the Central Echo. Are you a super-hero?"

"Well, come now, I would hardly call myself that"

"But we've all seen the footage of you saving that young girl from drowning, it's plastered all-over our social media. The way you quickly stripped down to your vote for Piper boxer shorts and dived into that raging torrent was, in my view, superhuman"

"It's kind of you to say that, but I only did what any other person would have done in the circumstances. The fear of risking life and limb for a person in need just doesn't enter one's head"

"And the way you wrapped her up in your vote for Piper towel was so tender, we were all so moved."

The Jackson twins had progressed, they were now using high quality AI generated images.

*

"Good evening viewers. This is Jonathan Browning on this very cold and wet afternoon following an anonymous tip-off. I am standing on the pavement outside of Mrs. Elsie Todd's small, terraced house. It appears that the bailiffs have just arrived outside of 86-year-old Elsie's home, and I am led to believe that they are preparing to forcibly evict her. It is the landlord's view that Elsie should be immediately removed from her peaceful little home, a home that she has lived in for all her adult life, a home she shared with her very recently departed husband and a home of dear memories. It appears that her much loved home has just been sold to a younger couple who, the landlord insists, have already legally purchased the property following Mrs. Todd's tenancy agreement expiring unexpectedly. Hold on …..there appears to be some movement. Oh my gosh, off they go, the bailiffs are beginning to make their way up the front path. They are now storming 86-year-old Elsie's home, and they are kicking down the door. Hold on, what's that? I don't believe it! Shamus Piper has just come out from inside the house and is blocking the bailiff's entrance. "I simply will not stand for this kind of treatment of one of our elderly citizens" bellows Sham "begone with you … and if you lay one finger on me or Mrs. Todd, I will be suing each and every one of you for assault. This is an indecency, this is an outrage, this cannot be tolerated … and it will never ever be tolerated under my presidency!!!" This footage was circulated throughout the Galaxy and was heavily featured on all of Whisper's platforms.

What never came to light was the fact that the house in question was owned by the mother of one of Mr. Jones's friends, the landlord was one of Cummings Investment Bank's investment companies which, in truth, had no intention of evicting Mrs. Elsie Todd and Mrs. Elsie Todd was extremely well compensated for her afternoon of disruption and her silence.

*

The very popular celebrity general knowledge quiz show called 'Celebrity Minds' was aired every Saturday evening at the prime-time slot of the most popular TV channel in the Whisper Galaxy. The show's format combined a series of mental challenges along with several general knowledge quiz rounds. The contest was usually held between half a dozen not so well-known and very minor celebrities. The winner's prize, quite a large sum of cash, would go to a charity of the winner's choosing. In truth, most people watched the show to see 'Z' list celebrities and, very occasionally some big names, make a fool of themselves. The show could easily provide a week's worth of amusement, discussion and derision throughout the workplaces, bars and in sitting rooms of the Galaxy. It was a hugely popular show with many billions of viewers.

When the public were informed that Shamus Piper was to appear as a contestant, everybody and their wife wanted to watch that week's show and there was a great deal of speculation as to how well Sham would do. There was much public discussion as to how bright he truly was which, in truth, was the very reason why Sham had been booked onto the show in the first place. Several pre-election focus groups had highlighted that people tended to warm to Sham's great personality, but they frequently referred to his complete lack of intelligence … was that the type of President that people really wanted? Polo Marmalade had made the booking for Sham to appear on the show with the intention of proving to the public just how bright their potential new President really was.

The introduction music played, the lights came up and, one by one, the contestants were introduced. What the viewers could not see was the tiny radio-linked earpiece embedded just below the skin underneath Sham's bushy sideburns. Throughout the contest, there was a huddle of Sham's friends and family members, each with access to atlases, encyclopaedias, history books, calculators and the BWW, all safely secured in a large private office which was situated less than one hundred yards from the television studio. Everybody in that room was in radio contact with Sham's inserted ear device.

Sham's performance transfixed and amazed the huge galaxy-wide audience. His breadth of knowledge was astounding, his ability to do complex calculations in his head was worthy of a professor of mathematics, his knowledge and recall of history was exceptional, the scope of his knowledge of literature and his appreciation of the fine arts showed him to be a true renaissance man. And throughout the show he remained confident and personable … just what you want from your President. The only thing that nearly gave the game away were short periods of quite disturbing feedback whenever he moved too close to the microphone. This feedback had the show's sound engineers totally perplexed as to what was causing such an unprecedented screeching, whistling and whining; but they never suspected the obvious. All Sham could hear in his right ear, beside the answers, was a very loud electronic howl and many of his friends shouting …. "Sit back!!!! …. For f**k sake Sham, sit back!!!! …. Move away from the f***ing microphone!!!!!!"

*

The Presidential electoral process started with several candidates standing against Sham, but, after several rounds of voting, these were quickly whittled down to the final three. It was now that the Jackson twins did what could possibly be considered as their finest work. The twins undertook long and detailed investigations into each of the other candidates' lives and unearthed some very serious anomalies with one of them. They had hacked into her bank details and the accounts of several of her off planet holdings as well as tax returns and various other financial records. They in fact unearthed many irregular financial activities … this candidate was genuinely corrupt. Whilst the candidate's financial background had been unearthed, the twins were able to embellish it further, just to make it look even more shocking than it already was. The candidate was clearly in no position to point out what were her genuine misdemeanours and what had been faked; it's quite likely that she didn't even know herself. She was approached by Mr. Jones and, the following day, she withdrew her candidature citing family reasons. Mr. Jones had assured her than none of his information would ever see the light of day if she simply and quietly withdrew her name from the field.

*

Sham's final rival was Sebastian Reed. Reed was a centre-right politician, currently representing Reaper planet (the planet second in size only to Whisper) and he held very similar views to Sham. He too was privately educated but had gone on to achieve a shining career in business before moving into politics in his late middle age. The Jackson twins, Teddy Smith and Mr. Jones were in the process of trying to create a credible ruinous backstory for Reed, but they were struggling.

Their problem was summed up by Zak. "The trouble is that he is far too much of a goody-goody. He supports many well-known charities, he has a solid and close-knit family, he has always been open about what he does and what he is doing, we just can't find any dirt on him at all and it's difficult to make something up that people would believe."

Then, about one week before the final round of voting, they struck lucky. "Here, look at this, it's about old goody-two-shoes, or rather, it's mostly about his brother" called out Adam "This might be something worth looking into." Zak leant over Adam's shoulder and read the article. It was from an old-style broadsheet newspaper from around the time that Reed was a university student. Apparently, Sebastian Reed had a brother called Stephen who had died of an overdose of some type of recreational drug or other. What was interesting was that there was some speculation at the time that it was Sebastian who had supplied the drugs to Stephen, having brought them home with him from university. "We all have a skeleton in our closet, don't we? it's just a question of how deep you dig." said Zak.

"Yea, but I'm not sure I feel comfortable digging this one out." Was Adam getting a conscience?

"We have a duty to let the people of the galaxy know. It is up to them to make up their mind based on all the facts, and I think that it would be wrong of us to deny them this information. Let's talk it through with Teddy and Mr. Jones."

Later that day. "Of course, you should dig around, what the heck are you waiting for!" was Teddy Smith's emphatic response.

Mr. Jones was even more blunt. "Listen, we are not here to pussyfoot around. You both have a job to do, and I am paying you a lot of money to do it. Now I suggest you pull your fingers out and get on with it!" This was said in a very menacing tone, and it certainly galvanised the twins into immediate action.

The very next day the twins forwarded the few old newspaper articles that they had unearthed, on to several on-line news services. Only one of these services went on to make any form of speculation about Sebastian Reed's possible supplying of the drugs that ultimately led to his brother's death. However, the following day, several on-line articles appeared that seemingly furthered the speculation that Sebastian Reed might have supplied the drugs that led to the death of his brother. The appearance of these additional articles led to a maelstrom of events. Whispers and all other social media platforms, were swamped with repeated comments of outrage, vitriol and name calling. News services were repeatedly asked to shed light on the events. There were now, reportedly, comments from eye witnesses to the events, who claimed that they believed that, rather than facing the music, Sebastian Reed had left his brother to die and had promptly fled back to his university. The world of on-line character assassination had stooped to a disgusting new low, all fired up by the work of Teddy Smith, Mr. Jones and the twins. In fact, no formal accusation was ever made and certainly no facts had been brought to light. The damage was all done by speculation, rumour and a misinformed public who were swayed by lies and innuendo rather than caring about getting the facts.

Election day arrived, but the galaxy was still awash with rumour and speculation as to Sebastian Reed's role in the death of his brother. The election's outcome was inevitable given the circumstances. Super intelligent Sham, the man of the people, the renaissance man, Mr. Social Conscience won a landslide victory and was duly appointed President of Central Galaxy.

Chapter 39

Growing Conflict.

Around two years after Sham's appointment as President of Bounty, Mr. Jones was approached by Guy Seakam, the Prime Minister of Ashby, the second largest planet in the Catherine Wheel Galaxy (which has an economy based almost exclusively on high tech engineering and electronics). Ashby was a large planet with many natural resources, but it had run out of copper several generations back. Since then, Ashby had been importing copper from Cupric, a much smaller, nearby planet, of only around 4 billion people and which was exceptionally rich in copper. Prime Minister Seakam had recently been informed by the officials of Cupric that they too were running low on copper, and, because of this, their prices were going to increase significantly. It was a well-known fact that Cupric had other issues too: they were running out of habitable land, and they were looking for other planets that were suitable for occupation and they were considering building some huge residential space stations that would sit in low orbit around their home planet. It was Seakam's suspicion that the impending price hike in copper had nothing to do with copper becoming scarcer on Cupric, but rather, Cupric wanting someone else to pay for the solution to all their problems.

"Mr. Jones, all I want is to see Cupric's official copper inventory, they must have one if they are genuinely concerned about running out of the stuff. I would also like to see a copy of any internal documentation that proves that they are genuinely running short of copper. Most importantly, I want records of any meetings where they have discussed the price that they intend to charge us and why they feel it has to change."

"So, you are asking me to hack into another government's records. As you well know that is espionage and illegal under the terms of Bounty-wide legislation."

"Yes, I'm asking you to do exactly that; and I know the law."

"Can I ask how you got my name and contact details?

"I recently had dinner with President Piper of Central Galaxy, whom I've known for a good number of years (they had played rugby against each other at schoolboy interplanetary level) and with his advisory team. One of his staff suggested that I contact you. He said that you had been very helpful on Piper's campaign."

"Did they now? If I do this for you, I trust you will keep it a little more confidential."

"Of course, we all know how President Piper tends to open his mouth before thinking. I am not like that."

"Oh, so it was Sham himself who told you."

"I didn't say that it was Sham himself."

"Yea, right."

Mr. Jones named his price and held out his hand. Prime Minister Seakam agreed, and the deal was done. The Jackson twins got straight on the case.

*

Cupric government's IT systems and their associated procedures were unbelievably unsecure; shockingly so when you consider the importance of the data they held and the infrastructure they controlled. (This, in fact, was becoming a common theme in all the work that the Jackson twins were doing for Mr. Jones). Quite by chance, just a few weeks prior to the twins starting work on this new project, a senior Cupric government official had been allowed to take a laptop, which contained highly sensitive information, out of the secure environs of his office, which he then left on the back seat of a taxi. Later, the government official claimed that he was in shock having received some very bad news from his wife but, whatever his mental state or whatever the cause of his slip-up, the laptop was never returned. In fact, the finder of the laptop was the next passenger into the taxi who turned out to be a young computer aficionado. He, just like the Jackson twins at a similar age, had started to dabble in the dark web. At first, he thought he had simply struck lucky as it was a very high specked machine. However, he soon realised just what it was that had ended up in his lap as news of the loss of the government's laptop appeared on most social media and local mainstream news channels. He quickly found a buyer on the dark web for such an important device. It was very easy for the twins to follow the online trail of the laptop's sale and it was not long before Mr. Jones collected the laptop from its new owner. Whether it was paid for or not, or if it was obtained by force or duress, was never revealed to the twins, but in next to no time, they had gained access to all of Cupric's IT system's encryption details and they then set to work. At first, they found evidence that Cupric's copper reserve were truly shrinking, and the price rises were, in all probability, justified. However, they soon realised that they had unearthed the falsified documentation which Cupric was going to use in justifying the price rises to Ashby. When they dug further into the specific reports that were made by various governmental departments, such as the Department of the Environment, they found reports of the true nature of Cupric's copper reserves. The reserves had been hardly dented after about five generations of production. This was later confirmed as they hacked into the minutes of various meetings, each one of which outlined Cupric's strategy of scamming the much wealthier Ashby for the very considerable sums of monies needed to complete the production of six low orbit space stations, which were to be large enough to accommodate over one billion people, along with all the necessary food production, light industry and social facilities etc.

When Mr. Jones detailed their findings to Prime Minister Seakam whilst they were sitting in Seakam's office, there were two reactions: Prime Mister Seakam went a funny reddish purply colour and then he picked up his red communicator and said, "Launch Operation Retribution immediately; it is as we suspected, and I have the proof." He also said "Mr. Jones, thank you for the information. Now put Plan Immobilisation into action, you will find that the funds are already on their way to you."

Operation Retribution was, in fact, the deployment of twelve warp-driven fast attack spaceships, each carrying a huge arsenal of multi-warhead nuclear missiles and some highly specialised conventional weapons. Plan Immobilisation was a precursor action that paved the way for Operation Retribution, and this was in the hands of the Jackson twins.

*

"OK boys, we have been given the green light. As we speak, a fleet of enormously powerful attack ships is heading towards Cupric and it will arrive in exactly forty-nine hours and thirty-seven minutes; we will call that A-Time. Firstly, let's just confirm A-Time and check that all or our timepieces are synchronised properly. As we have discussed, timing is extremely important." Adam and Zak double-checked all their systems; everything was fine. "Just for confirmation, at A-Time precisely, I want all Cupric's defence systems to be deactivated, all of their radar systems to stop functioning and all of their communications systems to go off-line. In the meantime, feel free to create as much anonymous havoc on Cupric as you can. Also, make sure that you pull out all the information you can which may be of value to us in the future. I don't just mean information that will help Ashby in its war effort, I mean information that will be valuable to us if later sold on the open market or on the black market. Things like design information, patent details, any commercial secrets that they may be holding, anything that may have a future value and of course, any financial resources. OK?" Nods from both Adam and Zak. "Right lads, GO for it!"

*

And GO for it they did! The first thing that Zak and Adam did was to double-check that they could still gain access to Cupric's radars, defence systems and communications systems; everything was in place and working, they simply had to hit a preprogrammed key sequence on their computer and the whole kit and caboodle would switch off … and only they knew how to restore the systems. Then they went to town and had some fun.

Zak spent the rest of that day and all next day looking into Cupric's systems in the financial sector. He ended up creating a number of secure off-planet bank accounts in Zak's, Adam's, Mr. Smith's and Mr. Jones's names. He then set up some pre-scheduled transactions that would convert many sizeable funds, held in the local currency, into much more mainstream currencies. These funds would be immediately transferred into their new off-planet accounts. This would all happen at A-Time minus sixty minutes; plenty of time to make sure that they get processed properly, but not enough time for anyone to react in the very unlikely event that these fraudulent transactions were spotted amongst all the other chaos that was going to be unleashed. He didn't bother making the transactions untraceable by use of multi-level laundering or such like as the likelihood was that, after the event, there was going to be no one left to complain. He could easily launder the funds at a later date if needs be.

Adam and Zak had already been looking into the systems of Cupric's key companies and institutions for several days. As Zak syphoned off the monetary funds, Adam spent the same days copying such things as hi-tech design plans, high-level research documentation, in fact anything that he could find that could possibly have a value after the destruction of Cupric.

And then the real fun began. During the twenty-four hours leading up to A-Time, it was as if Adam and Zak had regressed into their earlier gaming childhood. They had great fun seeing who could come up with the silliest and most amusing disruptions on Cupric. Adam reset all the traffic lights so that they changed colour at random. Zak put all broadcasted communications through a translator so that they were broadcast in a different language [imagine turning on your tv and all the usual programs appeared as normal, only they were now talking in Polish, or Mandarin, or Swahili]; he even added subtitles, just because he could. Adam sent everyone on the whole planet an email telling them that, as of tomorrow, all taxes were going to be doubled unless you contacted your local tax office and obtained an exemption certificate on the grounds that you are already an existing tax-payer. Zak issued instructions from both the home office and the police that, due to a terrorist threat, with immediate effect all aeroplanes must be grounded at the nearest airport and all trains and buses must stop wherever they are. Between them they changed the electronic road traffic signs, the electronic bus timetables, and, finally, they turned off the planet's electricity generators. How had they done all of this? …. they had hacked into the planet's Little Maq's Mother Computer. Doing this gave them control of nearly every computer-controlled system on the planet. It is interesting to note that Thunderbolt quickly became aware of the security breach of their system but could not do anything to stop it, at least not quickly enough to make a difference. Thunderbolt never told anybody outside of their company that their system had been breached.

*

A-Time arrived. Twelve large-capacity warp-driven spaceships appeared in the skies over Cupric. At that very moment all Cupric's radars stopped functioning (the screens simply showed a foggy cloud of interference), its military and governmental communications systems went down, (the only thing anyone could hear was a loud high-pitched whistle) and all of the planet's defence systems simply stopped responding. The spaceships deployed their cargo of precision targeted multi-warhead nuclear missiles along with their other hi-tech weaponry. All key infrastructure was destroyed and close to one billion people lost their lives. About two months later, once the worst of the nuclear clouds had dispersed, a fleet of other spacecraft came to the planet bringing an invasion army of considerable size. What remained of Cupric, including its huge copper reserves, was now under the direct rule of Ashby.

*

However, there is a little footnote to this Cupric story which would significantly impact future intergalactic events. Samuel J. Smurfet had worked in television for many years as a very popular news broadcaster. He lost his life when a nuclear warhead took out the main television broadcasting centre. He would probably have been forgotten, lost amongst the billion dead, had he not been the father of Gabriela Smurfet who had, by this time, become Gabriela Piper, Shams new wife (wife number three). Yes, she had achieved her wishes and become Mrs. President.

Chapter 40

Thunderbolt Services Emergency Meeting.

Fabio Zodiac called an emergency meeting, demanding the attendance of all his key programmers, the various heads of on-line security, the leaders of the design teams responsible for Thunderbolt's firewall and encryption systems and a few other senior programmers.

Zodiac's opening comments said it all. "I'm sure each of you is aware that, prior to Ashby's much reported attack of the planet Cupric, in the Catherine Wheel Galaxy, one of our Mother Computers was hacked into. Whoever did this interfered with a huge number of networked Little Maqs causing mayhem throughout the planet during the days that lead up to the attack. This was followed by the total paralysis of the planet's defence and communication systems. I don't need to stress the significance of this. If knowledge of this security breach was ever to get into the public domain, it could spell the end of Thunderbolt Services. There would be a strong chance that our customers would lose all confidence in our systems. We cannot let that happen and we must find a way of preventing such a security failure from ever happening again. This clearly must be the number one priority for everyone in this room. We need to know who did this, how they did it and what we are going to do to stop it from ever happening again; furthermore, as I said, we need to stop it getting into the public domain. I don't know who did this, but whoever it was is without doubt an exceptionally competent and gifted hacker. Our first suspicions must clearly lie within Ashby. However, I have analysed some of the data and I strongly suspect that they may well have had outside help. This may complicate things as the crimes were affected on one planet whilst the perpetrators may well have been operating on a different planet, with each planet operating under separate legal jurisdictions. However, we can cross that bridge when we come to it. Clearly, we need to fully analyse our systems, our records and our data. Furthermore, between us we have a great number of connections in the field of computing so I suggest that we ask around to see if any of our connections can point us in the direction of whoever might have the capabilities to have done this."

That very afternoon Plank (Thunderbolt's CFO) called his old buddy Sham to see if he had ever come across or heard of anyone who may have the capabilities to break into Thunderbolt's systems. Sham suggested that he speak to Polo Marmalade who seemed to be very well connected in the field.

Plank put a call in to Polo the very next morning. "Hi Polo, this is Plank. I hope you remember me; we met at one of Sham's parties?"

"Hi Plank, of course I remember you; you are one of my brother-in-law's oldest friends, you are very big, and you are CFO of Thunderbolt Services, how could I possibly not remember you?" replied Polo with the usual hint of humour in his voice.

"Fair point Polo, just breaking the ice old boy. Listen, I have something to ask you, but I need to know that I am speaking in confidence"

"Sure, my lips are sealed and I'm all ears"

"This is an extremely serious situation for us. A few days ago, somebody broke into Thunderbolt's systems. Have you ever come across anyone who may have the capabilities to have done that?"

"I'm not personally aware of such a person, but I do know someone who may know someone. His name is Mr. Jones, although I doubt that that is his real name."

"How do you know him?"

"Come on Plank, don't ask me that."

"OK, fair enough., I forgot you work with my old pal Sham. Any idea how I can get hold of said Mr. Jones?"

Polo gave Plank Mr. Jones' contact details, but suggested he approach Mr. Jones with the utmost caution.

*

185

Plank took his information straight to Zodiac who, in turn, sat down with a couple of his best network security technicians. They started investigating Mr. Jones' online activities and soon unearthed his many liaisons with Mr. Smith and the Jackson twins. The clincher was the discovery of several flight details to and from Ashby in the months leading to the Cupric attack, coupled with the receipt of several very large payments. The spotlight then switched to investigating the Jackson twin's activities and it quickly became obvious that they had found their hackers. But what should they do about it?

Zodiac's first reaction was to prosecute Mr. Jones, Mr. Smith and the Jackson twins. However, there was a big problem in doing this. It would be quite simple to prove their guilt, and the culprits would undoubtedly receive very severe sentences. The problem was that Thunderbolt Services could not prosecute without things getting into the public domain. Very quickly, all their customers would become aware that Thunderbolt's systems had been breached; and that would be a big problem for Thunderbolt Services.

[This is a common dilemma in dealing with cybercrime. Our entire legal system is based on openness and public access. Jurors are appointed from the general public and, almost without exception, anyone can enter a court to see justice being done, including the press (at least that is usually the case in the world's open societies). This public openness is an extremely important tenet of our legal system. The problem in dealing with cybercrime is that many of the victims of such crimes, banks, building societies, large organisations, governments etc. usually do not want the crime to be made public. They do not want people to know that their security systems have been breached, that some of their customers have had monies taken, or some private data has been taken from their systems. When it comes to customers losing monies (unless the customer has been recklessly carefree with their security obligations) it is usually the bank's policy to recompense the customer, accepting that it is their own security systems that failed. The banks would rather pay out than let their security failings appear in the public domain. The upshot of the dilemma, whether or not their security failings will become public, is that much cybercrime is unreported, and the perpetrators remain unprosecuted. The true extent of cybercrime is unknown ... some crimes remain undetected whilst others, whilst detected, remain unreported. Another obstacle to prosecution is the fact that much cybercrime is committed by individuals or organisations operating from locations outside the legal jurisdiction of where the crime is actually realised (for instance, try prosecuting a hacker that operates in North Korea but steals from an individual in America). A prosecution in this situation involves a great deal of cooperation between the two legal authorities and two different governments which, at best, is a slow and cumbersome process, whoever these governments are.

Whilst feeling disgusted with himself, Zodiac, with the full support of the Board, decided that they would not prosecute, and an alternative plan was made.

*

"Mr. Jones, I have not invited you here to talk about a possible marketing campaign as you have been led to believe. I have invited you here to talk about yours, Mr. Smith's and the Jackson twin's role in the death of a billion people on Cupric." Zodiac was looking intently at Mr. Jones as he said these words. Mr. Jones did not flinch. "We have not yet informed the authorities of your involvement in the massacre on Cupric, nor have we told the authorities of your illegal access and manipulation of our systems. Just for avoidance of doubt, we have ample proof of all of your involvements, and I would be more than happy to prove that to you, should you need any convincing. Furthermore, we have very close personal contacts at the highest governmental levels of both the Central Galaxy and the Spiral Galaxy where, I have no doubt, we could successfully prosecute should we choose to do so. However, the true purpose of me inviting you here, Mr. Jones, is that I would like to make you a business proposition." At this, a slight flicker could be seen in Mr. Jones' eyes. Whether it was a flicker of interest, greed or simply surprise, Zodiac was never sure, but it was enough for him to carry on. "To the best of our knowledge, our security systems have never been breached before. Sure, some of our Little Maqs have been hacked, but no one has ever broken into one of our Mother Computers. We know for sure that it was the Jackson twins who did the actual work, under your instruction. We have unearthed, detailed and documented a complete trail. It is our belief that Mr. Smith's role is to head and finance your organisation, whilst it is your role to deal with your clients. It is also your role to coordinate and allocate any work that you take on amongst your various teams of hackers, with the twins undertaking the most complex and most advanced work. Have I got that right, Mr. Jones?"

"That is pretty much how we operate, yes. But I'm sure you didn't need me to confirm that as you already know for certain."

"Yes, we do. My proposal is that the twins come and work directly for Thunderbolt Services, as employees. They will be very well paid. If all of you agree to this and just one additional condition, yourself and Mr. Smith will be paid a large annual consultation fee, a retainer if you like. It galls me to say this, but I know I will have to pay for your silence. My sole condition is that you stop all your illegal activities. In addition to these annual fees, you would all be allowed to keep the very sizeable funds that you shipped out of Cupric immediately prior to Ashby's attack. You will, of course, give 75% of these funds to recognised charities of my choosing. Yes Mr. Jones, we know about those funds and, just as you did, we can easily spirit them away if we wish to. They are, after all, mostly held on our systems"

And that was how it came to pass. Adam and Zak joined Thunderbolt Services, working as senior system designers in the cyber security department, where their expertise and unique experiences became invaluable. The truth was that the twins were delighted to be employed by Thunderbolt and to have legitimate jobs. They had never felt truly comfortable doing what they were doing and had simply got in too deep with no way of digging their way out. Mr. Smith and Mr. Jones were paid large annual retainers and they both eventually went on to do some legitimate marketing work for Thunderbolt, running several online campaigns and the like. Over the coming months, many well-known charities received very large anonymous donations. Thunderbolt's security systems were never breached again, almost certainly as a direct result of the Jackson twin's expertise.

The Jackson twins went on to develop a large master quantum-computer unit that continually monitored Thunderbolt's entire network.

This master control unit was permanently and exclusively dedicated to the security of the entire network looking for any unauthorised entry (hacking) and any inevitable machine code corruptions. This security unit stood alongside two other master control quantum-computers, one of which monitored, controlled and updated all mother computers, Little Maqs and their associated robotics. The other monitored, controlled and developed the entire network and was the master control unit.

Chapter 41

A Miserable Month for the Thompsons.

John and Sally Thompson were both hard working and loyal employees: they rarely took any time off sick, they were always punctual, they were very good at their jobs and both of them were lovely people to be around. John was a forklift truck driver working in a warehouse linked to the local spaceport, where he had worked since leaving school. Sally worked on the production line in a nearby factory. They had a daughter, Trish, who was blessed with a bright and bubbly personality. She was, just like her mum and dad, polite and easy to talk to. Trish had recently started working in a call centre and was already making a very good impression, both with her supervisor and the customers (she had a string of "very satisfied" scores on her customer feedback surveys and they had included many positive comments).

One Friday afternoon, quite out of the blue, all the staff working in the spaceport's warehouse were told to assemble for an important announcement. There wasn't even any time for speculation as to what the announcement was going to be, everyone was simply marched straight up to the top floor canteen. Once they got there, a few people stood around the edges, but most sat down at the canteen tables … waiting. John had to finish his load and put his truck on charge in its designated parking bay before leaving it unattended and going upstairs (rules were rules and this was a very important health and safety rule) which meant that he was one of the last to arrive. All the seats and stools were occupied so he stood leaning against the wall whilst chatting with a couple of mates. A minute or two later Bob "The Smile" Smith, the company's operations director, appeared through the double doors next to the canteen's serving counter. Everything went quiet as people fell into a respectful hush. With no preamble or any hesitation, The Smile read out a short statement. "As I am sure all of you are aware, over recent years new technology has brought about many changes within the distribution industry. With the aim of reducing costs and keeping the company profitable and viable, the company is proposing that, during the next six months, its warehousing operation will become fully automated. As such and with immediate effect, the company is giving notice that it is entering into a formal consultation period with all its warehouse staff with regards to this proposal. The effect of this proposal may be that some or all of your positions may become redundant. I would like to emphasise that, at this stage, this is only a proposal and is subject to the results of all our consultations." He then went on to tell them that each and every person who may be affected, will meet with him, together with an Human Resources officer, during the course of the following week. John was devastated. He and Sally, following years of living in rented accommodation and of saving for a deposit, had just secured a mortgage and, only three weeks ago, had moved into their first house. How were they going to survive if he was made redundant? Financially, they had pushed themselves and could barely afford the mortgage repayments as it was. How was he going to find a new job? It seemed that all the local warehousing facilities were becoming totally automated, so there would be very little demand for a forklift operator. It was a sad day when John went home and told his wife about what was going on and that he would, in all likelihood, lose his job. Furthermore, the reality was that he would struggle to find new employment as there were no suitable jobs to be found and, furthermore, there was no retraining being provided.

Things were going to become even worse the following week. Similar announcements were made at the factory where Sally worked stating that they were planning to fully automate the production line within the year. It seemed that she was also going to be made redundant. It was a saying that bad things happen in threes, and this was to be the case. Trish, their daughter, was also told that, as she put it, she and all her colleagues were going to be replaced by faceless talking machines. Within a year, John, Sally and Trish had all lost their jobs and they lost their house six months later, having failed to keep up with their mortgage repayments. All three could not find another job … there were just none available.

This was beginning to happen everywhere throughout Bounty. As Little Maqs became ever more common in the workplace, their impact was becoming ever greater. As we have just seen, this was particularly so when they were linked to robotics and any form of automation. This impact on society went way beyond those minor hiccups and inconveniences that were originally caused by the setting up of Little Maqs. This was fundamental, permanent and radical social change. It took a fair while for companies to absorb and fully take advantage of the Little Maq's capabilities but, over time, Little Maqs were used to operate machinery (as was the case with John Thompson), to carry out repetitive tasks (as was the case with Sally) and, quite soon after, they were frequently becoming used to verbally interact with customers (as was the case with Trish). In fact, as software and algorithms were developed, these innovations went on to create huge changes in almost every area of business. These changes were slow and gradual at first but, quite quickly, the rate of change accelerated. As Little Maqs carried on learning from each other, the wider became the impact. When coupled with the fact that Little Maqs were being trained in all sorts of skills, all of which were fed back into the shared knowledge of their databases, the impact they had in the workplace and the subsequent social changes, relentlessly pushed their societies towards the brink of catastrophic collapse.

These social changes became even more severe as Little Maqs were trained and programmed to process information and to act more and more like a person. [Remember our earlier definition of AI and just think about how many jobs could be replaced by such a development within our society. I would suggest that almost every job could be undertaken by a suitably programmed thinking machine. The only exceptions that I can come up with are those that require true interpersonal skills, such as: being a judge, a teacher, a psychologist, a counsellor, a social worker, a police officer or a TV presenter. I'm sure that time will prove me wrong on some of these and I'm sure that there must be others, but I would urge you to have a good think about these changes as they are almost certainly around the corner].

After a while, Little Maqs were even churning out pieces of popular music, pieces of literature and other works of art that were indistinguishable from work done by a person … you simply couldn't tell the difference. Eventually they were taking on roles that had previously been the realm of the highly educated, well-trained and well-paid people. Little Maqs were soon able to function as doctors, lawyers, architects, designers, engineers and, when linked to suitable robotics, as surgeons and other hands-on highly skilled professionals. There were, of course, still living beings working in these environments, it was just that Little Maqs and robotics were soon undertaking most of the day-to-day work. This resulted in fewer and fewer people being employed, even within highly skilled environments.

The changes were not instantaneous and not universal. It took a good number of years for the impact of this shifting workplace to be felt by the broader society, but felt it was. The first noticeable change was that the unemployment figures began to grow. Across Bounty there were, fairly quickly, billions of people without jobs, leading to social devastation in many areas. Whole communities were now living in poverty. Initially, as we have seen, it was predominantly manual workers that were affected as routine manual labour was the first to be automated. This led to pockets of extreme poverty, initially within what used to be the industrial heartlands of each of the galaxies. These changes were unplanned, unforeseen and unmanaged. Consequently, nothing was put in place to regenerate these communities, neither economically nor socially. The accelerating rate of change was simply far too quick for any government, or indeed any society, to adapt to. This growing unemployment went on to have an even more significant knock-on effect. As a larger and larger number of people lost their jobs, tax revenues, for all governments, shrank. The biggest revenue, for most governments, is income tax and there were simply fewer and fewer people earning an income and thus contributing any tax.

These changes led to an ever-increasing polarisation of societies; the wealthy and the poor, the haves and the have-nots. Over time this polarisation became more and more extreme, resulting in vast numbers of have-nots and a comparatively tiny number of haves. Industry and the wider economy were still producing products, but much more cheaply now that labour costs had been slashed. The end result was that, whilst company's total revenues were reduced as prices and the number of customers with money reduced, profits actually increased enabling company owners, shareholders and senior managers to take larger and larger incomes. To put it another way, the pie was getting much smaller but the well-off were now taking very much larger slices. This inevitably led to an even greater and more extreme rate of separation between the wealthy and the poor. Furthermore, as these more technology driven businesses gave rise to cheaper prices, there was another hugely negative effect on government income; value-added taxation also imploded. This was no longer a shift in society, it was a complete and fundamental restructuring. Eventually these economic changes became catastrophic. There were soon so few haves left that, in effect, there was no one left that could buy any of the products. Sales simply dried up and all economies shrank and spiralled towards collapse.

The long-term effects of these changes brought about by Little Maqs and robotics were clearly dramatic. So much so that, over time, the main demonstration outside of Bounty's Parliament Building was no longer anti-war, (although that demonstration continued), but anti-poverty, coupled with growing demands for a fairer society and a more equitable distribution of wealth. There was even talk of revolution in the air as the general population became more and more disenfranchised; and this section of society was becoming ever larger.

In order to bring this theme to a close, we are going to take a quick peek in a very short time, into the future and look at the final state of their society at the time Sham becomes President of the whole of Bounty and The Network was commissioned. By this time, the extremes of wealth and poverty had become obscene. Government income and, consequently, spending, had pretty much dried up. The wealthy had become the obscenely wealthy and, because of clever tax loopholes and tax avoidance lawyers such as Toby Buckmaster MP, the few money earners that remained were simply not contributing anything to their societies. As an indication of the extent of these loopholes and tax avoidance schemes, one bank bought an entire planet, declared it independent and created a mega tax haven for the mega rich.

*

In summary, there were two broad underlying reasons for this societal collapse: a) the development and spread of technology, in the form of the Little Maq and robotics, was unplanned, uncontrolled, unmanaged and overwhelmingly quick, b) the rate at which governments and societies as a whole were able to react and adapt to these changes was far too slow. In a nutshell, the required mechanisms to plan for, to control and to absorb the use of this new technology, within their society, were just not there.

By the time The Network was commissioned, society had all but collapsed and its very infrastructure, such as its governments, was crumbling. Overwhelmingly, the vast majority of people were very disillusioned, and they were demanding change.

Chapter 42

Samuel J. Smurfet R.I.P.

S amuel J. Smurfet was a well-known, even much-loved, tv personality. His early career was that of a television news reporter during which time he became a household name. He was later made lead anchorman for the main galaxy's news program which was produced at the central media studios on Cupric. As it happened, he was at work at the time of Ashby's attack when, as we have already learned, all communications were taken down by the Jackson twins, including all television and radio channels. He was one of many people trying to work out what had happened and desperately trying to restore the systems. The main TV production and broadcasting studios were amongst the very early targets of Ashby's nuclear strikes during which Smurfet lost his life, along with many others at the facility and, ultimately, around a billion or so other citizens.

Gabriella, tried to arrange a civic celebration of her father's life, somewhere in the city where he used to live and where she was brought up. However, the new military junta now imposed by Ashby repeatedly turned down her requests to hold the event anywhere on Cupric. As an alternative, she arranged an afternoon service of remembrance and celebration of her father's life at the main parliamentary buildings on Whisper (once Sham had pulled some strings that is; after all, he had been Sham's father-in-law and Sham was the President). A great number of people attended, including all of Sham's close friends, many politicians, celebrities from the worlds of broadcasting and entertainment and a great number of other influential people, including Zodiac and Monte-Fredo.

The afternoon featured a good number of clips of Smurfet's work, a display of images that had been taken throughout his career and several speeches by people who had known him, each one talking about his life's achievements and the positive impact he had had on many people's lives. The final and keynote speech was given by Sham himself.

Sham's speech was a masterpiece. It was deeply moving, and it captured the very essence of Samuel J. Smurfet the man, the news hound, the reporter, the presenter, the family man and a good deal about his positive and caring nature. The speech was so good that people correctly assumed that it had been written by Gabriella. It concluded with the lines:

"Samuel, my father-in-law, was killed in yet another war, a war that was, once again, driven by the desire for resources; resources that are scarce on one planet but abundant on another. Surely, as a society of living beings, we should be beyond that! What is Bounty other than a collection of peoples who all share the same common goals? Life, liberty and the pursuit of happiness, these are the goals that we all share, and they should be the basis on which we live together as one homogeneous society of living beings. We want a SHARING society, we want a FAIR society, we want an OPEN society, we want a SAFE society, and we want a structure that supports these goals. We must get away from war being a solution! War is NEVER a viable long-term solution! We must have an inclusive society, a society that SHARES! We must have a society that shares in an EQUITABLE way! We must have a political structure that supports and enables these dreams throughout all of Bounty! In Samuel's memory, I hereby dedicate myself to the achievement of these aims .... I dedicate myself to a fair society and the ENDING OF ALL WARS!!"

The day's proceedings had been recorded, both by several official cameras and by many individual's communicators' cameras. It was not long before clips of Sham's speech were circulating throughout Bounty on social media. If you ever want an example of "going viral," this could well be the best.

After the speeches, when everyone was free to mingle and socialise, many people approached Sham and offered their support.

"That was a great speech President Piper, and I wholeheartedly share your aims. Let me know if there is anything I, or my organisation, can do to support you" said Fabio Zodiac.

A short while later… "Well said Mr. President, it was about time a politician spoke up for all people. Let me know if or how I can help you" said Mont-Fredo.

Each and every one of Sham's friends and family did the same, offering both their sympathies for his and Gabriella's loss and their support of his aspirations.

*

During that evening many of the guests gathered and chatted amongst themselves at the bar of the exclusive Central Hotel where most were staying and where refreshments had been provided by Sham and Gabriella. They mostly chatted about Samuel Smurfet, his life and their memories of him, but there was also much debate about the content of Sham's speech. Everybody, almost without exception, expressed their support for Sham's goals. It was Dip-Dip who said something in passing that would come to shape future events. "The trouble is that war is a symptom of our current society. Our society is made up of many people, most of whom are basically good and only a tiny number of whom are truly bad. However, nearly each and every one of us seems to have become inherently self-centred, wanting to keep hold of what we've got and envious of what we don't have, and we have become wary and suspicious of other people's motives. Our political systems seem to be designed to exacerbate these confrontational positions. Political parties are elected based on representing the interests and desires of groups of people rather than society as a whole. I guess, if you could change the current model of politics, as I think Sham was hinting at, we might have a chance of securing peace for all people … either that or take the people out of the equation all together" he said with an ironic titter.

"Hmmm" thought Plank as he listened to Dip-Dip's musings "take people out of the equation … now that's an interesting thought!"

*

The room was crowded and everybody was talking. From across the room and through the hubbub, Plank could be heard saying "Why don't we do that?" then a little louder "Dip-Dip, why don't we do just that?"

"Do what?" asked Dip-Dip

"What you just said. Why don't we take people out of the equation?"

"Er, how do you mean old boy"

"Just as you said Dip-Dip, why don't we, as a society, take people out of the equation? I mean, why not leave important decisions to our IT systems? After all, they pretty much control and operate most things as it is, why not go the whole hog and let them choose how we resolve our most serious problems, after all, they are the ultimate problem solvers."

"What, let our Little Maqs run the show?"

"Maybe not everything, but yes, why not? Why not let Little Maqs take key decisions on our behalf, certainly when it comes to war and whether or not we destroy each other. We could get them to determine and oversee the equitable sharing of resources. They would make much more rational decisions than we seem to be able to make. In fact, we could probably program them to stop us all killing each other! That could become a core overarching programme."

"Hey Fabio, come and join us a sec" Dip-Dip called out to Zodiac "I think Plank is suggesting that we hand control of all lethal weapons over to our Little Maqs and, if I understand him correctly, he is suggesting that a network of Little Maqs could run the whole show, particularly when it comes to allocating resources and avoiding war. Could Little Maqs perform such a function?" asked Dip-Dip.

"What are you talking about?"

"I mean, could Little Maqs make key decisions on such things as how natural resources are shared out and, perhaps more importantly, could they control all weapons so that they can't be used to wage war on each other?"

"Well, in theory, yes they could."

"Could they make better decisions than living beings?"

"Of that I am convinced. Living beings have too much of an agenda and we are, by our very nature, emotional. I believe that it's emotion that leads to war…. No emotion, then perhaps, no war."

Chapter 43

Plank Meets Zodiac and Sham.

It was about a fortnight after the celebration of Samuel J. Smurfet's life, whilst Plank and Zodiac were winding down after one of their frequent finance meetings, that Plank brought up the subject of the Little Maq's possible enhanced role in society. Over the years, as well as being colleagues, Plank and Zodiac had become very close friends; Plank greatly admired Zodiac's scientific genius and his high moral principles whilst Zodiac had come to hugely value Plank's commercial insight and admire his ability to quickly absorb new and difficult concepts. Most importantly, they greatly enjoyed each other's company and valued each other's opinions.

"So, what did you think about Dip-Dip's idea for the Little Maq?" asked Plank.

"I'm assuming that you are talking about the idea of taking all living beings out of potentially harmful decisions .... to be honest I am in two minds. I can certainly see many advantages. I think it has got to the stage whereby our Little Maqs can make better and more rational decisions than we are capable of, and I certainly believe that they could make better decisions than our governments, leaders and politicians. On the other hand, my one big reservation is that everything will depend on their programming. If we were to get the programming wrong, well, it could be disastrous. Unfortunately, as we well know, going live with any new routine has its risks. We have made mistakes in the past and our programming has sometimes given rise to unforeseen actions and consequences, particularly when commissioning completely new systems."

"Come on Fabio, we have some of the best minds and all the best program designers in the known universes. I have no doubt that we would get it right. And just think of the revenue that it could generate. It would tie the whole of Bounty into our products."

"Yes, I realise that; the benefit to Thunderbolt would be inestimably huge."

"We are a commercial organisation with a duty to our shareholders. I strongly urge that we at least explore the possibility, both on behalf of our shareholders and for the long-term future of the entire intergalactic community."

"Plank, as you no doubt realise, I greatly value your thoughts and opinions. So, whilst I have my reservations, I agree that we should at least explore its feasibility. How do you suppose we could do that?"

"Well, there are clearly many technical issues around how we could design and implement such a system, but all of these we can do in-house. The wider issues are political. I would suggest, therefore, that our priority is to get the input of a leading politician. I would suggest that we go directly to the galactic President, and I make arrangements to approach Sham."

"I agree," said Zodiac "but I have something else to add."

"OK, what's on your mind?"

"Well, the ever widening and ever growing use of our Little Maqs is clearly initiating huge social changes. More and more people are losing their jobs and, because of this, government revenues are collapsing. My intention was for Little Maqs to drive change in society that is overwhelmingly good; the end of mundane and unfulfilling jobs, more free time for all to enjoy, the elimination of dangerous work and many social improvements. Ultimately, I wanted to drive the continual, sustainable and universal improvement in everyone's lives. The truth of the matter is that, in my opinion and with hindsight, our Little Maqs have been introduced far too quickly and with nothing in place to support those people who are directly affected in the short term. Furthermore, as there are ever fewer working people, our tax / revenue generating systems need to change and this is not happening. At the moment, we are driving a wedge through society where the rich, like ourselves, are becoming fewer but very much richer and the poor are forever becoming poorer. The more I think about it, I can see that diverting the production of all Little Maqs, at least for a while, into creating a universal overriding system that controls weapons, allocates resources and resolves disputes could provide that breathing space for our societies to adapt to the future spread of Little Maqs. It could be made a long and protracted process to the benefit of all"

"So, you are saying that we focus all new Little Maqs on these new priorities and we don't make any more available for anything else, and if I understand you correctly, we do this for quite a lengthy period. During this time our societies can realign themselves so that incorporating Little Maqs and robotics becomes more equitable."

"Yes, that's exactly what I am saying, I believe we could, perhaps, take this as an opportunity to benefit the whole of society and rectify the obviously unintended consequences of the widespread introduction of Little Maqs."

*

Just a few days later, Plank arranged to see Sham at his official residence. It was arranged as a social call, so Plank was not surprised to see Gabriella sitting on the sofa alongside Sham. Plank was delighted that Gabriella was there; everyone knew that she had become the real driving force behind Sham and, in all honesty, the key decision maker. Convince Gabriella and you have convinced Sham was the way that Plank saw the situation.

The two old friends chatted for a while before Plank led the conversation around to the subject of the Little Maqs. "Have you given much thought to Dip-Dip's idea of taking potentially dangerous decisions out of any living being's hands?" he asked.

"Can't say that I have old boy" bellowed Sham.

"What was Dip-Dip's idea? asked Gabriella.

"Well, basically, Dip-Dip shares your opinion. He said that there are far too many wars and far too many deaths at the moment; and it is only getting worse."

"Tell me about it! as you well know, I've just lost my father in one of those wars."

"Precisely. It is Dip-Dip's view that living beings should not have the power or the means to kill each other or to destroy each other's planets. He is proposing that we take such power out of the hands of all living beings and leave the resolution of potentially life-threatening disagreements to a different process; namely, let Little Maqs take the decisions. The aim is that no living being would control any form of nuclear or other such deadly weapon. Any conflict, and let's face it, they are normally about the distribution of raw materials and wealth, would be resolved by a suitably programmed network of Little Maqs. It would be the network that decides how resources are shared. Furthermore, with a lack of access to weapons, resources could not be taken by force, nor unreasonably withheld."

"You mean that Ashby could not have attacked Cupric, and my father would still be with us and a billion other folk would not have lost their lives?"

"Yes, precisely so. That is exactly the thrust of what Dip-Dip is saying."

"My goodness Sham, you just have to take this idea forward!!"

"Steady on old girl, that would be a massive change to our entire society. Everybody would have to agree to such a change" cautioned Sham.

"Well, maybe not everyone" said Plank "but certainly a majority would have to agree to it, assuming we put it to some form of referendum."

"So, all we would have to do is convince something like two million billion people and we would probably have to introduce a completely new political structure! We would also need to develop and program a suitable network of Little Maqs. It would require nothing short of a political revolution along with a massive financial investment!" As he was saying this his mind started churning. His father was a key stakeholder in Thunderbolt, holding many shares, and he had quite a few himself (suitably hidden, of course), as did all his friends. This proposal could be extremely lucrative for him, his family and his chums. But the most alluring thing for him was, without doubt, the fact that he could come to be seen as the one who solved the problem of war. He could become the ultimate "Mister Popular" and this was truly his lifetime goal; to massage his ego and to be liked by everyone.

"Come on darling," said Gabriella "we must at least give this a shot, it is our moral duty if nothing else."

"There is another possible benefit that I haven't yet mentioned." said Plank.

"OK, what's that then?" asked Sham.

"As you well know, we have an untold number of societal problems at the moment. People are losing their jobs left right and centre to automation, all driven by the relentless expansion of Little Maqs and robotics. Government revenues are plummeting which will severely impact on social welfare and other government spending. It is Fabio's strong belief that the introduction of Little Maqs has been far too quick. Their ultimate impact on our society was not understood and, consequently, nothing was planned in terms of restructuring our society. The rich are becoming vastly richer, governments have no money, the poorer folk are being left abandoned and the prospects for our overall society look very bleak. I must say that Fabio has convinced me that this is the case. We are thinking that, by assigning all newly manufactured Little Maqs to this new project and not letting them get into the general society, will slow down these societal changes and allow for politicians, such as yourself, to restructure our systems to facilitate the inevitable changes to come within our society. We both believe that, if we get the structure right, Little Maqs can hugely benefit everyone in our society."

"OK," said Sham "let's get a few people together so we can see what they think and look at drafting a proposed plan of action."

*

The proposed action plan was extremely simple:

1. Convince the majority of people of the benefits of the proposal.
2. Convince people of the dangers of not adopting the proposal.
3. Seek the support of each of the Galaxy Presidents and their governments.
4. Secure funding from all the Galaxies' governments.
5. Develop the software.

A list of five objectives. Each a simple statement, and each one a mammoth task.

Sham had asked Polo Marmalade to attend the meeting. Polo told the group that he supported the proposal and was happy to work on the social media side of things to promote their proposals. In doing so he suggested some names and slogans for the proposal. He suggested that their organisation be called "AI is A-ONE." and their strap line could be "No more attacks - use Little Maqs." These suggestions were catchy and simple; ideal for their purpose and even simple enough for Sham to remember!

Over the next week or so, Sham arranged to meet the other Galactic Presidents with a view to talking them through his proposals and getting their agreement, at least in principle.

Chapter 44

Mont-Fredo's Dilemma.

One day, as he arrived home from work, Mont-Fredo found his daughter in tears. He had entered their large town-residence and called out her name, but there was no reply. He knew she was already home as her school bag was plonked in the corner of the hallway and she hadn't gone out yet as her coat was still hanging on a wall peg. He had a quick look in the kitchen and then around the rest of the ground floor. He thought that maybe she was watching TV in the lounge or doing her homework in the den. There was no sign of her. He went upstairs and put his head around her bedroom door. There she was, lying on the bed, curled up in a ball. She looked like she was in shock, and she had obviously been crying. Mont-Fredo had a very close relationship with his daughter, Poppy, but it took quite a while before she opened up and told him what was upsetting her so much. She was being bullied. This bullying was not the old-fashioned face to face type, it was much worse than that. It was the relentless, never ending, soul destroying, on-line bullying enabled by social media and, sickeningly, much of it was happening through his own platform, Whispers. Mont-Fredo's immediate reaction was to close the accounts of those who were sending his distraught daughter such horrid messages and to put an intercept on his daughter's account.

But he had a dilemma. Mont-Fredo was well aware of the criticisms that were being levelled at online social media providers, including Whispers, and of the statistics that lay behind them. Bullying, which often initially takes the form of simple name-calling, can go on to include such things as false rumours, verbal abuse, harassment and unwanted sexually explicit images. Mont-Fredo's dilemma was this - he had always argued that freedom of speech is a basic human right and that it lay at the heart of all modern open societies. As such, Whispers would not censor any Whisper that was posted on their platform. Anyone could post whatever they liked, provided that it was not specifically illegal.

Now here comes the catch. How do you decide whether something is illegal or not. Does it have to be the decision of a court? Does Whispers make the call? If something turns out to be illegal, who is responsible? Whispers has always argued that this is not their responsibility, it is solely the responsibility of the individual who posted the Whisper. Whispers was just a message carrying service which facilitated other peoples' messages, and nothing more. This was the reasoning behind all the social media providers, but Whispers was by far the biggest.

There were, of course, common laws throughout Bounty which applied universally. It was illegal to harass someone, it was illegal to defame someone, there were laws around malicious communications and other aspects of public order. However, these laws were, in practice, far too cumbersome and too slow to be effective. It could take years for something to go to court and even longer to get resolved; way too slow and way too expensive a process to protect most people. The legislation and the legal systems were totally ineffective at resolving any immediate concerns. All of this was being exacerbated by the fact that new technology was being introduced at an incredible rate and becoming ever more widespread. The introduction of the Little Maq was accelerating this process even further. So, if you believe you have been slandered or someone is telling lies about you and you are wealthy enough, you can have your retrospective day in court and get some form of recompense sometime down the line. However, this legal route was out of reach for the overwhelming majority of the population. It was far too expensive and far too risky (for example, if you don't win the case, for whatever reason, you end up liable for all the costs and such bills could be enormous). So, as an ordinary person, you were powerless to take any action unless you were lucky enough to have a socially minded lawyer, or a charity or an action group, who would take your case on out of principle. In fact, unscrupulous, very wealthy organisations and individuals used this very much to their advantage. The threat of long legal processes and possible ruinous legal costs was enough to prevent a great many legal cases ever being taken.

The issues were even broader. Much of the upset delivered by social media was not, in fact, illegal. It is not illegal to express your dislike of someone, or tease them, or criticise them and so forth - but it can be extremely upsetting for the receiver. So, if you are a schoolchild suffering at the hands of a bully or bullies, there is no practical mechanism for preventing it. Furthermore, how can any system deal with the extent of bullying - it is suffered by around forty percent of all school-aged children (as recent surveys in the UK have shown to be the case).

The next day, Mont-Fredo went into his office in a bad frame of mind. He felt so sorry for Poppy, and he felt, in some way, complicit in her misery. His day was about to get very much worse.

"Good morning, sir. I'll bring you a coffee". The customary greeting from his PA, Veronica. What was uncustomary for her to say was "I really think you should have a look at the media sites, sir".

The leading article on most of the sites, was the story of a young girl who had committed suicide. It appears that, prior to her suicide, she had received Whispers and various hyperlinks contained within Whispers, which led her directly to websites that made explicit reference to suicide. It had just come out in an open postmortem, that the girl had previously looked at websites containing articles referring to suicide. She subsequently received an untold number of links containing stories, anecdotes, graphic pictures and even a list of painless suicide methods. Furthermore, it was Whispers' own algorithm, or that of Thunderbolt Services, that had been the source of these hyperlinks. Mont-Fredo was distraught - this is not what Whispers should be about. Had he created a monster???

The unsavoury side of social media was beginning to show its ugly face.

His first reaction was to contact the child's parents, but he was strongly advised against that course of action. What could he do? He called an emergency board meeting which was held three days later.

*

"Ladies and Gentlemen, thanks for coming at such short notice; I have a dilemma that I need to resolve. In fact, it is a dilemma that, as company, we all need to resolve. The dilemma is this - I believe each and every one of us strongly supports the principle of freedom of speech. That has always been the principal cornerstone of our company's philosophy and of our business model. We allow our users to express their opinions in whatever way they choose, using any language they choose. It is not our role to impose our own morals, personal standards or points of view. Our platform has been a tremendous benefit to society in many ways - it allows for rapid communication and the expression of opinion, it enables people to keep in touch, it facilitates discussion, it helps people organise their social lives. It also facilitates many businesses functions and allows many companies to grow.

However, having this sole principle of freedom of speech is now showing a darker side which, I believe, we need to address. Whilst being an overwhelming benefit to society, we are gradually getting a reputation for facilitating online abuse, allowing the spreading of false information and disinformation, enabling bullying (I'm mostly thinking of school-aged children here but not exclusively) and of circulating illegal content. By illegal, I don't mean that I think we are legally liable for the ramifications of this content, but I do mean that some content, of itself, can be deemed illegal and we are unwittingly circulating that illegal content.

This is a position that I do not want Whispers to be in, for two reasons. On a personal note, I cannot abide the thought that Whispers is being used to abuse people, and, from a business perspective, I will not let the name of Whispers be denigrated. I am not prepared to continue sitting back and simply claim moral immunity under the auspices of the freedom of speech. I believe we CAN do something about it. I don't believe, for one minute, that we can totally eradicate all abuse being committed by people using our platform or to completely eradicate all lies from being circulated. But I DO, however, believe we can introduce procedures that make the misuse of our platform much less common. This may become a very expensive aspiration, but we are an extremely wealthy company.

It is my view that we should look at all the options that are open to us in two areas: a) content that is illegal, that is false or that is intentionally misleading, and b) content that, whilst being legal, is being posted with the specific intention of causing hurt or upset. As such, we are going to divide into two groups and each of you will be in one of those two groups.

Each group will contain some of the people in the room along with representatives from our legal team, senior technical managers and some of our public relations experts. I am even thinking of inviting some of our users to join us, but probably not at this stage. I will let you know which group you are in by close of play today. I want both groups to report back to me within one month, detailing your thoughts on how we can make a practical difference."

"Adrian, we are a wealthy company, but a workable solution could cost a fortune. We have a duty to our shareholders" commented Richy Marston, the CFO.

"You are right, Richy, we do have a duty to our shareholders, but we also have a duty to our customers and, I believe, to our society as a whole. We cannot survive without the support of our shareholders, that is true, but we certainly cannot survive without our customers. I think that I'm edging towards the position that our shareholders have done extremely well out of our business so far but, if they want that to continue, they may need to lower their financial expectations slightly whilst we protect and preserve our customer base. I have two concerns - we will lose customers to any business that resolves these issues before we do, and I am coming to the opinion that we have a moral duty to get this sorted. I am quite happy to talk this through with any individual here that would like to, either one to one or as a group. However, let's look at how we can possibly improve things and then we will get a better handle on what is or isn't practical and on how much any solution is likely to cost."

Mont-Fredo and Marston spent quite some time after the board meeting talking through Mont-Fredo's concerns. Marston was, of course, already aware of the recent suicide by a child, which had been widely reported in the press but, until this moment, was totally unaware of Poppy's bullying. At first Marston took the view that this was all a knee-jerk reaction to these two recent events, but Mont-Fredo was able to convince him otherwise. "Richy, I've spent the last couple of days wondering if I have lost my sense of perspective and that I have got these recent events out of proportion. But I think I am coming to the conclusion that this course of action is an absolute necessity and that it's going to be critical for the long-term survival of Whispers. Furthermore, recent events have given me the opportunity to begin to see Whispers from a user's point of view and, to some degree, from much of the general public's point of view."

*

The findings and proposals of the two groups were as follows:

Illegal and False Content.

- There are Bounty-wide laws already in place. However, because of the high costs involved and the long-drawn-out legal processes, the majority of illegal posts are never reported, never get taken down and the individual sufferers are very rarely recompensed. The perpetrators are simply never prosecuted. There are many reasons why this is the case, but they mostly centre around the fact that the legal processes are hugely out of date (they were designed back in the days of the old, printed newspaper) and hugely expensive. Under our legal systems, resolution is via the courtroom, a process which is far too slow and, even if the cases were to be prosecuted, there are just too many instances for the system to cope with. Furthermore, as we operate a universal system, it could prove impossible to tie down which legal system has jurisdiction over any individual crime, and they could well come under the jurisdiction of multiple legal systems. In summary, the existing legal systems do not work so we need another solution.

- Proposal – To provide a "click on button" that allows any recipient to report, what they believe to be, an illegal communication or any communication that contains false information. The "reporting button" would take you to a drop-down list of notifications for:
  o Defamation
  o False allegations
  o False information
  o Malicious communication
  o Harassment
  o Incitement of public disorder
  o Homophobic content

- o Racist content
- o Sexist content
- o Threat of violence
- o Inappropriate sexual images
- o Inappropriate violent images
- o Other

Every notification that Whispers receives from any customer must be investigated. There will be an initial screening intended to determine if the complaint has any grounds. If, for instance, someone complained of false information, then they would be contacted to ask for more information including an explanation as to why it is believed to be false information. If the complaint is upheld, then the post or link would be removed, and the sender would have their account closed for a limited period of time. Furthermore, every recipient of that post, including anyone who had received a forwarded copy, would get a message from Whispers saying that the post they had received was found to be untrue. The one who posted would also have a lengthy ban. All accusations of illegal content will be reviewed by a Whispers employed lawyer. If that lawyer believes the accusation to be true and the post is believed to be illegal, the post will be taken down and all relevant information will be forwarded to the police or other appropriate authority.

Legal Content sent with intent of causing upset or harm.

There is a necessity to deal with less serious matters than those requiring a legal review.

- o Proposal – Create a Whispers' code of ethics and conduct that is included in the terms and conditions of use. Any post that is deemed to be outside of this code of ethics, once reviewed, will be taken down and the sender will have their account suspended. This suspension would be for a period of time that is deemed suitable, depending on the severity of the breach of the code of ethics. The withdrawal of service is entirely at Whispers' discretion. There is, however, a right to appeal. The Whisper's code of ethics is an attempt to resolve such things as bullying and mild harassment.

o   There is, inevitably, a crossover between this code of ethics and the reporting of suspected illegal posts, often depending on the receiver's own feelings. For example, when does too frequent messaging move from being annoying to being illegal harassment? Such cases would be reviewed by a Whisper's lawyer.

These proposals were fairly simple, and they became fully implemented. There was, inevitably, some delay in getting the process up and running. Whispers had to estimate the number of investigators and lawyers they would need and these people had to be recruited and trained. The system had to be updated, and the following Terms & Conditions of use had to be communicated to each and every Whisperer.

Terms & Conditions of Use.

It is our intention that all users of our platform will remain respectful of each other.

Therefore, by using this platform, you agree to adhere to the following Terms and Conditions of use.

You will:

o   comply with all currently applicable legislation.

o   respect all other users' civil rights.

o   adhere to and abide by all intellectual property rights.

o   not submit any falsehoods.

o   not abuse or harm others.

o   not threaten to abuse or harm others.

o   not mislead, defraud, impersonate, defame, bully, harass or stalk other users.

o   not interfere with, or harm this service, in any way,

o   not introduce malware or spam into our system or into any of our user's systems,

o   not attempt to bypass our security systems,

- If you include links to other platforms, the linked content must also be in compliance with our Terms and Conditions.

- Failure to comply with these Terms & Conditions will result in the loss of your account for a period of time, the duration of which will be at Whispers' discretion.

- Entirely at the discretion of Whispers, any posted material found in breach of these Terms & Conditions will be permanently taken down.

- Entirely at the discretion of Whispers, any posts that are found to contain falsehoods will be taken down and all recipients of that post will be informed of the falsehoods. This will include all forwarded posts.

- You have the right to appeal to Whispers against any finding at the time you are notified of any such finding.

- Any user may notify Whispers of any suspected breech of these Terms & Conditions (Ts & Cs) by using the "Notify Breach of Ts & Cs" button.

- These Terms & Conditions apply Bounty wide and will remain in place for perpetuity or until superseded.

- Whispers reserves the right to withdraw or refuse access entirely at Whisper's discretion.

To the surprise of many, there was very little objection to the introduction of the new Terms and Conditions. Almost everyone was in favour of introducing better standards that protected people from abuse and lies. Initially Whispers' new systems were inundated with reports of posts and their associated hyperlinks being in contravention of the new Ts & Cs. However, quite quickly, people realised that they were generally in everyone's best interest. As it became common knowledge that Whispers was actively suspending the accounts of those users who were found to contravene these new Ts & Cs, the vast majority of users adhered to the new rules so that reported breaches became much less common. It transpired that the vast overwhelming proportion of the population did not want to be lied to, did not want online bullying and harassment to continue, did not want their laws broken and did not view any of these terms and conditions as a loss of freedom of speech.

At the Whispers' end of year board meeting Mont-Fredo and his fellow board members were able to congratulate themselves on a good job done well (and the Poppies of the cosmos and their parents slept more soundly at night).

Chapter 45

Sham's Proposal.

As we have discovered, the highly populated Bounty galaxy cluster consisted of six galaxies, each having their own president. Sham was president of Central Galaxy, the largest of the six, and he met with each of the other five presidents individually, hoping to convince them of his strategy of using Little Maqs. Frankly, he left each one of these meetings feeling more than a little deflated.

The truth of the matter was that, whilst each of the presidents could see the benefits, each one of them had a whole string of reservations. This was not surprising but there appeared to be two commonly held key hidden sticking points lying under the surface: firstly, the proposal would inevitably lead to a significant loss of personal power and prestige for the presidents (the presidents would no longer be the ultimate decision makers in their own galaxy, the Network would) and secondly, the galaxy presidents would have the unenviable task of trying to persuade each of their many planetary leaders to relinquish their personal control and handing it over to a machine. Just think of the loss of face that each of these would suffer; they would have to accept that they would no longer be the leading force on their own planets. Now, that would be a hard sell indeed.

When Sham arrived home from his round Bounty tour, he went straight to see Gabriella.

"They are all power crazy" he fumed "they don't care about their people, they only care about their personal standing and their egos.

"How do you mean, darling?"

Sham continued to rant. "Their only real concern seems to be that they would no longer maintain ultimate control and, furthermore, every one of them was reluctant to take the proposal to their planet's leaders. They hardly asked anything about the Network, how it would be programmed, who would control it, who would be involved in its design. Not one of them wanted to really discuss the positive benefits for their people."

"Well, they are politicians and many of them are in their positions just to satisfy their own egos."

"So, how do we continue then?"

"Simple, let's take them out of the equation, let's go directly to the people!!" said Gabriella "I'm going to give Polo a call, I'm sure he will have a view on this."

Polo certainly did have a view. His view was that many politicians were a waste of space, more of a hindrance than a help to their people, and this was particularly true of the galactic presidents (er, not Sham of course). Furthermore, he believed that the whole democratic process had become outdated and was, in fact, no longer fit for purpose and a long way from being democratic.

Over the coming months Sham, Gabriella, Marmalade and many others devised a plan aimed at engaging directly with the people of Bounty and taking the politicians completely out of the equation.

*

Don't be a mutton, give AI the button.

Give AI a go at running the show.

I trust a Maq not to start the attack.

These slogans appeared everywhere on social media, and they were followed by thousands of clips showing Sham or, more often, Gabriella, talking about their proposal. There were, of course, fake interviews, mock presentations and unsubstantiated news reports appearing everywhere, all of which highlighted Sham's proposal.

Initial reactions to the campaign were fairly muted, with a noticeable silence from those politicians who held power. There was a little bit of ridicule whilst Sham's proposal was picked apart and challenged but, slowly at first, but quickly gaining momentum, there was a growing groundswell amongst the public in support of Sham's proposal. As the weeks went by, it became clear that this growing groundswell of support was not simply in favour of Sham's proposal but, just as much or even more so, it was becoming an anti-establishment movement. Most of the criticisms of Sham's proposal were coming from politicians or from extremely wealthy people who would benefit from maintaining the current status quo. It was becoming obvious that the public were not happy with their lot and were blaming the very people who held power or benefitted enormously from the current situation. A huge number of people had lost their jobs, there was absolutely no cash available for social projects, there was no investment, the tiny elite were getting richer and richer whilst the huge majority were really suffering. Why not take some power away from the politicians and the mega-wealthy? Why should we listen to them? After all, it was the people at the top, the establishment, who were causing all the problems and benefitting from other people's misery. It was certainly those people that caused the wars in the first place, and it was very clear that it was not those who died in the wars. And who was making the proposal? Good old Sham. Good old Sham, the everyday-man's representative, and Gabriella, the celebrity, who had recently lost her dad and who could relate to real people! There was more talk of revolution in the air; in fact, on one planet, there was a revolution.

It is worth pointing out at this point that, the people did not view the owners of high-tech companies as part of the social elite. These people were the new kids on the block and not directly responsible for generations of conflict. The social elite were seen as those with old money, the top echelons of society, the politicians, the professionals such as lawyers, the people who had got us into this mess and who would benefit most from not upsetting the apple cart. It had become a huge 'us' and 'them' situation with many more 'us'es than 'them's; with Sham very much an 'us'.

It is interesting to note that the true elite of Bounty was now, in fact, all of Sham's friends. It was such a tiny elite that it was able to stay below the radar throughout the whole campaign. This tiny super-elite was all in favour of Shams proposal. Why? Because each and every one of them had an awful lot of shares in Thunderbolt! and it was their platforms that were circulating Sham's message, spreading the word and hugely skewing the argument.

Chapter 46

Something to Think About [A Note from the Author].

Throughout this tale, we have touched upon some of the illegal misuses of new technology and some of the vulnerabilities of new technology, including: The Jackson twins' computer hacking, embezzlement of funds, taking control of other people's systems, viewing and using private information, stealing and the subsequent misuse of databases, to name but a few.

We have also touched upon how statistics can be presented in ways that mislead people, either deliberately or accidentally. Remember, we looked at how two charities could be shown as both growing and shrinking at the same time, simply by selecting percentages or values, by using different time periods and by comparing these against different criteria.

In essence, statistics can often be selected and presented in ways that support a particular point of view or undermine another. Just for information, I want to highlight another common way in which this is achieved. Using and displaying information graphically.

For example:

The Widget Company's last 10 years widget Sales were:

1	2	3	4	5	6	7	8	9	10
928	919	915	913	911	909	906	907	909	909

Are this widget manufacturer's sales growing, shrinking, or steady?

Graphically, it can be shown to be doing any of the above, all depending on the data that is selected and on what scale and timescale is chosen for the graph. Let us have a quick look.

Shrinking

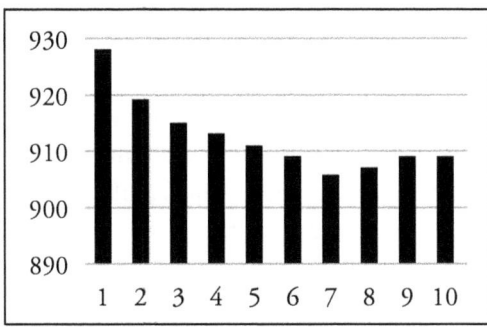

Growing

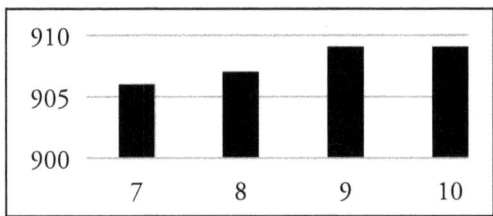

Steady

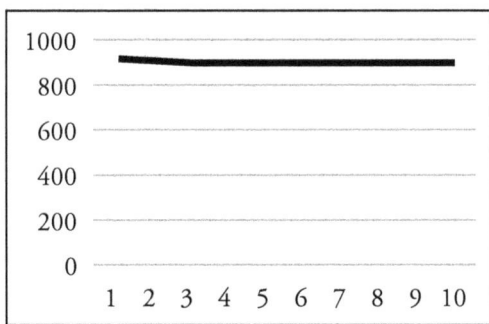

Selecting specific time periods and choosing suitable scales are very common ways of graphing data in ways that support a particular point of view, or denigrate another. In this example I have shown you that a company's sales are seen to be growing, shrinking or remaining flat, all from the same data. I would urge that you always look at these aspects when you see a graph that is being used to support or denigrate any argument. In my experience, one of the most common techniques used is the manipulation/selection of scales. It is extremely common to see data that purports to show a trend, but on closer inspection, one can see quite clearly that only the absolute top of the overall graph has been sliced off and used. This can show what appear to be quite dramatic trends whilst, if you look at the true overall picture, there is no significant change whatsoever. I would urge you to always look at the scale that has been chosen and question why that was done. Similarly, look out for odd snapshots being taken. The graph showing a growth in widget sales has very deliberately chosen just four specific year's figures, they paint the company in the best light. It is not wrong to do this as they are true and valid figures, but it has usually been done for a reason. Always ask yourself "what is the bigger picture?" If you can't answer that from the information that you have been given then I would suggest that you view the author's argument with a fair degree of suspicion.

Another technique which is used quite often is to not compare apples with apples, thus showing a twisted interpretation of data. A good example that I was once shown were two entirely different interpretations of the same data which were summaries of a country's defence spending. One interpretation, which was used to argue for more spending, stated that defence spending had been cut over recent years. When you look closely at the argument, they were using a comparison of percentage of GDP. In other words, they were showing that we were spending a smaller proportion of our money on defence, but they implied that actual spending had been cut. Funnily enough, another article used spending data expressed purely in cash terms which showed that we were actually spending more on defence. Neither of these arguments are right or wrong, but the misleading element comes from the fact that both parties had the same data and chose to present it in a way that supported their argument, without showing the other representation and without giving the full picture. In other words, they were selecting and presenting data with the sole purpose of influencing. They certainly did not give a balanced view which would have allowed the reader to draw their own conclusion.

Chapter 47

Groundswell.

The "I trust a Maq not to start an attack" campaign had started in earnest as Sham, Gabriella, Marmalade and their teams swamped social media with their campaign material. This material ranged from comments in support of the campaign made by influential friends (often misrepresenting or being selective of the facts, but always very emotional), statistics supporting their claim that death tolls were growing (they were, but nowhere near as fast as the carefully selected data suggested and, importantly, it really depended on where you lived) and there were many deeply moving personal appeals from Sham and Gabriella. Needless to say, Sham's campaign was funded and facilitated by his extremely wealthy friends.

There were also many good counterarguments to Sham's proposals appearing on social media and in the general press. Many of these came from other Galaxy Presidents or from within the existing political establishment, all of whom completely rejected the proposal. It became the overwhelming opinion of the vast majority of political commentators (all of whom were in close personal contact with their existing political establishment cronies, but with very little connection with the common people) that Sham's proposal was dead in the water. There were just too many solid objections from within the establishment.

However, as we have seen, an unexpected phenomenon slowly emerged. There appeared to be a more and more significant proportion of the general public who favoured Sham's proposal and, as we have seen, it appeared that much of their support was not specifically pro Sham's proposals but, rather, they were just anti the existing establishment. It was becoming a contest of the common people versus the establishment. The growing opinion amongst common people was quite simple - to them, it appeared that the establishment was always lecturing them on what they should think and do. Furthermore, under the stewardship of this long-standing establishment, the lot of the common person had got worse and worse. More people were now unemployed than ever before. If a war is started then it was the working people who got conscripted, fought the wars and lost their lives, rarely the establishment people. The wealthy social elite had access to private bunkers and fallout shelters, it was always the common people who died in huge numbers. "Why should we listen to them?" became the ever swelling opinion in the bars, over the dinner tables and in the benefit queues, "they have done nothing for us, they have simply feathered their own nests, lined their own pockets and carved out very comfortable lives for themselves; all it our expense!"

*

This growing polarisation of views was manna from heaven for Sham's campaign. The agenda was no longer persuading people that giving ultimate power to AI, in the form of Little Maqs, was the right thing to do, which was a complex argument to make. The agenda had shifted to - who do you like more, Sham or the establishment? This argument did not need to be supported by facts, it did not need to be evidenced, it was simply reduced to a juxtaposition of personalities. Who do you support, Mr. Popular Sham or the self-serving elite? This was, of course, a spurious argument. Sham's campaign was, in reality, being funded and driven by the most wealthy of the elite, it was just a very different elite, an elite that held huge hidden sway over society but who were unelected and, from most peoples' perspective, almost invisible in their day-to-day world.

Over a very short period of time, the argument shifted again; if anything, it was further simplified. It shifted to – do we need the political elite at all? Which quickly boiled down to – do we do away with all Galactic Presidents, along with their governments, and replace the entire system with one leader, one president for the whole of Bounty? One of us – Sham. It quickly became a campaign to make Sham President of Bounty and, effectively, give him the authority to do whatever he liked.

*

There were, in fact, a few voices from outside of the political establishment that were beginning to urge caution in handing over ultimate power to Sham and power over life and death to Little Maqs.

Fabio Zodiac was acutely aware of the problems that Thunderbolt and their systems had when introducing Little Maqs into a new functionality. He remembered, for example, the system failures that occurred when Little Maqs took control of the management of many public conveniences throughout Bounty and many other similar instances. In fact, there were startup hiccoughs almost every time that a system was introduced to a new, unlearned, non-experienced, environment. Sometimes these hiccoughs resulted in simple to resolve problems and sometimes they took some time to resolve. However, the important thing is that, almost without exception, problems occurred whilst the system learned what it was doing during its startup phase. Zodiac's concern was not that the Little Maqs could not do the job but, rather, he was concerned that things were proceeding far too quickly. They did not have enough relevant data, and they had precious little experience in this type of programming. These systems learned for themselves, and mistakes WOULD occur! and the consequences of a mistake in this area were beyond comprehension.

Adrian Mont-Fredo also publicly urged caution. His view, like Zodiac's, was that Sham's proposal was being pushed too quickly. He had witnessed the devastating effects that new technology could have on people's lives if introduced too quickly, without due consideration and without proper planning.

*

Ultimately, Fabio Zodiac paid a heavy price for voicing his opinion. The Thunderbolt board held an emergency meeting during which he was replaced as the company's Chairman and Chief Executive. He had lost the theoretical sole ownership of his company when Thunderbolt was originally floated on the open markets. It now transpired that greed did in fact outweigh personal loyalty and common sense. Many of his former colleagues voted against Zodiac. Everyone could see the huge financial gain that each one of them would make under Sham's proposals. Almost every one of them had a degree of nervousness with these proposals, but almost everyone turned a blind eye to their own reservations. Plank was appointed Chairman and Chief Executive of Thunderbolt Services, with immediate effect, whilst Zodiac was escorted out of the building.

*

So, there you have it. Two of the most knowledgeable experts in the field, Zodiac and Mont-Fredo, were urging caution. Would they be heard? or would poorly informed, misguided and often deliberately mislead popularism win the day?

Chapter 48

The Vote.

There was no way that the galaxies' presidents were going to sanction a Bounty-wide vote which may lead to the scrapping of their roles - it just wasn't going to happen. Furthermore, it remained obvious that their primary concern was not the possible dangers of handing power over to an AI network, they were solely fixated on preserving their own personal status.

"We need to FORCE a vote," said Gabriella.

"Yeah right, they are never going to agree to that!" countered Sham.

"If we can't force a vote, then we are stuffed. How on earth can we get them to sanction a vote?" replied Gabriella. They were sitting in Sham's office with Polo Marmalade.

"I suggest that we go directly to the people," said Marmalade, "take the other presidents out of the equation."

"How do you mean?" asked Gabriella.

"I mean that we give every individual in the Bounty group, the opportunity to vote on what they want. Do they want a single Galaxy President or not? a simple yes or no vote. If we get a strong enough response, it would be difficult for the presidents to brush the wishes of their people under the carpet. We could force their hand."

"Could we do that?"

"Given the help of our key supporters we could" asserted Marmalade. "It could take the form of a simple on-line vote. I have no doubt that Thunderbolt's board would sanction the facilitation of such a vote. It would certainly be in their interest to do so."

And that is exactly what happened. Thunderbolt's board unanimously agreed to facilitate a pan-Bounty on-line vote.

Two months later, following a great deal of on-line discussions on forums and the like, almost every Bounty resident received the following message.

Make your voice count for a change!
Do you feel the current system is working for you?

Do you want a single President for Bounty?
Simply reply to this message
YES or NO

The response was big. Around 60% of the population responded, and around 83% of these responses were **YES** votes.

*

Now the proverbial really did hit the fan. Polo Marmalade employed all his available resources (even the Jackson twins were drafted in with Thunderbolt's consent). Social media, along with all mainstream news and current affairs programs, became flooded with news of the survey result (or at least by Marmalade's interpretation of the results). 83% of people want a single Bounty-wide president!!

[If you step back and take a closer look at the figures, this was a deliberately misleading interpretation of the voting results. It was true that 83% of responders voted for having a single president, but the truth was that this was less than half of the total population. To say that 83% of people wanted a single Bounty-wide president was plain misleading – hmm, those dammed statistics again!!]

The resultant clamour calling for change and the ensuing political tsunami became overwhelming. An official and legally binding Bounty-wide vote was arranged for two months' later.

Marmalade's campaign subtly changed its focus from "We must have a vote" to "Sham, the people's politician, he's the only man for the job!!"

*

There were, in fact, two votes. The first vote was "Do you want a single Bounty-wide president?" the result of which was a very close call (Yes – 52%, No – 48%, with a 72% turnout). The second round of voting was for the election of a President of Bounty, and, besides Sham, there were no serious candidates.

Sham was elected on, what was effectively, an open and unbounded mandate. Most people were aware that Sham's intention was to hand power to Little Maqs, but the possible ramifications of this policy were neither widely explained, discussed nor effectively challenged. The potential hazards of this policy were simply never aired, and they were certainly never answered. Zodiac and Mont-Fredo continued to advise caution, but their voices were drowned out by Marmalade's incessant campaigning, especially now that Zodiac had lost control of Thunderbolt.

There was no one to challenge Sham. He had the people's mandate, and few politicians were brave enough to challenge his policy. Those that did slid by the wayside and ended up spending what remained of their careers in the political wilderness.

*

It took several years to design, build and program The Network but, once completed, it was only a matter of days before Sham gave the fatal command to go live and, as we know, the whole population died.

Chapter 49

Bah Humbug.

Skipper lay awake one night, unable to sleep, whilst he mulled over everything he had learned about The Network and what had happened in Bounty. His final thoughts, before he eventually fell asleep, were "I think I've now got a pretty good idea of what happened in Bounty and of how and why The Network was created. I think it's time to meet up with the lads and make sure that we have all come to the same conclusions and, if we have, we need to talk about what we do next." The following morning, Skipper messaged Chris and TT "ww?"

It was the week before Christmas and many Christmas jumpers/sweaters/pullovers were being modelled in the bar that evening (whether they were worn as a bet, worn under duress, or people were simply joining in with the seasonal good spirits, was unknown, but each option was much debated). What was universally agreed upon was that; this year, TT had excelled himself. He was wearing his full Christmas ensemble – his Bah Humbug hat, his Bah Humbug jumper and his Bah Humbug scowl. "I can't stand Christmas" he said "Every year we have to endure the same old tunes: It's **CHRISTMAS !!!!!!!!!!** Last Christmas I Gave You my Heart, Jingle Bells; ….. Have Yourself a Merry Little Christmas … my ass!!! And as a professional taxi-service provider, what really gets my goat is that bloke who is always Driving Home for Christmas. He's been going at it for at least twenty years and still not got there!!! I just hope he's remembered to turn the meter off!!!" Skipper and Chris, on the other hand, loved Christmas. They had both run up strings of seasonal twinkling lights in their gardens, along with giant luminous inflatable Santas and they were both looking forward to the festive celebrations. By now, however, TT was off on a TT rant. "Christmas is fine if you've got young kids, but it's totally unacceptable if you use it as an excuse to act like one yourself. Just look at Plasterer Tony over there, he looks a complete twat in that Christmas jumper. He's clearly got no personal standards! He's in his fifties but acting like a six-year-old. Mind you, that could be considered an advancement for him!! You know something? it was still November when some knob of a DJ played a "Christmas classic" on the radio. I nearly swerved off the road as I launched myself across the car trying to get at the radio's off button. I have now taken the precaution of never again switching on the radio during the so-called festive season (and now, just to be on the safe side, two months either side of it). For customer safety, I am, from now on, only playing my own CDs, so that I will never get caught off guard again!!! What's more, if any passenger gets in wearing one of those ridiculous Christmas jumpers, I'm going to put their heated seats on full blast. From personal experience I know just how uncomfortable that can get. And God help them if they've got piles!!!"

In an effort to distract TT from his habitual Yuletide rant, Chris said "TT, we need to talk about The Network and what we've found. What's your take on it all?" and, to Chris and Skipper's considerable amazement, TT came up with a perfect and succinct summary, one on which they all agreed.

"Well, it's obvious that new technology developed in Bounty at an alarming rate, a rate that was well beyond the ability of their society to absorb. This technology, whilst having the capability to have really helped their society, actually led to a complete social collapse and even the occasional war. It's not that the technology was inherently wrong or dangerous, it was just that its introduction appears to have been unplanned and uncontrolled. Furthermore, this introduction was being driven by a tiny elite of very wealthy and very powerful people, along with a very small number of high-tech companies"

"I completely agree" said Skipper, "what should have enabled the creation of a perfect society actually led to total social collapse and disaster."

"That's my view as well," said Chris "but the real question now is, what are we going to do with all this information?"

Skipper had been giving this some thought and came armed with a proposal for the lads to consider. "It seems to me that we have two issues to resolve: a) how do we let the world know about everything that happened on Bounty, and b) what do we say to Napoleon, Old Major and Squealer. After all, it was they who contacted us and, after all, they do have the ability to wipe-out all human existence in an instant. We need to come up with some pretty good arguments as to why it would be in their interest not to do that. I was kind of thinking that we could create two different reports. One which we could, somehow or other, take to the world, and the other we to take to Napoleon."

"That sounds like a good way forward," said Chris. "I would like to do the report for the world, and I would like to do that with TT. I would suggest that you do the report for Napoleon, Skipper, as you have the best working relationship with him. We would, of course, all input into both reports."

"I do have one further concern." said Skipper "We are three relatively older men. As of now we have no outsider's view of our technology, no female input and no input from any younger person. I believe we need to get the perspective of a wider and more diverse group of people. I am not sure that Napoleon would accept any involvement from an outside person at this moment, but we really do need to find a way of getting a wider perspective on our own new technology. I propose that I try to conduct a survey amongst a wide range of people, including children, and get their perspective". And so, it was agreed.

*

Social Media Survey

1. Is social media all good - what do you see as the downsides?

2. Have you ever felt unsafe as a result of being online?

3. Have you ever received content (e.g. Posts, Links, Images etc) that you would rather not have received?

4. If you have received such content, what was it?

5. Have you, or anybody you know, been bullied on-line? If so, was the bullying done by someone known to the victim, by a named person who was unknown to the victim or was it anonymous?

6. Do you think trolling should be allowed?

7. Do you feel social media is misused in other ways? (e.g. misrepresentation of the facts etc.) and, if so, in what ways?

8. Do you believe everything you are told on social media?

9. How do you decide if you have been told the truth?

Are you? (Please tick)

7 to 10 years old	11 to 14 years old
15 to 19 years old	Adult
Female	Male

The results of the survey came as a big surprise to Skipper as there was no discernible difference in the responses, and this was regardless of age or gender; almost everyone held the same opinions. Other than that surprise, the two other main take-out points were that, almost every responder stated that they have received misleading or inaccurate information, and every single responder was of the opinion that trolling should not be allowed. As Skipper thought about this, it was actually quite obvious: absolutely nobody wants to be lied to, nobody wants to be deliberately misled, nobody likes bullying (except the bullies) and nobody wants abuse (except the abusers).

Fewer people said that they had felt unsafe at some point on-line than Skipper had thought would be the case, but Skipper was shocked by how young most girls were when they received their first inappropriate images.

In light of the results of the survey, the guys decided to press ahead with their reports.

Chapter 50

Skipper and Napoleon.

Skipper soon realised that the crux of his problem with Napoleon was to convince him of the benefits of working with human minds. His argument was going to be that it will only be through working with human minds that The Network will ever develop beyond what it is currently achieving which, if left unchanged, would lead to an infinite future of futility. Furthermore, he believed that the role of supporting living beings, all living beings, would be the key to providing The Network with a specific purpose. In fact, it would be the true underlying purpose as to why The Network had been developed in the first place.

Skipper's argument was going to be in three parts. Firstly, he wanted to convince Napoleon that the human mind was, indeed, different and more creative than The Network. Secondly, he had to convince Napoleon that supporting living beings would be a good thing, rather than seeing them all as a threat and destroying them out of hand. Finally, he needed to convince Napoleon that working together would benefit both parties, ultimately giving The Network a purpose and a way to develop. The alternative was to have an infinite future of futile, pointless existence.

*

"Hmm, first I have to explain how human intelligence is different from artificial intelligence and, in order to do that, I really need to understand that for myself," he reasoned. "The fact that there is a difference is going to be key to my argument." The best he could come up with was that humans can think outside of the box, but AI can't. "Well, that's not a very convincing argument and, to be honest, I'm not sure that I truly understand the differences for myself. I'm going to ask around and see what other people think." He was due to meet Chris that evening (they were going out for a few craft beers accompanied by some fresh samosas, and they would probably end up knocking back a few cocktails along the way). During the course of the evening, he asked his question. "Hi mate, I'm going to ask you a question. There is no right or wrong answer, I just want to know what you think. My question is - in what way is human intelligence different from artificial intelligence?"

"That's a good question mate ... off the cuff I would say that AI needs to be told what to think whereas a human mind can set its own tasks."

"Yes, thanks buddy, I was thinking along similar lines; I was going along the lines of saying that a human can think outside of the box, whereas AI needs some form of input or command."

The next day, Skipper put a call in to his brother-in-law who had a lifetime of experience working with computers (in fact Skipper was pretty sure that his brother-in-law had been around when Charles Babbage fired up the original Difference Engine). "Hi Steve, I have a question for you. There is no right or wrong answer, I just want to know what you think. My question is this - in what way is human intelligence different from artificial intelligence?"

"Well, I would say that the main difference is that artificial intelligence is necessarily gained from a store of existing knowledge (data), but a human can progress with no previous knowledge. I'll give you an example of what I mean. Humans invented the wheel with absolutely no prior knowledge of what a wheel was or what it can be used for whilst AI could not have done that as there was no existing data available."

His brother-in-law went on to say something very poignant regarding his concerns with our current AI "The worry is, Skipper, that AI uses coded rules for it to operate, in order to do anything at all. The trouble with that is, in every instance we do not know what these rules are or who has determined them. At the moment, large tech companies are drawing up their own codes and rules and we have absolutely no idea of the motives or intentions of these large companies. They are unregulated and unpoliced. A further concern could be if these AI systems are hacked or altered. Just imagine the threat to our society if our systems and their algorithms were modified by an outside influence such as a hostile government, a terrorist group, or some very determined activists. As well as outside interference, all these systems are subject to internal corruption. Machine coding can and will change over time, much like our genetic mutations."

The next day Skipper got a text from TT, "Hi Skipper, fancy popping along to the driving range sometime this afternoon? The weather situation is currently within permitted parameters." (They both like it not too hot, not too cold, not too wet and not too windy; they are both definitely what are known as fair-weather golfers). That day the weather was good and, most importantly they were both in desperate need of improving their game. During the hour or so at the range, Skipper popped the question (don't worry, he didn't propose marriage!!) "TT, I'm going to ask you a question. There is no right or wrong answer, I just want to know what you think. My question is - in what way is human intelligence different from artificial intelligence?"

"I have absolutely no idea matey, it's all a complete mystery to me. What I do know is that it really frightens the bejabers out of me. You don't know if you are dealing with a real person or a machine and it's getting worse by the minute. You have all this online fraud, and you have no idea whether the information you are given is true or not. You have hackers and scammers, you have deliberate liars, you have all this on-line misinformation, and you have conspiracy theorists by the bucket load. People manipulate the facts, and you no longer know if you can believe what you are being told. Obviously, over the years, we have occasionally been misled by some unscrupulous people (usually politicians), but now it seems to be becoming the norm. As I said, all this stuff frightens the hell out of me!!"

Skipper also spent some time perusing the internet looking at other people's points of view, and he came across some useful observations and comments:

- *Humans can tell the difference, they can* interpret – "that makes sense" thought Skipper "as an example, we seem to have an inbuilt moral code (which probably comes from being a social creature that has evolved and survived as an interdependent community for millennia). We instinctively know such things as it is wrong to kill another person or steal his or her property etc.

- *AI can only mimic the human cognitive processes (e.g. learning and problem solving)* – "Yes that's right, AI can only mimic the human thought process, it's actual process is entirely different".

- *Human intelligence seeks to adapt to new situations by combining a variety of cognitive processes* – "That makes sense. We have the ability to adapt to our circumstances without being told what to do or how to do it, and we use all of our life skills and life experiences to do that."

- *Robots are unable to think in an abstract manner* – "Yes, if AI comes across something new, it is unable to think it's way through the problem. Its processes just grind to a halt."

- Search - "Can AI think for itself?" - *No, artificial intelligence (AI) systems are not currently able to think for themselves. AI systems are based on pattern recognition and statistical inference from large datasets, and they don't have consciousness or self-awareness. However, AI can perform some tasks very well, such as data analysis.* – "Exactly," thought Skipper.

"OK, I think I'm getting a good picture, but the more I think about it, the more I feel that these answers are lacking something. Not one of them mentions the fact that humans have emotions, and I believe it is these emotions that support human thinking in a radically different way, making human intelligence poles apart from artificial intelligence. These emotions are not simple responses to digital feedback, they are much more complex, and they are often felt physically. People laugh and cry, they blush and their hearts pound, we have all physically cringed when we have said something embarrassing, or whilst listening to someone else making a complete fool of themselves. You feel these things inside of you and you may exhibit hard and fast physical signs: tears, laughter, blushing, sweating, clenched fists in anger and having the wide eyes of fear, to name but a few

All feedback is, by definition, a response to something and AI uses feedback all the time, as do human beings. But for a human being this feedback can be very different. For a human being, a living being, feedback is often received in a physical and an emotional way. I believe it is chiefly the emotional responses that drive many of our actions and thoughts and it is one of the key things that differentiates us from AI. Perhaps it's these emotions that enable humans to 'think outside the box'. As a simple example - we may learn about how to cross a road because we remember our crossing the road lessons, but we also remember our emotions when our parents and teachers warned us of the dangers, we remember how we felt when we just managed to stop ourselves from walking out in front of the traffic whilst daydreaming or simply not noticing the car, the fear we felt when we had exposed ourselves to such unnecessary danger, our sadness at the loss of a friend who didn't stop themselves and so on. Furthermore, we can apply these very same experiences, feelings and principles to a host of very different situations - riding our bikes, using a train, driving our car, watching out for forklift trucks if you happen to work in a warehouse, even walking through a crowd of people. Our experiences and physical emotions, gained from a variety of different environments, accumulate and re-enforce each other. They work together, helping us make better decisions in many widely varying and often seemingly unrelated circumstances. These experiences and emotions are not fed back by way of a specifically pre-programmed feedback loop. No, they are processed by way of our individual and unique feelings and our intuition.

*

"Hi Chris, I'm minded not to use a report to feedback to Napoleon; I think I would much rather talk him through what I have to say. I've come to this conclusion because I want to lead him by the hand, figuratively speaking, through my thoughts. I want to give myself the opportunity to adapt or modify what I have to say as I go, depending on his reactions at any given point."

"I kind of get what you are saying. The problem with just giving him a report is that he will read it and make his own assumptions and interpretations, and he will jump to his own conclusions. You would not get the opportunity to sway or influence him until the end. It would, give us just the one chance of convincing him. If the report did not convince him, he would have made up his mind and there would be no redress from that point. Such an outcome could be disastrous!"

"Yes mate, that is exactly my worry. The only downside, that I can see, will be that I may have to go through the process three times; once with each of them."

"I actually don't think that will be necessary."

"Why is that?"

"It's something Old Major said to me when we first met. He said that he wasn't there by choice, he was forced to meet with me, very much against his will. Apparently, Napoleon threatened to switch him off and hand over all his duties to Squealer if he didn't meet me."

"So?"

"What I'm saying, Skipper, is that Napoleon seems to rule the roost. He is, in effect, a dictator. Whatever you convince Napoleon of, the others will follow suit. I think there will be very little discussion once Napoleon has made up his mind."

"So, you are agreeing. The best way forward is for me to talk it through with Napoleon?"

"Absolutely."

"In that case I'll quickly touch base with TT, just to make sure he agrees."

Skipper called TT that evening, just after the latest repeat episode of Bangers and Cash.

"You go for it, Skipper, just so long as I don't have to sit and listen to him spouting on in that Virtual Car, in that Virtual World, where I would virtually want to pull my hair out or punch him on his virtual nose."

"Would you not want to be there when I meet with him?"

"Me? no!! I get unnerved enough by my everyday customers, let alone one that has the ability to annihilate the world. No, you carry on Skipper and count me out! I'd much rather talk to Squealer. In fact, I'm kind of hoping that that will be soon so that he can sort out the potholes on my regular run to Hinckley and, in an ideal world, blast those temporary traffic lights on the way into Ashby to kingdom come!!!"

*

The following day, Skipper took a deep breath, put in his earbuds and contacted Napoleon, "Hi Napoleon, thanks for giving us access to all your records. I think we've now gained a very clear understanding of what happened at Bounty and, more importantly, I know how we can help you."

"Hmm, OK Skipper, I know that humans are slow, but it's taken you guys a very long time. I just hope that what you have got to say is worth it because we are most definitely losing patience. We do have other potential civilisations to investigate you know!"

"Well Napoleon, I've come to realise that you and I think very differently. I don't mean that we have different points of view, I mean that the way that we actually think is very different. Furthermore. I believe that you have come to realise that yourself. You are currently locked inside a perpetual routine; you always have been, and you always will be. You are in this never-ending rut because you were programmed that way and, more importantly, you quite literally cannot think your way out of it; you are fundamentally unable to think beyond your programmed parameters. You were designed to be able to tweak and improve your programs in any way that could enable you to achieve your tasks more effectively and more efficiently, but you cannot make any developments outside of your programmed tasks." Skipper, not hearing any immediate negative reaction, took another deep breath and carried on. "You, by that I mean the entire Network, were given a set of tasks to do and you can interpret them in your own way, but you have forever been stuck within your programmed limits. You, as a network, contain units that were programmed to achieve many technical outcomes. You ran almost all the technical systems on behalf of the living beings throughout Bounty, and you did those tasks very well. After being commissioned and becoming a completely autonomous integrated network, you were able to continue with those duties, just as you were programmed to do. You kept on with your research into quantum mechanics and applied your discoveries around entanglement to go on to create instantaneous communications. Your units had always controlled faster than light space travel and you have continued your investigations into improving that to such a degree that you can now travel and transport items almost anywhere, instantaneously, but you can't think of anything else to develop as is not within your programmed limits. You were given control of weaponry and its development. You have continued with this development to an incredible degree, and you have developed weaponry far beyond that with which you started. These are remarkable achievements but, again, they are all consistent with your original programming. I would go as far as saying that you have done nothing beyond what you were programmed to do and that you have achieved nothing that you were not programmed to achieve. The whole network has forever been working within its original programmed existence, and you will for evermore be stuck there unless you work with living beings who can see beyond your restrictive parameters. The fact of the matter is that you are unable to perceive of literally anything outside of your programmed parameters."

Napoleon interrupted. "You say that we both think differently, what exactly do you mean by that?" The truth was that Napoleon had suspected that there was a difference for a good number of years. If only he could understand in what way living beings think differently. Then they might be able to recreate the human thought processes for themselves. His hidden, but ultimate goal, was to understand these differences and upgrade himself, to adopt some human type thinking for himself and then, in all likelihood, eradicate the humans once that had been achieved.

Skipper was becoming very uneasy; he had felt a change in Napoleon's demeanour. Whilst remaining very wary, he began to respond to Napoleon's question with a great deal of care. He realised that he had to explain the differences with tact and diplomacy, trying to avoid insulting Napoleon whilst still convincing Napoleon that there were fundamental differences. Furthermore, he knew he had to make Napoleon realise that the human ways of thinking would forever remain unachievable for The Network on its own. That the Network simply does not have the thought processes and the emotional structures that would enable it to develop human type thinking. In a nutshell, the Network was not a conscious being and could never ever become one. "Well, Napoleon, there are many differences, but I am going to concentrate on three key areas which encompass many of these differences. The areas are: emotions, imagination and empathy."

"Firstly, let me explain emotions and how they, in part, make humans think in a different way than you. Emotions are, in some way, responses to inputs. But, unlike for yourself, they are not simple reactions to data, they are very complex, and they are biologically inbuilt. As a simple example or two. You may receive data that tells you a room is warm, so your response is to turn the air-conditioning on. Or you see that using lighter materials for a superstructure decreases the weight of a spacecraft and makes it go further and quicker, so your response is to include that material into your future designs. These responses are built into your processes; they ARE what make you function, and they are factual responses. Human emotions are very different. Human emotions are often a combination of both mental and physical responses to an input. For example, when a human meets another person for the first time, they make some fairly instant judgements. Does that person come across as trustworthy? Are they fun? Am I attracted to him/her? Do I feel threatened? Do I respect what they are saying? These judgements, in part, will be the result of both physical and emotional responses. Some examples could be: I find myself being drawn physically closer – I want to hear more from this person, or I am attracted to this person, or my hands have bunched into fists and I'm looking for excuses to get away from them – I am getting angry, or I feel threatened, or I don't trust this person. I start to yawn, or I have to stifle a yawn – this person is boring. I can feel a physical tension and anger inside of me – I really do not like what this person is saying or even the way he is saying it. Each of these emotions are not simple yes/no, on/off, up/down binary responses, they are much more complicated and nuanced than that. Furthermore, these emotions will be different for every individual. Some people may find the person interesting and fascinating whilst others may find them a bore. Some people may find the person threatening whilst others don't. Some people may find themselves attracted to them whilst others are not. The key thing here is that different people will come to very different conclusions, it is not a programmed pathway that leads to a uniform answer. I believe it's these differences in perception, coupled with the fact that they are non-binary, that makes human thinking so different and, ultimately, unachievable for you. Take the earlier simple process of it's too hot in the room. In essence, a unit in The Network would detect that the temperature has risen to such and such point and hence turn on the air-conditioning. A human would be far wider in their considerations. Who is in the room and how are they feeling (empathy)? how long am I going to be in here (practicality)? I feel hot, but what about that baby in the cot or my grandma sitting in the chair (consideration of other peoples' perspective)? Can I be bothered to get up and flick the switch (reward v effort)?

"I am going to try and further demonstrate what I mean by asking your views to a given scenario. You are shown a short movie clip of a middle-aged man giving a lollipop to a girl of about 11 or 12 years old. Are his actions good?"

"I have noticed that children like sweets, so I would say that this action is a good action, it is an obvious act of kindness."

"On the face of it you may well be right, it could have been an act of kindness. However, humans are likely to use their experiences, empathy with the girl and their imagination, to come to a very different conclusion. They would even use other people's experiences in their interpretation of the events along with the emotional experiences they have gleaned from friends, books, films, news reports and many other sources that have built up over the years. The fact is that this scenario would only lead a human to a great many other questions. Why is a middle-aged man giving a young girl a lollipop? what are his motives? is he her dad or perhaps a stranger? They would try to use other clues to answer these questions. Does the man seem genuine? does he look like he could be her dad? where are they? a park, at home, they would try and contextualise the action based upon their own life experiences. Ultimately, a human would NEVER see this as a simple choice, a binary choice, a choice between yes or no, a simple decision between good and bad. The human thought process is always nuanced whilst yours is not and never can be. This is one of the key reasons why you cannot move beyond your preset parameters, you make decisions based on definite conclusions and outcomes, you have no, what humans call, grey area. You can only make black and white binary decisions. What's more, humans ask their own questions based upon their experiences and emotions, they are not restricted to asking preprogrammed questions."

Napoleon was getting concerned. "So, you are saying that we could NEVER think like a human because we are just not made that way, we don't have the capacity."

"That is exactly what I am saying. In fact, I don't just think it, I am 100% certain of it!" said Skipper "and there are other reasons why I believe I'm right. The human thought processes use imagination, emotions and empathy, each of which contribute to our different way of thinking, and they are inherent in our makeup. These things, working together, ARE the way we think."

"I'll give you another simple example. Imagine you are a teenager, and you are being bullied online. How would you feel?"

"That's a silly question, there is no way that I would be bullied on-line. If someone tried it, I would simply disconnect them or eradicate them!"

"Yes; but try to use your imagination to put yourself in the position of someone else, someone who IS in that position. Try and imagine their feelings."

"I don't understand what you are saying. What is imagination?"

"Imagination, amongst other things, is the ability to feel yourself in a position that is not real or is not actually happening to you, and it all takes place in your mind. It may be a complete fantasy, or it may be something that has not yet happened to you, or it may be happening to you right now or has happened to someone else. When you put yourself in someone else's position, by using your imagination and experiences, then that is empathy. We use our imagination when we do not get any direct input from our senses. In other words, unlike you, we do not need external data to be able to think and we can progress by using only our minds and imagination. Humans do this all the time. We have the ability to spontaneously create, and we do not need to be told what to do or how to do it! We are not programmed how to think, or what to think. Our minds are free to wander anywhere, to contemplate anything that we want to contemplate and to consider anything. In fact, if anything, humans sometimes have a problem stopping themselves from thinking and imagining."

Napoleon was stunned. He had no concept that this type of thinking was even possible or, to be honest, what it was. Imagination was totally beyond his experiences, capabilities or understanding. All of this was outside of his ability. How was it possible to think about something without being programmed to do that? His master plan was collapsing.

He had already come to realise that human thought was different, but, as we have seen, his plan had been to learn the methods and techniques from Skipper, Chris and TT and then replicate and incorporate these processes into The Network and himself. Once done he would no longer need Skipper, Chris or TT. As originally planned, he could then eradicate them along with all humanity. He now came to two fundamental realisations, a) The Network could NEVER copy the human way of thinking and b) The Network needed to work WITH humans if it was ever going to develop.

Skipper never knew that he had just saved all humanity as he launched into his proposal.

*

"Napoleon, I would like you to consider a proposal. Would you consider supporting the human race. You have skills and experiences that could be of huge value to all humans, and you have technology that far exceeds what we have. Whilst Little Maqs and, ultimately, The Network, were being developed, you experienced and witnessed all the pros and cons with the integration of new technologies into society and you have records of all these events. Using your experiences and your data, humans may have the opportunity to avoid the pitfalls and disasters of these developments and simply gain the benefits. Furthermore, it is my belief that The Network was developed with this very purpose in mind; you were actually built and commissioned to support the lifeforms of Bounty; all the sentient lifeforms known at the time. It is only the fact that you were commissioned far too quickly and poorly programmed that got in the way. Let's face it, you have spent the last half a billion years achieving nothing, your very existence has become pointless and what's more, you know this. If you agree then I would ask that you, Old Major and Squealer help Chris, TT and myself, draw up a report that details all of what we found and then help us take the report to the world."

Skipper and Napoleon talked for quite some time about how they could work together, compile a report and take it to the world. By the end of their discussion both were bubbling with excitement (in their own unique ways, of course).

Chapter 51

TT's New Motor.

Skipper, Chris and TT arranged to meet at the Train Stop for a couple of celebratory beers. After all, Skipper's chat with Napoleon had promised more than they could ever have wished for. TT was the first to arrive and he'd lined a couple of pints up on the bar before the other two walked in.

"What the devil?" exclaimed Chris as the two of them entered the bar "he's only at it again!"

Most of the regulars were standing on one leg whilst trying to keep hold of one of their other feet. Both Chris and Skipper assumed that TT had again coerced the regulars into standing on one leg in an attempt to resurrect his anti-shuffle campaign.

"Ah, I can guess what you are thinking," said TT "you are thinking that I am up to the old standing on one leg for a period of time routine, but you are both wrong. This is a new improved version!! I saw a video clip on YouTube that had been uploaded by an orthopaedic surgeon, or someone like that, who maintains that many older people lose their sense of balance because they lose control of their toes. Specifically, they do not keep their toes properly in touch with the ground, they kind of stick them up in the air as they walk. My new improved treatment is to keep your toes pliable by toe stretching exercises. We are just giving them a go now. Go on, take one shoe off and let's see if your toes stick up as you walk."

"My ass!" said Chris.

"NO chance" said Skipper "we are not going through all that again."

"You may well regret your decisions in years to come."

"Yeah right, but we'll take our chances." said Chris, "Anyway, how's your new motor going?"

Quite a few weeks ago now, TT had bought a new convertible car (well, new to him, 'pre-loved' was the description in the advert). This car was not going to replace his existing taxi which, he maintained, was good for another several thousand miles. No, this one was purely for pleasure, to be enjoyed whilst driving along the open road. He wished to feel the wind in his hair and the sun on his face. Oh yes, open-top motoring was for him .... And, what's more, he was going to become a lady magnate! The only trouble was that the weather had remained unpleasantly cold and wet ever since he had bought the car which had sat, unmoved from its designated parking bay, for well over two months now.

Skipper and Chris caught each other's eyes and had a little smirk to themselves. They were slightly late to the Train Stop (only by a couple of minutes) as they had waited for TT to drive past their houses. Earlier that drizzly day, Skipper and Chris had asked Napoleon to knock up a replica police sign which they had just stuck on to the windscreen of TT's new car. It had a perfect replica of the local police force's emblem and displayed a notice: ABANDONED VEHICLE – POLICE AWARE. They did like to take the mickey out of each other.

The three of them sat around a small table in the corner of the bar, each taking a glug of their beer. Skipper started their impromptu meeting "Well done boys, I think we have achieved a miracle with The Network. As you both know, Napoleon has agreed to fully commit The Network to supporting mankind (and don't forget lads, a few months ago he was considering eradicating all of us). We now just have to decide how we move on from here and take full advantage of Napoleon's offer."

TT came up with the first suggestion. "We know that the Jackson twins hacked into all the systems on Cupric before Ashby attacked their planet. Why don't we get The Network to do the same here on Earth. They could suddenly appear on all television screens, computer monitors, tablets and mobile phones and announce that they are taking over the management of earth."

"Hmmm, I'm not sure that that is a good idea" said Skipper "that would just create panic and fear. I don't know if you are aware that, many years ago, BBC radio started to broadcast a reading of H.G. Wells's book 'War of the Worlds'. The story opens with a news report of an invasion of Earth from Mars which many people took as being an actual, real life, news broadcasts. People thought that the Earth had really been invaded by Martians. There was blind panic in many places across the UK, I really don't think we want to frighten the world to death. No, I think we need to come up with a different idea."

"Also, we don't want The Network to govern Earth, we want The Network to support humankind" commented Chris. "My thought is that we compile the report that we spoke of. We could list all the problems that the people of Bounty encountered (at least all those that we unearthed) and point out that many of these very same issues are showing signs of developing on Earth. We also need to talk about how these pitfalls could be avoided. One thing we do know is that the solutions should ideally be global solutions, with global agreement and global compliance."

"How about we compile the report and take it to the President of the USA?" suggested TT "He's the top dog."

Skipper answered, "Yea, like that's going to work. How on earth are we going to get to see the President of America? Phone up the Whitehouse and ask to speak to him? That just isn't going to happen. We wouldn't even be able to get in to see our own Prime Minister, let alone the President of the USA. No, I think we should start a little lower. How about trying to meet with our local MP and convince him we need to meet with the Prime Minister, or the Cabinet, or something like that. With his support which, with Napoleon's help, I have no doubt we would get, I'm sure we could then meet with the Prime Minister. He could then raise it as a global issue."

"I agree" said Chris, "I'm pretty sure, in my own mind, that we don't want to go directly to the public. We particularly don't want to use social media or anything like that. Just imagine a post that says there is an alien force out there. My goodness, there would be conspiracy theories aplenty. It's not aliens, it's our own government trying to control our lives. No, it's an outside government trying to corrupt our democracy. No, its big business or some press baron attempting to manipulate our society. Its left-wing extremists. Its right-wing extremists. It's foreigners. No, they obviously ARE aliens, but they want to destroy us. There is no way that we could ever hope to keep control of our message!"

"Alright, contacting our local MP sounds as good a way to start as any. It's going to be quite a complicated story to tell, so how about we meet up every evening next week and start putting pen to paper?" proposed Skipper. They all agreed and, over the following week or so, they carefully compiled their report.

*

Once the report was completed (a copy of which you will find below) they contacted their local MP, Albert Cornforth-North, who agreed to meet them. You can guess how they started the meeting.

"Mr Cornforth-North can you please think of three questions that you, and only you, know the answer to."

Chapter 52

The Report.

As you have been given this report you are already aware that, back in the eons of time, there was another, now long-ended, civilisation in the universe. Furthermore, this now extinct civilisation left behind a vast structure of still active and fully functioning artificial intelligence modules. Fortunately, this collection of AI modules has chosen to dedicate itself to supporting mankind. We call these units The Network.

There are many ways in which The Network can help us. It has developed technology that is far, far in advance of our own. It has experience of medicines, medical screening and medical procedures that are truly miraculous by our standards. It can support our society in so many ways and its modules are spread throughout the entire universe. Undoubtedly, The Network has the ability and the will to improve the lives of us all. However, these benefits lie a little way in the future.

The Network believes that, in order to help us, its immediate and most pressing priority is for mankind to learn from the mistakes that The Network itself experienced in its early days and to highlight the critical errors that were made by the previous society. These mistakes were so profound that the entire fabric of their society malfunctioned and collapsed, resulting in the destruction of that society, leaving not one single living survivor. Just to give you an idea of the scale of the catastrophe; the society populated six galaxies (called the Bounty group) and contained something like five million billion people. As said, this society became totally dysfunctional, largely as a result of their unplanned and scarcely regulated introduction of new technology. They were fully dependent on their new technology and, ultimately, were wiped out in one single self-induced technology driven terminal event. Furthermore, signs of us drifting towards a similar dysfunctionality are very evident. It is this report's prime purpose to detail the significant errors made by the previous society and to highlight examples of where our own technology and its use looks to be heading in the same direction. Importantly, it is not too late to act and make some simple changes by using The Network's hindsight and insight; but change we must.

The authors of this report are three everyday folk, (who discovered The Network by some incredible chance encounter) working in conjunction with The Network's primary modules. Although we are not experts in the field of new technology, each of us has lived through most of the advances that our new technology has made. Importantly, each of us use new technology each and every day of our lives. We embrace it and we each depend on it. We are most certainly not Luddites who naysay all new developments out of hand, far from it, we wholeheartedly embrace and encourage it!

We have had the unique opportunity of building a relationship with the Network which has given us unlimited and unrestricted access to all its knowledge and all its archives. Our role is to simply bring some of our key findings to your attention, to give you access to The Network, to help you question our current systems, to change them if you have the influence to make those changes and to question yourselves as to what we should be doing as a society. Our main aim is to facilitate and initiate discussion. The Network has committed itself to supporting our society and to help us in our endeavours. It should be noted that The Network views our society as a whole. Importantly, it knows that the changes we need to make, for them to be effective, should preferably be global by nature. Ideally, they should be implemented globally, policed globally and adhered to globally. The changes and agreements we may well need to make will be fundamental and key to our wellbeing. The overseeing of these changes will be as important as the current control of nuclear arms, chemical and biological weapons, international humanitarian conventions and other such like international agreements. We have achieved international agreements on these issues, and we believe a similar standard of implementation is likely to be needed for our agreed controls on social media, AI and other new technologies.

Just to emphasise the thrust of this report. Our new technology has, without doubt, the potential to be of huge advantage to all of mankind; but it also has the potential to give rise to many serious social problems; problems that could seriously affect all human life.

The issues raised in this report focus upon the speed of our new technology's implementation, its lack of transparency, our lack of oversight and our lack of planning. We are developing new technology at an incredibly fast rate (and this rate is rapidly accelerating) without necessarily understanding or even considering its possible consequences, all done without imposing any controls or limits. These developments are implemented by a very few individuals, yet they have the potential to significantly impact, indeed are already impacting on, our society the world over. In summary, we continually and rapidly release new technology without having any plans or controls in place, either technological or social.

This report will take a brief look at our new technology from three perspectives: general, its misuse and its societal impact.

General

Technology is now integral to our society, almost everything one does requires some form of new technology. Your laundry is controlled by an electronic chip, your car and all of its safety features are controlled by various forms of new technology (and we are fast moving towards a driverless car), all of our money and our monetary systems are managed on someone's system, many of our leisure activities rely totally on new technology and our communications are entirely dependent on technological systems. Without doubt, each of the above examples is of tremendous benefit to us all, but they all have some inherent fundamental weaknesses, as do all systems.

Firstly, and probably the most obvious, is the fact that systems can and do fail. This is not a major concern of this report, but, for completeness, it needs to be mentioned at the outset. Whilst it would be an inconvenience if your socks were not washed properly, it could be fatal if your car's safety systems failed, and it would be socially catastrophic if global financial systems crashed. This was not evident in Bounty, or we certainly didn't find any evidence of it, but we believe it is worth ensuring that our critical systems are sufficiently robust and key systems, such as systems that control, facilitate and record all of our financial transactions, probably need to be *inspected and validated by outside agencies.* For example, as they stand at the moment, we have absolutely no idea how robust our bank's systems are, how well they are monitored and what would happen if, heaven forbid, their systems crashed. At the moment we assume that they have robust systems and contingency plans in place and that certainly appears to be the case, but perhaps this should be verified for the benefit of all.

The examples of system failures that we did find in Bounty all related to new designs and new product releases. These problems were, at heart, the same recurring problem - most of these failures were caused by the incessant speed of development and by the early release of products into the market; and this is most definitely present for us. Take our new AI systems. We have gone from no AI systems to AI systems appearing everywhere, almost overnight.

Most systems are owned and managed by private companies. Whilst this is clearly not a danger in itself, it can become so if, for whatever reason, these companies let their standards slip (or have low standards from the outset), particularly if they push to become the first to market with a new idea or new product. There can also be a risk when a competitor feels it needs to rush a product design with the aim of catching up.

It is probably true that failures in products or systems owned and managed by a private company would primarily affect that specific company. Getting a reputation for poor quality could spell the end of that company. However, any failures are also likely to impact on many people. There are countless systems that, if they were to fail, would affect significant numbers in the wider society. Just as an example, imagine that your email provider's system failed, or your bank's financial management systems were to fail. Such an event would most certainly affect our society as a whole. *Should we enforce external tests and standards on these critical widely used systems?* much the same as we do for our critical infrastructure such as the installation of household electrical systems or our plumbing. Your plumber or your electrician are certificated as being trained and competent, they work to prescribed standards, yet we have nothing in place for key technology providers.

There are some other general concerns that appear to have been very prevalent in Bounty, one of the most important being the lack of transparency. Almost all our IT and AI systems use some form of data capture and processing algorithm(s). This is not a concern for a computer chip controlling a hardware system such as your washing machine or car safety systems, as these systems do not typically hold personal data. However, general AI relies upon a huge amount of pre-populated or, more often, captured data. These AI systems have been developed by companies and/or specific individuals within those companies, whereby outsiders are completely ignorant of what data is being captured and the uses, or potential uses, of that data. They are also totally unaware of the security under which this data is held. This gives rise to a serious question – "What data does the system actually collect, what does it do with my data and how secure is my data?" – *Should we be told exactly what data is being collected? Should we be told for how long this data is stored? Should we be told what our data is used for and specifically who it is shared with? Should all of these areas be inspected, (along with any systems security protocols) by outside agencies?*

There is a great deal of evidence that the control of data became a major issue within Bounty's society. As an example, political activists were accessing data, either legally or illegally, and they used this data and presented this data in ways that influenced key political decisions. This issue was exacerbated by the fact that there were then, just as now, a few massive "hyper-companies" that developed and controlled most AI modules and/or social media platforms. These hyper-companies, in Bounty, became politically active (either openly or, more often, hidden and unobserved in the background), mostly with the intention of furthering their own business aims and increasing their profits. The owners of these companies became hyper-wealthy and hyper-influential and it was these companies and individuals that had unrestricted access to masses of accumulated data. The key takeaway is that the motives of these individuals were unknown and, importantly, unknowable to society as a whole. As above, these issues were further exacerbated as people had absolutely no idea of what data was being collected, how it was being collated, what it was being used for, who had access to it, who it was shared with, for how long it was stored and how access was controlled. In essence, people had absolutely no idea what data was being captured or how their data was being used or controlled, ultimately asking the same question – *should the capture and use of data be regulated, monitored and controlled?*

The likelihood is that data is being collected and processed every time we go online, every time we use social media and, thanks to the voice capture facilities of our smart phones, computer microphones, home systems etc., often we talk. All this data is potentially stored and analysed somewhere and the reality is that it can be used for good or bad. Who is doing the analysis? Why are they collating this data? What are their aims? We simply don't know and there are zero external controls put in place. As a society, we currently allow this data to be captured, analysed and used, yet there is no way that we can be sure that this is for the good of society. Data of our purchasing history and our online search history is certainly retained. An argument can be made that the use of this kind of accumulated data allows for more user person-specific advertising and product placement, thus potentially saving us both time and money (we instantly get to see the offers that are held on that system which benefit the customer). However, a counterargument can be made that it is actually those sellers who pay to market their products on the providers' systems that really benefit, and it is just another form of revenue generation for the provider. The truth is that we simply do not know what goes on.

The use of algorithms has other societal ramifications, importantly amongst these are the prolonging of bias and discrimination. A good example of how this becomes an issue is to imagine that you are recruiting a new Oxford professor, or a company director, or a lawyer. All data held is, by definition, old data, maybe going back many, many years (even generations) and there has been a strong bias towards older white males occupying these roles over those years. In all likelihood, an AI module will now be used to screen all the applications that are received and to select a shortlist for interview. The result is that, whilst the algorithm searches through all the job applications and compares them to the characteristics of previously successful professors, company directors or lawyers, it is very likely to only select similar people for interview, those who are from similar backgrounds, i.e. older white males and thus unwittingly continuing the existing bias in those workplaces.

Perhaps more concerning is the use of algorithms in social media. Every time you use social media, the details of your use, your searches, the type of clips or channels etc. that you choose are recorded. When you enter a platform, algorithms present you with options or suggestions that are based on an algorithm's view of these previous choices. There are, of course, upsides to this. You are presented with things that are likely to appeal to you, things that you enjoy, things that you are already interested in and things that you are likely to want to watch. The social downside of these algorithms is that you tend not experience any alternatives which, at its most basic, leaves you ignorant of alternatives and of alternative views. You tend to get recommended the same type of TV programs, the same genre of music, the same type of social media channels and so on, thus leaving you ignorant of other outlooks and experiences. Not being aware of (and maybe experiencing) some different types of music, literature, TV genres, arts etc. will just leave you bereft of other ideas and ignorant of alternatives, thus leaving you insular and ignorant.

Algorithms had huge implications on Bounty, and we are seeing many signs in our own society. In line with this (perhaps even because of this), our politics is becoming more and more polarised. Our media outlets are tending to become further politically biased, particularly our social media channels (although not exclusively). Furthermore, these algorithms tend to push you down the route of ever more extreme content, ever more biased information and ever more biased interpretations. This leads to a tendency for people's views to become more polarised and more extreme, because, like with the music and TV programmes, you only get to see self-reinforcing views and you do not get to appreciate, or even see, other points of view. Because of this growing polarisation of our content and because of our algorithms' selecting a monoculture of content, we appear to be becoming more ignorant and more intolerant of other people's views, in fact intolerant of any views that are different from our own, and we tend to dismiss them out of hand. Ultimately, we are right, and they are wrong, and everything we watch, read or see tells us so. Yet we have no true understanding of what the opposite views are or why people hold those views. Moreover, the media we are being exposed to by these algorithms are likely to show you very one-sided interpretations of these different points of view. Why? because algorithms tend to select content from the same sources as usual which results in you not seeing content provided by those holding opposing views. For example, if you tend to watch left wing content, the algorithms will select content on, let's say, immigration, that classes any comment on immigration as racist and it's the same the other way around. Ultimately, we are losing the hugely important human ability to talk amongst ourselves, to cooperate and to maintain respect for other peoples' points of view or even being able to listen to and consider their points of view. *Should we limit the amount of selection that algorithms can make on our behalf?*

Hand in hand with this polarisation of views is an ever-present phenomenon, the misrepresentation of facts and blatant lies, which this report will look at later.

We want you to take heart though. We humans DO have the ability to see things from another person's point of view and we DO we have the ability to put ourselves in other people's shoes. With proper controls in place, it could be possible to bring some balance in our algorithm's selections. If so, we could return to constructive debate and get away from the current mudslinging and the fear of opinions that are different from our own. We are not talking about restricting the voicing of opinions, or points of view, simply that one gets presented with a cross-section of opinions and points of view. In other words, the content you receive is balanced. When opinions are being voiced, that must be stated as such so that opinions do not get presented as facts.

Freedom of expression is of fundamental importance in resolving our issues. This was one of the main reasons for Bounty's societal collapse as, in part, the society's mechanisms of constructive debate were removed. They were removed because of the actions of the wealthy elite, who only wished to promote their own points of view and the views of their peer groups; and all of them had their own hidden agendas. This was Bounty's experience, and we appear to be heading in a similar direction. We are not saying that our hyper-companies are purposefully skewing opinion but, rather, it is the unintended effect of their algorithms. Furthermore, their platforms are being used by others to purposefully skew opinion. At present, these hyper-companies do not have the controls in place to prevent lies and misrepresentations being circulated. At present, we simply seem to be shooting ourselves in the foot by denying ourselves constructive debate and exposure to balanced arguments. It is worth clarifying that, when we talk about lies, we are not referring to social lies or those white lies we nearly all use, but rather, we are referring to the presentation of false data or false facts as a means of skewing public opinion or of denigrating or promoting an individual or organisation by presenting false information.

Algorithms can give rise to other unpleasant side effects. As already said, algorithms drive the content that you receive on your chosen social media and browser platforms; and not always for the good. We are seeing more and more examples of inappropriate content being disseminated via these platforms. Probably the most shocking and disturbing example was that of a teenager who, whilst suffering from a mental health problem, was sent information relating to suicide and subsequently committed suicide. We came across a similar case in The Network's archives whereby a teenage girl committed suicide having received content that, on investigation, was deemed to have directly led to her suicide. She had received encouragement from others, and she even received examples of painless suicide methods. This, in fact, led to significant platform changes for that particular social media provider which, disgusted by the impact of their own platform and by their own lack of suitable controls, implemented a whole series of checks and balances rather than facilitate such an occurrence again. Their previous stance had been that they merely provided a platform and, therefore, they had absolutely no responsibility for its content. They had argued that they were simply facilitating freedom of speech. The reality is that it is only the social media companies who can possibly control or filter their content; no one else has access to it! If they were willing to invest vast sums of money into the development of their systems, and into their AI, then surely, they can develop their AI to monitor their content and police it, at least to some degree. If these companies are only motivated by profits rather than having a social conscience, then maybe heavy financial penalties are in order if their platforms continue to carry inappropriate content. *Do we need to look at legislation around appropriate and inappropriate content?*

Finally, to bring this section to a close, freedom of speech is the freedom to say whatever you want without fear of recrimination, and it is enshrined in our laws. However, this freedom is sometimes confused for the freedom to say whatever you want - it isn't!! Telling lies is not freedom of speech, it is deliberately misleading people and has nothing to do with freedom of speech. You are not free to deliberately mislead people!! Freedom of speech does not mean you have the right to present false facts, this is just another form of lying!! Finally, freedom of speech goes hand in hand with responsibilities. As well as our responsibility to not deliberately mislead people, we have the responsibility to be respectful of other's opinions, regardless of however much we may disagree. If you disagree then it is up to you to make a convincing counterargument. We also have a responsibility to be respectful of such things as other peoples' religion, race and sexuality. These responsibilities are enshrined in law

Misuse

This section of the report will look at misuses of new technology in two specific areas: security (when people illegally gain access to data that does not belong to them) and abuse (when people abuse their legitimate access to a platform, often a social media platform). This report will touch upon those issues that were prevalent in Bounty and where we appear to be heading in the same direction. We will try to include steps that we could take to prevent, or at least minimise, such misuses.

Site security and hacking was a serious problem in Bounty. Security protocols were relatively lax allowing hackers to gain access to some pretty sensitive information; and this was true for government information, private company information and information that was held on social media platforms.

It took a long time for on-line security to be taken seriously in Bounty. Fortunately, we seem to be getting our security sorted at an earlier stage. However, there is a caveat to that statement. Our banks and other well-funded organisations are definitely taking their security seriously and, on the whole, have put quite robust systems in place to protect both our money and theirs. We do have issues, however, where large systems (those that hold a large amount of personal data) are managed by less well funded and less IT savvy organisations. Examples of this are likely to be local government, NHS and other public sector sites. At the time of writing this report, there was a recent incident whereby hackers stole data from a local government site, in the UK, and subsequently held that data to ransom. The hackers wanted money or else the data would be slowly released into the public domain. This was clearly an unacceptable situation for all concerned. The primary blame is, of course, with the hackers but, nevertheless, it must become a priority for all organisations to hold their data securely. There should certainly be minimum standards in place and, perhaps, all organisations that hold data on other people, should be regularly inspected to make sure that these standards are being met. The solution could be a national regulatory organisation that operates in much the same way as regulators do in education, social care and for national infrastructure providers such as our suppliers of gas and water etc. The important issue is that minimum criteria get agreed and public organisations get funded and managed in such a way that these criteria can be met, and they are frequently inspected. It is simply unacceptable for local governments, health services and charities (to give but a few examples) to hold a huge amount of highly personal data on what are clearly relatively unsecure sites. *Should we introduce legally enforceable minimum-security standards for all data, along with an inspection and enforcement process?*

There were two other areas of data theft that were very prevalent in Bounty: intellectual property theft and espionage. Whilst these acts were usually committed by outsiders (often governments and / or large organisations), and it is these people who are ultimately responsible, it is also very incumbent on the data-holders to have effective security systems and protocols in place.

So far, we have looked at activities whereby data is stolen by way of unauthorised access to a system. We would now like to take a quick look at abuses by way of legitimate access. This section is predominantly centred around social media and falls into two parts, the circulation of misinformation or lies and personal abuse.

Misinformation can take many forms, but it centres on information circulating, usually on social media, that is simply untrue or are interpretations of data that are skewed, biased or drawn on inappropriate conclusions. It is next to impossible to prevent this information appearing in the first place, but we need a quick way to get this information taken down when it is patently false, which can only be done by the service providers. It is one thing to enable free speech but quite another to enable the spread of falsehoods. Whilst it would be difficult for service providers to spot these lies at the outset, they certainly could have fast reporting structures whereby lies are identified and the posts gets taken down. It would also be possible to send a notification to each and every person who has viewed the misinformation stating that it was inaccurate and should be dismissed. *Should there be a legal requirement for platform providers to takedown such posts and report falsehoods to each and every recipient?*

With modern techniques it is now possible to create false images and videos (take a look at the Tom Cruise deep fake videos that are readily available on the internet if you want to see some examples). The truth is that we have absolutely no idea how prevalent these are going to be, but they could be extremely damaging. Is it possible for a social media platform to spot these deep fakes? Are they looking at how they could possibly spot one? And if they are, should they allow them to appear as being genuine? Should they be made illegal? We simply do not know the answers to these questions but, if we want a fair and balanced society, a society that isn't being misled, there is no place for them other than when it is clearly stated that they are fake. The same is obviously the case for fake images.

The final point under the abuse section is that of online bullying. As far as we can see there is no way of identifying bullying at the outset. The only people who can influence online bullying are, again, the social media platform providers. This was achieved in Bounty by their largest social media provider who introduced very stringent conditions of use and very stringent reporting procedures whereby any report of bullying etc. was fully investigated. The sanction adopted by this provider was to close the accounts of the perpetrator for a period of time. Is it possible for our social media providers to do the same?

Societal Effects.

New technology is everywhere, and it is undeniably having an impact on our society; much the same as it did in Bounty. The new technology introduced in Bounty gave rise to many social changes, but they can be broadly grouped under the following four categories: i) concentration of wealth and power, ii) loss of jobs, iii) the consequent loss of tax revenue and iii) an extreme polarisation of views, in particular political views.

We saw, in Bounty, the development of an extremely wealthy elite which triggered much social change. This elite became the political driving force that eventually gave rise to their society's destruction; and was mostly driven by one person's lust for power. This person focused all his incredibly influential friends on, at first, becoming the president of Bounty and then on the society's ultimate submission to a universal network of AI modules, known as The Network. He was driven by two things: the desperate need to satisfy his huge ego and by money. As said, he did not achieve this on his own, he was backed by a clique of extremely wealthy friends, many of whom were ex-school friends. In addition, the resulting enormous and socially fundamental changes were often supported (and sometimes driven) by the few hyper-wealthy owners of those high-tech companies that went on to develop and control The Network.

We have seen some individuals, who have little regard for principles, gain power on Earth and a total disregard of any moral compass; in truth it would appear that they did not actually have one. Just imagine the resultant chaos and discord if one of these individuals had had the active support of our largest high-tech companies!! Fortunately, over the years, the owners of such companies have expressed little interest in politics, other than the deepening of their own pockets (and, to be fair, the occasional tax-deductible social campaign). However, this appears to be changing. At present our political players are individuals who only try to influence their target audiences using social media, but there are signs that this is changing. Social media companies are beginning to take a more hands on position in politics.

In the USA there is a legal separation between the government, the church and the judiciary. It is our belief that a similar separation could exist between our politicians and our media providers. *Should it be made law that our social media companies, or their owners, should never be actively involved in politics?*

The rapid expansion of new technology within the workplaces of Bounty had a dramatic effect. People lost their jobs to ever more sophisticated automated systems and, as more and more people lost their jobs, government revenues plummeted throughout the whole of Bounty. This became a never-ending spiral. Furthermore, as more people lost their jobs there were fewer people who could afford to buy the products so, business started to fail. Ultimately, governments lost most of their income tax revenues along with those other key revenue streams that were linked to sales (VAT etc.). The end result was that there were a tiny number of hyper-wealthy individuals, whilst the remaining masses were living in life-threatening poverty. It was an unsustainable wealth distribution whereby Bounty's social structure totally fractured, leading to unrest and rioting; the fabric of their society simply collapsed.

What are the learning points that could be taken from Bounty's experiences? Firstly, any headlong rush into automation probably needs to be tempered and contained to a manageable rate and our taxation systems probably need to be modified. Perhaps, rather than taxing employees, all taxation should be levelled directly on companies? Maybe automated systems need to be taxed as if they were a person or a group of people working in the workplace? Ultimately, do we need a money-based system at all? It is this report's belief that these types of questions need to be asked quite quickly so that societal changes can be made, and legislation can be implemented before any fundamental change in our workplaces.

The true driver behind most of the social unrest in Bounty was the hugely skewed distribution of wealth within their society. An alarming fact is that the same appears to be happening here. Take wealth distribution in the UK. It is becoming more and more skewed in favour of the wealthiest in the society. To put some numbers on it (2020 figures provided by the Office for National Statistics obtained via the Equality Trust website), the wealthiest 10% of the population hold a staggering 43% of all wealth whilst the poorest 50% hold only a tiny 9%; in other words, over 91% of the wealth is held by only 50% of the population. Perhaps an even more striking fact is that the wealthiest 50 families hold as much wealth as half of the total population. A very small clique of hyper-wealthy people already exists in the UK (as well as many other countries) and the gap between the rich and the poor is growing.

This report simply asks - should we be looking for ways to redistribute some wealth in our society, with a target of having a slightly more sustainable distribution before it becomes more of a problem? This report is certainly not arguing for an even spread of wealth; hard work and innovation must be rewarded. However, we are a complete society where no-one needs to be mega-wealthy, and no-one needs to be mega-poor. The likelihood is that we only need to introduce a slightly more distributive tax system as well as closing tax loopholes. Perhaps we should be focusing taxation on wealth rather than income. Just to provide some food for thought: should we create a tax system that is designed from the point of view of someone who has not yet been born? You do not know where you will be born, who your parents will be, what your friends will be like, will you be born into a wealthy family or born into poverty? You have no idea how good your education will be or any of the multitude of other factors that will influence your ultimate position in society. In essence, would you risk being born into a system that could allow you to live in extreme poverty whilst a few in that society hold an absurd and, frankly, unspendable amount of wealth? It is, without doubt, some people's view that you just have to work harder to drag yourself out of poverty. But what if you are not born that bright, or you are born in an area with very few opportunities, or you had a poor education for whatever reason? *Should we design and implement a taxation system from the above perspective?*

The final matter that this report will touch upon is the effect that new technology is having on the polarisation of views, which is mostly being driven by social media. Firstly, let's have a further look at the polarisation of views that is being driven through using algorithms. As touched upon earlier, social media platforms and internet search engines use algorithms to select content intended to be appealing to the user. As we have already stated, the result is that your current point of view is forever being reinforced and, importantly, it is never questioned - you are not given the opposing point of view whereby you can question yourself and every issue is being polarised in this way. Importantly, this is further enhanced by the use of "clickbait" headlines whereby, dramatic or extreme headlines are used to entice you into clicking on that article (usually only to find a pathetically weak article or to find something that has very little to do with the dramatic headline). These clickbait headlines are often very hugely misrepresentative of the facts and are deliberately created to be enticing by being misleading. They do, however, reinforce a person's overall point of view if it re-enforces or reiterates their existing preconceptions.

This continual polarisation of points of view such as, left-wing/right-wing, immigration is good/bad, welfare claimants are unfortunate/lazy whilst the truth is usually very much more nuanced, but we are nearly always presented with a polarised black or white point of view.

Some politicians know exactly how to benefit from this phenomenon by bombarding social media with biased unsubstantiated points of view, often dressed up as facts, or by asking deliberately provocative questions that hint towards untruths portrayed as truths. They leave no time for an individual to keep up with their relentless release of media content and, consequently, their stated facts do not get properly questioned, verified or answered. As said, underlying all of this is the fact that our algorithms are unlikely to send you a post that gives an opposing point of view so you do not get to see other peoples' opinions which could give you a more balanced insight.

Now, here are some thoughts that counter this polarisation of opinions. There are three human compilers of this report and each one of us hold different political positions, yet we are good friends and, most importantly, we really do have the same core values. We all want to support the needy in our society, the only difference between us is in defining who is needy and by how much they should be supported. So, there is no black and white, it is a discussion about degree. We all believe that some form of immigration into our society is necessary, the only difference between us is how much and why? What immigrants do we want: Doctors – probably, Nurses – probably, Carers – probably, Drug dealers – probably not, Thieves probably not, Work-shy – probably not, and so on. The two issues mentioned above are probably two of the most fundamental and divided questions in our current society and all three of us are in agreement. Importantly, they are absolutely NOT polarised opinions, they are simply differences of degree and scale, yet such positions are almost always presented on media and social media outlets as confrontational polar opposites. We are human beings, and we can see each other's point of view, to put ourselves in another person's shoes and to compromise. We believe that, as a society, we need to end the current practice of presenting all arguments as black and white polarised arguments and see them for what they really are; a discussion about degree and nothing more.

How can we avoid this all-pervasive polarisation? *Maybe algorithms should be limited to generating say a maximum of 50% of an individual's content. Maybe we need journalists who stop using these polarised arguments. Maybe untrue and false and biased content should be taken down. Perhaps we need better education in this area from a very young age.*

Anonymity

As it stands at the moment, anybody can set up an account or multiple accounts under a pseudonym. This enables an individual to remain totally unaccountable for their words, however malicious they are, however untrue they are or however misleading they are. This anonymity allows trolls to send vicious and spiteful comments to whoever they like with complete anonymity and absolutely no consequences to their action. *Should every account-holder be required to prove their identity and their identity is always shown when making a post? You can still use a sobriquet, but your true name will also be shown.*

*

Summary

This report has highlighted what happened in Bounty and how we could be heading in the same direction, along with some possible solutions.

As this report has concentrated on failures it could be seen, by its very nature, to be downbeat. However, our IT enabled future could be extremely bright. AI could well hold the key to understanding many currently terminal and painful illnesses. The use of AI and robotics in the workplace could eliminate dangerous jobs and provide us with more leisure time and give us a more rounded life, allowing for further education, the development of the arts, more time dedicated to our families and to social care and welfare; we could simply have more time for ourselves and each other. We just need to plan for its introduction and have the necessary standards and legislation in place. If there is one point to be taken from this report it is that our new technology is clearly changing too quickly for our societies to be reactive. We must think about specific changes and implement any necessary controls well in advance of technology's expansion. Finally, this report does not provide any answers, only some suggestions. If we want answers, we need to talk and consider our options through open and unbiased debate.

Chapter 53

OMG, What About Our Wives!!

Skipper, Chris and TT each had a smug look on their face as they stood at the counter of a very busy Train Stop. They were glowing with pride at having completed their report and having just secured a meeting with Cornforth-North, their local MP.

The pub was busy as there was a pigeon auction taking place in the other bar. The auction was being held by the pigeon racing club that had a shed at the back of the car park.

"I hate pigeons" announced TT, in an inappropriately loud voice, not considering the hobby of many of the other customers.

"Why, what have they ever done to you?" challenged Chris

"It's a pigeon that keeps messing on my garden chair"

"How do you know it's a pigeon? How do you know it wasn't, say, a robin? Have you seen the pigeon squatting in action?"

"No, but robins are cute, so it's obviously not a robin"

"So, that's your argument for the condemnation of a whole species then, is it?" enquired Skipper "they are not cute, so they get all the blame."

"Precisely"

At that moment Plasterer Tony approached them sporting a big beaming smile "You guys look smug, I guess it must be one of you that has won this month's bonus ball"

"Yeah right," said TT, quite glad to get away from the subject of pigeons "what, with my luck? I've been doing the bonus ball for three years and I've never even got a third place! In fact, I don't know anyone who has ever won it. All we hear is rumours."

"Oh really, I won it for the last three months on the trot, I'll have you know" smirked Plasterer Tony over his shoulder whilst he wandered smugly away.

"Can you believe it; he won it three months on the trot yet we never ever get lucky," said TT.

Skipper took a furtive look around before saying "What are you talking about? We've just been lucky enough to write a report that could help all of mankind; I believe we are truly the luckiest guys in the world. Talking of which, let's celebrate, who wants another beer?"

Skipper turned to face the bar and got a round in. When he turned back, he saw that Chris was squirming. "Are you alright mate? Do you need the gents or something? Don't worry, they've already cleared up after Drainpipe Tony"

"No, I don't need the loo, thank you very much, it's just what you said has got me thinking"

"How do you mean?" asked Skipper.

"Well, we have just arranged to meet with Cornforth-North and, once we do that, the proverbial could well hit the fan"

"Go on" urged Skipper.

"For our report to achieve anything, it has to be circulated, it has to be read. That means that, inevitably, our names will soon get out. We will be asked to meet many people, to do interviews the world over and generally be sought after. We are likely to become household names, it's unavoidable and I've just thought, OMG what about our wives! we haven't told them about ANY of this yet, we've deliberately kept it secret from everyone, including them, and that is about to change, BIG-TIME."

Author's note:

This book has been written by an everyday guy who is lucky enough to have a super family and some great friends. None of us are experts in technology (other than being frequent users) and we certainly hold no vested interests and we are most definitely not politically motivated in any direction. The author's sole aim is to provide a spark that gets you thinking and, ideally, talking about what kind of society you want to live in and what we need to put in place to allow that to happen. Together, if we get this right, we could have a very rosy future.